The King of Whitechapel

BARBARA RUSSELL

OLIVERHEBERBOOKS

one
Dartmoor, 1891

ELIZABETH WAS TIRED of being told she lacked focus and was easily distracted because she was perfectly capable of concentrating on her history class without—hey! Was that a carriage?

She craned her neck to take a better look at the driveway.

"Elizabeth." The sharp tone of her governess's voice jolted her. "Would you please listen? Why do you always get distracted when we study history?"

"I'm following every word you say, Miss Martin. But see, a travelling carriage has just arrived." She pointed to the window overlooking the front yard where a dark carriage was approaching.

Miss Martin didn't share her interest. She didn't even glance outside. "What was I talking about before you got distracted?"

Elizabeth went through her notes filled with ink stains and blobs of wax. History, unlike mathematics, was a messy affair. People did irrational things for questionable reasons. No logic at all.

"The war between the Guelphs and Gibberish ..."

"Ghibellines." Miss Martin narrowed her eyes behind her round glasses. "History is an essential subject. You can't study only what you like, and I seriously doubt that algebra will be of any importance in the life of an earl's daughter. I'm a forty-year-old governess, and I've never needed algebra."

"Of course you have. Measuring ingredients for a recipe is all about ratios, proportions, and other algebric concepts."

"As I was saying." Miss Martin straightened her glasses. "The Guelphs—"

The noise of the carriage stopping in front of the house distracted Elizabeth again.

"Did you hear that? Please, Miss Martin, may I go and see who's arrived?" she said. "I need to stretch my legs as well."

She'd been locked into the schoolroom with her governess for hours, listening to the story of a twelfth-century conflict in Tuscany she wasn't sure she cared about. Now, that was a subject she would never need in her life.

Miss Martin exhaled, lowering the hefty history book. "You might take a break for ten minutes."

"Thank you, miss."

Elizabeth didn't need to hear more. She scraped her chair backwards and made a dash for the door. Being the daughter of an earl included enough rules and restrictions to exhaust her sometimes. It would be wonderful if she could study only what she found fascinating or spend more time outdoors.

She slowed down at the end of the long hallway and paused in a dark corner at the top of the sweeping stairs from where she could see the entry hall.

A cold gust of wind swept up the first floor when the front door was opened, causing her skin to pebble. The weather in Dartmoor didn't seem to care that the winter was ending. The scent of wet soil and the pungent smell of the moorland thickened the air.

She crouched and peeked through the balusters as two men in dark travel coats entered. One wore a tall hat, but the younger one wore his unfashionably long, pale-blond hair loose on his shoulders. She'd seen hair of that colour, so blond to seem silver, only on the Duke of Grafton, her father's friend.

The young man walked with his hands shoved into the pockets of his coat with a swagger and a sullen look gentlemen didn't usually have. He cast a disinterested glance around, clenching his jaw.

After the men's entrance, there was a flurry of activity from the servants, with loud voices and hurrying footsteps. Then Mother arrived at the entry hall, followed by the butler and housekeeper.

The older man removed his tall hat and bowed to Mother before handing her a letter. Elizabeth shifted her position to hear what they were saying, but only indistinct mutters reached her. Mother nodded a few times while the blond young man's face remained tense.

Mother's chest rose and fell quickly as she kept throwing glances at him.

He looked up and found Elizabeth as if her stare had warned him of her presence. Their gazes locked. If his hair was the colour of silver, his eyes were the colour of an ancient glacier and just as cold. The cheeky stranger stared straight at her in a challenging fashion that made her feel like an intruder ... in her own house!

Another shiver went down her neck, and she moved back from the balusters.

When the two men and Mother walked up the stairs, she rushed to her bedroom lest Mother catch her spying.

A young man with silver hair and cold eyes, here at Spencer Hall. She didn't know what to make of that. The clock on the top of the chests of drawers informed her ten minutes had passed since she left the schoolroom, but she had no intention of returning to the Guelphs and Ghibellines's fight without learning more about the guests.

She inched the door open and listened.

"... follow me," Mother said.

Elizabeth slid out of her room and searched the corridor.

Mother and the small group stopped in front of the sitting room sandwiched between Father's personal study and the library.

Elizabeth waited in her bedroom for a few moments before coming out again.

"Elizabeth?" Miss Martin called from the other side of the corridor.

She sped up and slid inside the dimly lit library. Miss Martin's voice came muffled through the thick door once she shut it. The library was connected to the sitting room through a second door. Careful not to hit the table and chairs, she tiptoed across the room and pressed her ear on the wooden door.

"... His Grace is aware he's putting you in a difficult situation," the man said, "but it's an emergency, and this arrangement won't last long."

"We understand." That was Father. "Christopher can stay here, of course. You may reassure His Grace."

"Charles," Mother said. "Perhaps we should consider an alternative before making a decision."

"No." Father's reply didn't leave room for a debate. "William knows he can count on me. I won't disappoint him."

William, yes, it was the Duke of Grafton. And that hair! Christopher had to be the duke's son. Or perhaps a relative. The name of the duke's son was Pearce. She'd never heard of Christopher, and Pearce was the duke's only son.

Her parents lowered their voices, and she couldn't grasp any words.

"My lord," the man continued. "His Grace kindly requests your absolute discretion on the matter."

"Absolutely," Mother said. "Besides, here in Spencer Hall, we rarely see any visitors."

None. Absolutely no one ever came to Spencer Hall in winter. Or summer. Or ever.

"Thank you, my lord, my lady." The relief in the man's voice was loud. "His Grace told me you have complete freedom in how you wish to deal with the boy. Your comfort is of utmost importance to His Grace."

The rest of the conversation was a quick exchange of half-whispered words she didn't understand. Pity. Her parents would tell her only a fraction of the chat, if none at all. She straightened and smoothed down her skirt. Miss Martin was going to punish her if she didn't return to the schoolroom soon.

She turned around and gasped, clamping her hands over her mouth. Christopher, the very young man whose presence was being discussed in the next room, was sitting on the armchair, his chin resting on his fist and his long legs crossed at the knee, looking like a bored king.

"Anything interesting?" he asked in a deep voice that matched his harsh features.

"I didn't hear you coming."

"I was already here in that corner when you sneaked inside, and I didn't think it was polite to point out my presence."

How embarrassing. "Who are you? Christopher?" Surely she was allowed to ask that, given the circumstances. "The Duke of Graft—"

"Shush." He pressed a finger to his lips. "I didn't hear what Mr. Weston said to your parents, but I'm sure he mentioned the importance of being discreet," he dramatically whispered the last words.

She pointed a finger at the sitting room. "Why aren't you with my parents and Mr. Weston?"

"They asked me to leave and wait here, so they could talk about me in private. I guess it's more polite than talking about me in front of me as if I weren't there."

"May I ask why you're here?"

He reclined his head, exposing his strong neck and Adam's apple. "What's your name?"

She was about to tell him he shouldn't answer a question with another question when it occurred to her he was still sitting while she was standing, but he would stand up when he learnt who she was, wouldn't he? Although he couldn't have mistaken her for a maid. But Mother always said to be polite, no matter what.

"I'm Lady Elizabeth, the daughter of the Earl of Lincoln." She bowed her head just to show him how to be civil.

He didn't look impressed. "I doubt we're going to see each other again, Elizabeth. There's no point in introducing myself, and you already know my name."

A heated flush flamed her face. The cheek of him! Where to start? He'd addressed her by her Christian name, hadn't stood up, and hadn't acknowledged her nod with any form of greeting.

"Why would you say that?" she said in a clipped tone without addressing him properly. Served him right.

"Your parents will do their level best to keep me away from you. Nothing personal. They'll likely keep me away from everyone."

Well, she found that intriguing despite herself. "Why?"

He stood up, the dark coat flowing down his legs. With those broad shoulders and that ruthless face, he had a future as a highwayman.

"Don't worry. I have a hunch that I'm not going to stay here for long."

"You make no sense."

"I hear that a lot."

Her next observation of his behaviour was cut off by Miss Martin flinging the door open.

"Elizabeth." She shifted her gaze from Christopher to her. "What's happening here? Who are you, sir?"

Christopher shook his coat, causing pieces of dry mud to fall onto the carpet. "No one. Officially, I don't exist."

He brushed past Elizabeth and left the room, leaving behind a trail of astonishment.

two

*Y*OU'RE NO ONE, *Christopher.*

Christopher had lost count of how many times he'd heard that. Everyone around him seemed eager to remind him who he was and wasn't. Especially his half-brother Pearce. '*You're no one*' was Pearce's motto, repeated religiously twice a day. The only good thing about the constant repetition was that the insult lost its meaning the more Christopher heard it.

After he strode out of the library, leaving an astonished Elizabeth behind, he didn't know where to go. Mr. Weston had told him to wait in the library. He'd be angry to learn that Christopher had disobeyed him. Good.

The Earl of Lincoln's country house was just like the duke's country house—ridiculously big, cold, and filled with useless items no one liked but that were supposed to impress guests no one cared about.

He wondered where his bedroom would be. If they were going to give him a proper bedroom and not the barn, that is.

Elizabeth and the older woman came out of the library and hurried away. Elizabeth shot a fleeting glance at him, her cheeks reddening. He returned the glance.

He might be the bastard son of a duke, recently expelled from the prestigious Eton, but he'd never sneaked into a room to eavesdrop on ... no, actually, he had. Several times. He and Elizabeth had something in common.

He stopped in front of a floor-to-ceiling window that overlooked the grounds. Beyond the manicured flowerbeds, trimmed hedges, and the wall surrounding the house, the moorlands stretched out for miles with those tufts of grass stubborn enough to defy the wind, the cold, and the rocks. He felt an immediate kinship with those plants.

"Christopher." And here it came, dear Mr. Weston. He always made Christopher's name sound like a hiss. "I told you to wait in the library."

"Shall I meet the earl now?"

Mr. Weston brought two fingers on his temples as if he were exhausted. That made two of them.

"Would you please do as you're told for once? Follow me." Mr. Weston glowered at him. "The earl and countess agreed to let you stay here. Do not make them regret their decision and don't take advantage of their generosity."

Generosity? The earl and countess were too scared to defy the mighty Duke of Grafton—a war hero, successful investor, and one of the queen's favourites.

Mr. Weston's scowl vanished when he stepped into the warm sitting room.

Christopher glanced at the door opening to the library where Elizabeth had eavesdropped on the conversation about him. There was something intimate about that, a sort of bond between them.

She was the essence of autumn with her glossy chestnut hair, rich brown eyes, and dark red gown. Pretty much the opposite of her parents, who were the essence of winter with their almost matching blue clothes, blond hair, and frosty expressions.

Mr. Weston cleared his throat.

Christopher bowed to the earl and countess without enthusiasm. "Lady Lincoln, Lord Lincoln. Thank you for your kind hospitality."

If they could detect the sarcasm in his voice, he didn't give a damn.

To his credit, Lord Lincoln didn't look disgusted. "The duke is an old friend of mine. We were in the army together. My wife and I are more than happy to have you here."

"On the condition," the countess said, "that you avoid contact with the household, family members, and the locals when possible."

The translation was: don't talk to us, don't talk to anyone in our family, don't glance our way, and just pretend you don't exist.

He'd heard variations of those rules quite often. But the alternative was to be sent to Grafton House in London, and it was the least appealing option. Also, it was potentially dangerous. The duke's wife would strangle him with her pearl necklace if she saw him. He'd rather be mistreated in the country than in London. At least Dartmoor had plenty of fresh air.

He offered a shallow bow of his head. "I'll do my best to be non-existent."

The countess frowned, but Mr. Weston shot him a glare.

"I understand the reason you were expelled from Eton is thievery," the earl said.

The reason was more complicated than thievery; it had to do with Pearce being an ass and his determination to get his disgraceful half-brother as far away as possible from him. A lie had been all that Pearce had needed. The headmaster's prejudice against Christopher had done the rest. Christopher had professed his innocence with no result.

"So you stole from another student," the countess said.

"Technically, no, my lady. My dear brother, Pearce, whom you surely had tea with many times, wanted to get rid of me and thought accusing me of stealing from him would get me expelled. He was right, of course. The headmaster didn't even bother to ask for my version of the incident. Who was to be trusted? The prim son of a duke, or a bastard who officially doesn't exist? Decisions, decisions."

The earl and the countess looked horrified.

"Christopher," Mr. Weston said. "Mind your language."

He shrugged. "A bastard by any other name would stink as smelly."

The countess gasped.

"Enough!" Mr. Weston straightened to his full height, failing to intimidate Christopher. "You'll show respect while in this house."

He had always to show respect, but curiously enough, he never received it.

Mr. Weston clenched his fists before stepping back, likely pondering if slapping him in front of the earl and the countess was a good idea. Not that Christopher minded one way or another. He was used to being beaten.

"You'll stay here until the duke orders otherwise," Mr. Weston said in case Christopher was thick enough not to have grasped that.

Interestingly, no one used the words 'your father' in front of him, only a generic 'the duke.'

"I thought so." He brushed off a piece of dirt from his jacket.

"Apologies, my lord, my lady." Mr. Weston bowed again.

The earl clasped his hands behind his back, regaining his composure. "Let's try to go through this moment together without causing any further inconvenience for the duke."

Of course. Heaven forbid the duke had to experience even the smallest of inconveniences. Meanwhile, his illegitimate son could be shipped across the country like an unwanted parcel.

Never mind. Christopher would leave Spencer Hall in a matter of hours, a day at most.

He guessed no one would miss him.

AFTER A RATHER BORING afternoon during which Elizabeth had learnt more about mediaeval Tuscany but nothing about Christopher, she went down to the dining room for dinner.

Her evening gown left her shoulders almost bare, causing her to tremble. Perhaps the weather was still too cold for such a light gown.

She checked every corner for Christopher, hoping to exchange a word with him before dinner. But nothing. He'd vanished. After he'd left the library, Miss Martin had dragged her to the schoolroom and hadn't let her out for another couple of hours. Every question unrelated to the Guelphs and Ghibellines had been ignored.

But she'd see him at dinner. Surely her parents would want to dine with a relative of the Duke of Grafton and introduce him to her properly.

Before stepping into the dining room, she straightened her skirt and tugged at her satin gigot sleeves. She didn't care about making an impression on Christopher, but he'd been so unorthodox to her that she wanted to show him she wasn't upset by his behaviour. Although she was. But that was the point of being a lady—to always be composed, even in front of rude people.

And she did want to impress him a little. The winter was so long and boring at Spencer Hall that she longed for a companion who didn't blather about centuries-old wars.

Her hopes were crushed when she entered the dining room and spotted only her parents talking in hushed tones in front of the warm hearth. With her older brothers and sisters married and away, her family had become depressively small and quiet.

"Darling." Father flashed a quick smile upon seeing her.

"Father, Mother."

George, the footman, held out a chair for her.

She couldn't bring up Christopher because, officially, she hadn't met him, but she could talk about the carriage.

A few glances were exchanged between her parents as they sat at the table and the soup was served.

"I noticed a carriage coming up the drive this morning," she said, taking a small spoonful of soup. "Did we receive a visitor?"

Mother put her hand on Father's. "We should tell her."

Father nodded at the butler, and the servants left the room, closing the double doors behind them.

Despite Elizabeth knowing about Christopher, her anxiety spiked. "What is it?"

"We have a guest," Mother said. "His name is Christopher Blackwood."

"Blackwood? But I—" She coughed in her fist. "Sorry, Mother."

Father leant closer. "What I'm going to tell you is not to be disclosed to anyone. Christopher is the Duke of Grafton's son, a child born without benefit of clergy. And ..." He paused. "His mother was a fallen woman."

"Charles." Mother huffed. "You didn't need to tell her that detail."

"Oh." An illegitimate son. That explained the familiarity with which everyone treated him. "Why is he here?"

Mother raised her eyebrows. "The duke was generous enough to send Christopher to Eton. Unfortunately, his generosity wasn't repaid in kind. Christopher was expelled from the school after repeatedly breaking the rules." She paused before adding, "He stole from another student. The headmaster couldn't ignore that."

Elizabeth stopped eating the soup. She'd been in the same room with the illegitimate son of a duke and a criminal. How exciting!

"Christopher will stay here until the duke decides his future," Father said. "Meanwhile, you won't have anything to do with him."

Mother gave a serious nod. "He's staying in the guest wing. We won't see him anywhere in the house. You will not talk to him, and, of course, you won't talk about him with anyone, not even the servants. Should you see him, you'll ignore his presence and pretend he doesn't exist."

Elizabeth sipped her glass of water, trying to find the right words to express her disapproval of such behaviour. "I understand the need for discretion, but he's our guest, and we're treating him like a plague-ridden prisoner."

Mother huffed. "Nonsense. We simply don't want to get involved in any rumours about this unfortunate affair."

So Christopher was only an unfortunate affair?

Mother continued, "We must think about our reputation as well. We couldn't refuse the duke's request for help, but we aren't going to become associated in his horrible affairs."

Father nodded. "Had we been in our house in London, I'm afraid I wouldn't have agreed to keep Christopher with us. Too risky."

She refrained from making a comment. Her encounter with Christopher had been brief and rather upsetting, but she couldn't deny feeling sorry for him. He wasn't an unfortunate affair only because he was born out of wedlock, and he had feelings that could be hurt.

Surely having a chat with him wouldn't cause any trouble. Her parents didn't need to know. But she would show Christopher not every member of her family considered him a disgrace to be ashamed of.

three

T HE GUEST WING of Spencer Hall was so detached from the main family rooms that Christopher essentially slept in another county. He could scream bloody murder and no one would hear him.

Had he suffered from leprosy, they wouldn't have sent him that far away. But no matter. He had a huge, four-poster bed all for himself, a room twice the size of the one in Eton, a study, a small dining room, and a spacious corner for dressing, washing, and shaving.

The earl had also allowed him to be served by a footman and a maid, who likely had been instructed not to talk to him, judging by how silently they'd drawn a hot bath for him and left without a word.

He removed his clothes, wincing as his tired muscles burned. He and Mr. Weston had travelled mostly by carriage from Eton. Nearly two hundred miles of bumpy roads and awkward silence. Not to mention the headmaster's beating had left sore bruises on his body. They didn't hurt as much as his pride. At least he hadn't begged for mercy, even though the headmaster would have let him stay if he'd knelt and begged.

Sod him.

He sighed when he sank into the hot water. The servants had filled an old Oxford hip bath to the rim. The bathtub was deep and large enough for him to sit comfortably, but the water closet at the end of the corridor was so bloody cold that he'd asked to place the bathtub in the bedroom in front of the fireplace. It'd been the right choice.

Finally loosening his muscles, he reclined his head, water dripping from his wet hair, and closed his eyes. His past wasn't free from mistakes and bad decisions, but he hadn't minded studying at Eton. He'd liked it, actually. Damn good teachers. Father had to be furious about the expulsion.

Christopher had no idea what would happen to him. Or rather, he'd had enough of obeying whatever Father said and being sent around the country whenever it was convenient for his father. He was nearly old enough to do as he pleased, like find a job and live on his own terms. Find a place where he was only Christopher and not the ducal bastard no one wanted to be friends with.

He let the hot water wash away his tiredness. As for his frustration, he had to wait.

"Oh, good Lord!" The high-pitched, feminine voice jolted him so hard he kicked the bathtub, hurting his knee.

"What the hell!"

He flung his eyes open. Elizabeth stood in the middle of the room, holding a candle in her trembling hand. Her deep brown eyes, the colour of warm brandy, were fixed on him. Shock or curiosity froze her.

"What are you doing here?" he asked, wiping his face.

"I'm sorry," she stammered. "I just wanted ... I didn't know you were ... I'll leave."

Watching him, she took a few backward steps before pivoting with the speed of a spinning top and promptly tripping on the ottoman. She fell over, face first, with a strangled cry and a smacking thud against the floor. The candle toppled on the Hessian carpet, and the flame hissed with a flare.

Before he could yell a warning, the jute caught fire at an impressive speed, and the worst thing was that Elizabeth remained motionless on the floor.

"Bloody hell!" He jumped out of the bathtub and grabbed the tin bucket next to it.

After sinking it into the tub and filling it to the rim, he tossed the water on the burning carpet. Another bucket was needed to quench the blaze.

"Shit." He covered his nose as the stink of burnt fabric filled the room. "Elizabeth?" He crouched and rolled her over. "Elizabeth?" He patted her cheek lightly.

When she didn't reply, he gathered her in his arms and laid her on the bed. Some of the water had ended up soaking her, and half of her gown was drenched.

He opened the window to let some fresh air in and wrapped a towel around his hips. Just to cover the mess that was his scarred back, he donned a shirt as well, not bothering to button it, though.

She didn't stir. He'd try to wake her up one last time. If she didn't come around, he had no choice but to search for a servant, thus revealing her presence in his bedroom.

How in the hell he was going to explain the earl's daughter was unconscious and wet in his bed, he had no idea. Not to mention the fire. No one would believe she'd come to his bedroom uninvited and had started a fire. He risked more than a sermon from his father.

He lit a few more lamps and leant over her. "Elizabeth, please wake up."

A red spot marred her forehead, promising to become a large dark bruise. Great.

He exhaled in relief when her eyes fluttered open.

"What happened?" She touched her head but paused when she saw him. Sheer horror flashed across her gaze. "What's this smell?"

"You fell, hit your head hard, and started a fire. I put it out and lifted you from the floor because you were unconscious. You're welcome. Now please leave before the situation becomes more complicated than it already is."

Wincing, she propped herself up on her elbows. Her gaze skimmed over the large burnt spot on the carpet and paused on his naked chest.

"You're naked!" she said.

"Well, I tried bathing with my mackintosh, but it doesn't work."

She blinked and averted her gaze. "I feel dizzy."

"Then wait a moment before going, lest you faint in the corridor," he said. "If you pass out in the corridor, no one will find you until the next morning, and it's better for you if I don't escort you to your room."

"I'm sorry. The surprise of catching you in the bathtub shocked me."

"Trust me, I was shocked as well. Why did you come?"

"Goodness, it's cold." She rubbed her arms. "I wanted to talk to you and see how you were faring."

He closed the window although the smell of smoke still lingered. "Why do you care about me?"

"Because everyone ..." She pressed her lips together and brushed a wet curl from her cheek. "You're a guest and ..."

"Yes?"

"Would you mind putting some clothes on?" she said.

"You came here, and I was—oh, never mind."

She cried out when he lifted the towel to put on a pair of breeches.

"I beg you!" she said.

"Don't look, for crying out loud!" He donned his dressing gown for good measure as well although he was still wet. "There." He tied the sash on the front tightly. "I'm decent."

She sat on the edge of the bed, her cheeks flaming crimson and her back straight. "I'm sorry about the carpet."

"It's yours. And I still don't understand what you're doing here." He folded his arms over his chest.

"I simply wanted to be friendly. That's all."

"Friendly at night? Sneaking into my bedroom alone? I wish I had more lady friends like you."

She shot him a glare. "I didn't sneak. Not really. The problem is that my parents forbade me to talk to you."

He nodded. "So you decided to disobey them for a nocturnal thrill."

She flushed a deeper shade. "No. I genuinely wanted to know how you were faring."

He closed the distance between them and loomed over her, annoyed that he was nothing but an entertainment for her.

"I have a theory. You wanted to talk with the ducal bastard again after your parents told you how deranged and dangerous I am and ordered you to stay away from me. Curiosity won, and you decided to take a look at me as if I were a circus freak, just to have something to gossip about with your friends."

"No." She shot up to her feet, ending up an inch from him. Her rosewood scent eluded the thick smell of smoke. "I ..."

She tottered on her feet, and he held her by waist before she fell again. "Careful."

She blushed a fierce red when she eyed his hands on her waist.

He released her. "What were you saying?"

"I felt sorry for you because the way my parents talked about you was so horrifying it made me wonder if you felt alone. They relegated you here, in a room at the end of the guest wing, forbidden to talk to us, and with no company. I didn't think it was a compassionate manner to welcome you, and I wanted to show you that not everyone in this house was rude. Now move."

Still unsteady on her legs, she bumped into him when she

brushed past him. He was caught off guard, and he nearly lost his balance on his slippery, wet feet.

He suppressed a groan of pain as he hit the bedpost with his back and hurt a sore spot.

"I'm sorry." She withdrew her hands. "Did I hurt you?"

"It's nothing. You'd better leave now."

"But—"

"Leave. Please. For the sake of both of us." He stepped aside as she brushed past him.

She reluctantly did as told, casting glances at him.

"It was a pleasure meeting you." He couldn't completely remove the sarcasm from his voice.

She paused at the door. "I've never thought you were a curiosity to sneer at. But you obviously have."

She shut the door behind her, leaving him stunned but not in a terrible fashion.

He put his hands on his hips, surveying the disaster that hurricane girl had left behind. A burnt carpet, water everywhere, and the smell of smoke in the air.

And they said *he* was a menace.

four

ELIZABETH'S HEART GAVE a solid kick of sheer terror when she stared at her reflection in the mirror the next morning.

A large blue-and-black bruise marred her forehead, the afternoon gown she'd worn to see Christopher was still wet and wrinkled, and a tiny burn darkened the hem of the skirt.

How was she going to explain the bruise and the ruined gown to her parents? More importantly, how was she going to explain to herself the riot of emotions that had bothered her since last night?

The image of Christopher in the bathtub with his eyes closed, his head reclined, his strong neck exposed, and his slick, wet skin would remain forever in her memories even if she didn't want it to. No, she didn't want a half-naked Christopher in her mind, but he had been, quite vividly so, and there was little she could do.

He was handsome, no point in denying that, but as for his attitude, she wasn't sure how she felt. Not to mention the questionable reason he'd been expelled from school. And once again, she hadn't learnt anything about him.

The maid entered, carrying a pile of fresh linens. She frowned at the discarded afternoon dress. "Your gown is wet, my lady."

"Yes, I dropped a glass of water on it last night." Elizabeth sat at her vanity.

The maid's eyebrows knit together likely because she'd brushed the gown and put it aside in the armoire yesterday before Elizabeth had taken it out again.

"I'll take care of it. What happened to you, my lady?" the maid asked, standing behind her to comb her hair.

"I fell." That was true.

"Heavens." The maid frowned again, staring at the bruise. "It must have been a painful fall."

"Quite painful." And embarrassing. Not her finest moment. "Will the face powder cover it?"

"We can try. I can style your hair in a different way as well."

"Great."

Not so great.

Half an hour later, after breakfast, she couldn't convince her mother to stop asking questions about the bruise. Layers of face powder and a curtain of curls weren't enough to deceive Mother's keen gaze. The sunlight on that crisp morning didn't help either.

"I don't understand how you got such a large bruise," Mother said for the umpteenth time.

Elizabeth rubbed her arms, walking along the path in the garden. Frost covered the ground, making it slippery and threatening to cause her to trip again, and she didn't need another bruise.

"It's chilly," she said. "Can't we forgo our morning walk today? The air is freezing, and it might start snowing again."

"Why didn't you call for help? That bruise is too big for a simple fall. You must have hit your head hard enough to have lost consciousness. And you're quite pale."

Botheration. "The bruise didn't seem that terrible last night."

Mother shook her head. "I will send for the physician." She narrowed her gaze, staring at a point behind Elizabeth. "There he is."

"The physician? That was quick."

Mother strode past her, heading towards the cypress trees where Christopher sat on a sunny bench. Elizabeth's pulse sped up as she followed her mother. Try as she might not to think of him, another vision of him in the bathtub came unbidden to her mind. To her defence, she had never, ever seen a shirtless man. So, of course, she found the novelty interesting. All normal.

"Countess." He rose when Mother stopped in front of him. He gave a quick bow as if performing it only because he had to.

Elizabeth gave him a curt nod, her knees weakening. Last night, she should have told him not to mention anything to her parents.

"I need a word," Mother said. "The maid told me she found the Hessian carpet in your room half burnt and the floor wet. Would you care to give me an explanation?"

Elizabeth trapped her bottom lip between her teeth to stop it from quivering. That was it. She would have to confess to her stupid decision to see him last night and face the consequences, which would likely be living in Spencer Hall for the rest of the year, studying mediaeval wars.

Christopher didn't flinch. "I accidentally dropped a candle but put out the fire immediately after."

He lied for her. She hadn't expected that. "But—"

"Why didn't you call a footman?" Mother said.

He shrugged. "It didn't seem necessary, my lady."

"So it was an accident." Mother's tone lacked kindness but made up for it with suspicion.

Elizabeth had never heard her mother using that sharp, accusatory tone, not even with a servant.

"Don't you believe me, my lady?" He lifted his chin, his icy blue eyes glinting.

"I simply find it difficult to believe it's all a coincidence."

"I don't understand."

Mother stepped in front of her as if to protect her. "You're forced to leave your school because ... of certain circumstances, and the next thing that happens, a carpet in my house catches fire."

"I honestly don't see the connection."

Mother glowered. "Then allow me to be blunt. Are you an arsonist in addition to being a thief?"

His glacial eyes turned colder. The temperature must have dropped a few degrees. "I'm not a thief, much less an arsonist. It was an accident."

"I'm not sure I believe you," Mother said.

"You're entitled to your absolutely wrong opinion," he gritted out.

Mother gasped. "How dare you!"

Elizabeth couldn't let him take the blame for something he hadn't done. His situation in her house was already precarious without the added crime.

She cleared her throat. "Actually—"

"Elizabeth," Mother said, raising a commanding finger. "Please don't get involved."

"But I already am. See, I—"

"You should listen to your mother." He shook his head.

"Do not tell my daughter what she should or shouldn't do!" Mother said.

He shrugged. "I wouldn't dare. Besides, she seems perfectly capable of making her own decisions."

"The way you speak to my daughter is outrageous." Mother gripped Elizabeth's hand. "I hope that no more *accidents* will happen while you're staying here, Blackwood."

"I hope the same, my lady." He bowed, keeping his gaze on Elizabeth and silently warning her.

"And refrain from taking promenades in the garden from now on. If you need a walk, go to the forest. Let's go." Mother led her away. "Honestly."

"Mother, that's harsh." She was ignored. She glanced behind

her. He was still staring at her. "Perhaps he told the truth, and it was an accident."

Mother didn't slow her pace until they were inside the house. "I told you not to get involved with him. Don't intervene ever again. Don't encourage him. Don't stand close to him. His kind can't help itself."

"What do you mean?"

Mother was flustered. "Many experts claim illegitimate sons are particularly prone to attacking young girls, being violent, and lying. And they have this ... inappropriate appetite that never diminishes, if you understand what I mean. Give him the opportunity, and he'll attack you."

"Nonsense."

"It's in the illegitimate sons' nature. They can't help themselves. And he's also an arsonist."

"But I started the fire," she blabbered out, tired of all the poppycock.

Mother handed her coat to the maid absentmindedly. "Your attempt at helping him is pathetic, and, quite frankly, I don't understand it. Go upstairs. Your class is about to start."

"Mother, I'm serious." Pointless conversation. "Mother!"

Mother had gone already, firing orders to the housekeeper.

Before going upstairs, Elizabeth glanced out of the window. Christopher was sitting with his shoulders hunched and his elbows propped on his knees. She couldn't see his face, but a sense of loneliness radiated from him.

He might pretend he didn't care about what Mother had said, but being continuously mistreated must take a toll on him. And if he were as dangerous as Mother believed, he would have attacked her last night. He'd had plenty of time and the opportunity to do so. Instead, he'd been kind to her. And he'd lied to protect her.

Finally, she learnt something about him. He was kind and honourable.

If focusing on history had been hard yesterday, it was twice as hard that day.

Guilt gnawed at Elizabeth. She'd tried to tell the truth, but she couldn't deny her cowardice had played a part in her failure at being believed. The least she could do was to apologise to Christopher and thank him for having covered her mistake.

"Elizabeth, you aren't listening," Miss Martin said, sitting in front of her.

"Apologies." She caressed the bruise.

A bump had also swollen, and the skin was sensitive to the touch.

Miss Martin lowered the book. "Is it the bruise? Goodness, you must have hit your head really hard."

"I did. My head hurts, to be honest."

"Why don't you lie down? We'll resume later if you feel well enough, or tomorrow."

"Thank you, Miss Martin. I need some rest." After she talked to Christopher.

Elizabeth headed straight to the guest wing. Her breath turned into mist in the long, wide corridor, and the sound of her footsteps echoed off the domed ceiling. She paused in front of a frosted window. In the garden, snowflakes drifted down slowly.

She rubbed her cold hands. The guest wing had a different climate than the rest of the house. The marble floor didn't help keep the warmth, and with only one room occupied, the servants hadn't lit any fireplaces.

She knocked on Christopher's door. "Christopher? It's me, Elizabeth. May I come in?"

No reply. She inched the door open. Surely, after what had happened between them, he wouldn't be surprised if she entered uninvited. But the bedroom was empty.

She grimaced at the dark stain on the floor. The flames had marred the wooden planks as a permanent reminder of her shock at seeing Christopher in the bathtub. The study was empty as well.

Since he wasn't exactly welcome in the house, he had to be outside. She looked out of the window. The snow was falling faster as the wind picked up speed, shaking the trees. But through the white flakes, she spotted Christopher in his long dark coat, heading towards the path that led to the village. She wouldn't have a better opportunity to talk to him. They'd be alone, and officially, she was in her room.

After quickly grabbing her scarf and coat, she avoided the main corridor to exit from a French window opening to the garden. She sped up once the evergreen hedges blocked the view of the house, but the snow made the ground slippery.

After she rounded a corner, the path to the village stretched in front of her, white, silent, and empty. With his long legs, he must have walked beyond the curve of the road.

Clenching the lapels of her coat, she soldiered on. She was getting more distant from the house than she'd planned, but she needed to see him.

The strong wind made it difficult to keep her eyes open, and the snow was falling in earnest now, thick white sheets that blurred the view. Her feet were numb, and she was halfway to the village by the time she spotted a lonely dark figure ahead. She forced her legs to speed up, but he'd taken a lateral path that headed north towards the small lake where the sheep gathered in summer. If he wasn't heading to the village, where then?

"Christopher!" She waved a gloved hand, running towards him. "Christopher."

He stopped in the middle of the snowed path and spun towards to face her. She sped up in his direction.

The snow and wind agreed with him. The white expanse exalted the glacial blue of his eyes and turned his blond hair into pure silver, and the wind ruffled his tendrils. But his expression wasn't exactly friendly. The closer she came to him, the harder he frowned.

"You." He shoved his hands into his pockets. "What is it now?"

She breathed hard. Each inhale brought icy air down to her lungs. "No need to be so sour. I want to talk to you."

"Do your parents know you're here?"

"No. They think I'm resting in my bedroom."

"Then you should leave." He turned around and marched on.

"Wait." She had to stride to keep up with him. "I'll return to the house, but I want to apologise for last night and to thank you for protecting me. Why did you lie?"

He stopped walking. "My reputation is already terrible. There was no need to ruin yours as well."

"But now my parents believe you set our carpet on fire."

"I'm the ducal bastard. Everyone thinks I'm a rogue anyway, no matter what I do."

She cringed. "Would you please stop saying that word? It upsets me."

He shot her a glare. "Apologies if I'm hurting your feelings."

She rolled her eyes. "I mean, that word is insulting towards you as well."

"I'm a bastard. I'm not scared of a word. Besides, everyone keeps saying it."

"If you really have to be so crass, then do go on."

"Fine." He held up a hand. "I appreciate your concern, but you needn't worry about me."

The wind grew in strength, howling through the treetops. Snowflakes slapped her face, and she had to close her eyes against them. Goodness. Even the inside of her nostrils was frozen.

"Go home, Elizabeth," Christopher yelled over the wind. "The snowstorm is getting worse."

"Come with me."

"I need to go somewhere else first."

"It's freezing. In a moment, the path will be buried under the snow. You won't go far." Her teeth chattered, and tremors went up and down her back. Her legs were numb, too. "Let's go."

The tip of his nose was red, and his breath turned into fog that the wind slapped promptly away.

He gazed around, the gusts ruffling his hair. "You're wasting precious time."

"I won't go without you. Seriously. The temperature is dropping too fast. You'll freeze if you don't go home now."

His eyelashes were covered in frost. "All right. I'll come with you."

Except there wasn't anywhere to go. The wind was too strong. It was a force shoving Elizabeth back at each step, a freight train hitting her chest. The loud howling of the wind hissed in her ears.

The cold was paralysing, and the snow piled up too quickly on the ground for them to wade through it at a decent pace. She wasn't even sure if they were following the road.

She clenched the lapels of her coat together, but the freezing gusts of wind sneaked underneath her clothes anyway, stealing her warmth.

"Watch out!" Christopher grabbed her arm and pulled her back before a tall tree crashed down on the path, lifting a wall of fresh snow.

She closed her eyes as snow covered her and slipped under the collar of her shirt. A chilling trail went down her back. She didn't feel her lips, cheeks, and hands anymore.

"This weather isn't normal." He wrapped his arms around her, and she was too tired not to find the closeness comforting. "We'll never make it to Spencer Hall," he shouted over the wind. "My house is closer."

"Your house?"

"Come." He took her hand firmly and ploughed through the snow at a steady pace.

She couldn't see anything through the storm aside from his

back, and keeping her eyes fully open hurt. Even her tears were likely turning into ice.

He trudged wearily through the snow, pausing now and then, until they arrived at an old cottage. She couldn't see much of the place aside from a white wall and a diamond window. Still gripping her hand, he unlocked the front door using a key he produced from his pocket.

"Almost there." He led her inside and had to shoulder the door to shut it against the gale.

Complete darkness fell into the house. She didn't feel any difference in terms of temperature, and all the questions she meant to ask were frozen, too. At least the wind wasn't a problem anymore.

He stared at her with concern, holding her cold hand. "Let me light a fire."

five

CHRISTOPHER'S HANDS WOULDN'T stop shaking as he tried to light a match.

The wind battered against the shutters and the door as if wanting to bring down the whole house. Frost covered the windows, and everything he touched seemed carved out of ice, so cold it was.

Finally, the reassuring sizzling of a flame came from the tip of the match. He lit all the candles he found and a couple of oil lamps, granted they would last. Elizabeth shuddered in the middle of the room, so pale he worried she might pass out.

If he had to be honest, he feared they might both die. The snowstorm had arrived without warning and hit hard, and they might have been exposed to the cold for too long, surely enough to develop pneumonia, and he wasn't sure they would get warm enough in the cottage.

When he'd planned to spend some time in the cottage the duke had bought for his late mother, he hadn't thought he'd need the place so desperately.

The draughts caused the candlelight to quiver as he placed a few cobweb-covered logs in the fireplace. Every time he flexed his fingers, stings pierced them. Thank goodness the duke always made sure the cottage was stocked with wooden logs and food supplies.

The wood seemed too damp for the fire to catch, but when the logs produced a fiery blaze, he exhaled in relief. If the wind was too strong, though, there might be back draughts, and smoke would fill the room. So many dangers.

"Come here," he said.

Elizabeth didn't move. She didn't even blink.

"Elizabeth." He held her by the shoulders and sat her on the worn sofa in front of the fire. "How are your feet?" He rubbed her arms, brushing iced snow from her coat.

"Co-cold." Her lips had a blue hue he didn't like.

"I'll boil some water in a moment." He rose to search the house for dry clothes and blankets. "You need to change into something dry."

She didn't nod or give him any signs of having heard him.

He searched the room that had once been his bedroom where he kept spare clothes. Instead, his mother's belongings were reduced to a couple of gowns and shawls. The wardrobe held plenty of blankets, but the bedroom was so cold that black ice caked the floor.

He gathered every quilt and warm and dry piece of clothing he found and rushed back to the sitting room. The blazing log fire slowly spread warmth through the room.

He dropped the clothes on the armchair. "You must change. Our clothes are wet and frozen."

"Y-yes."

"I'll change in the other room. Don't worry."

It took him a couple of attempts to unbutton his coat and jacket. His fingers felt like clumsy sausages—swollen, numb, and stiff. His shirt was wet, and his socks had ice on the top. There was no relief when he slid on the dry clothes, not at first at least. The fabric was a slab of itchy ice. No sound came from the other room.

"Elizabeth, are you all right?" He walked into the sitting room, keeping his gaze low in case she wasn't dressed yet.

"I can't unbutton my shirt. My fingers hurt."

"I'll help you if you want."

"Yes." She was sitting on the sofa where he'd left her, fully clothed.

He faced her. She opened and closed her hands that didn't seem to work.

"May I?" he asked.

She nodded.

He crouched in front of her and undid her coat. Wet patches stained her shirt where the snow had melted under her coat. Slowly, he went through the tiny buttons. The little buggers were slippery, and his clumsy fingers couldn't hold them. Her breath felt cold on his skin. Bad sign.

He pulled it open, revealing the swells of her breasts and her pretty pink corset with hooks on the front.

"Can you manage from here?" he asked, hoping she said yes.

She shook her head.

"Right." He exhaled, pretending everything was fine and that he wasn't undressing the beautiful daughter of an earl. Hell, her parents would chop off his bollocks for that.

The only good thing about the embarrassing situation was that a little blush coloured her cheeks. Good. Her blood was flowing.

He unhooked the corset, accidentally brushing her breasts through her chemise in the process and cursing himself for that.

"Sorry. I didn't mean to touch you."

She shrugged, or maybe she just shivered.

He hated she might think he was despicable enough to take advantage of the situation.

When the corset was fully open, it sagged to her hips. He averted his gaze from the wet, flimsy fabric of her chemise sticking to her skin and hiding nothing.

"Can you do the rest?" he asked, staring at the rug, aware of the scent of her skin.

"Yes." Her voice sounded low.

Thank goodness.

He turned around to stoke the fire and add another log. The slow swish of fabric came from behind him as she got dressed.

"I've finished," she said.

When he turned towards her, he was relieved to find her fully covered.

He brought the sofa closer to the fire while she hugged herself. She disappeared inside his old jacket and trousers, quivering.

"You'll feel better in a moment," he said, hoping he sounded confident. He draped a blanket around her shoulders.

"Th-thank you."

"I'll brew some tea."

The wind didn't stop hammering against the windows as he searched the kitchen for supplies. Tea, dried meat, nuts. Almost a feast.

He put the kettle on the fire in the hearth, keeping an eye on Elizabeth. She was too pale and trembled too much.

"May I hold you?" he asked. "You'll get warm faster."

Another blush. "Yes."

"I won't do anything else with my hands." *Crap.* He had no idea how a gentleman would behave in a situation like that or what he should say. "I mean, I'm not going to ... do those things ... that people ..." *Shut up.* "You know."

A little crease appeared between her eyebrows. "It's all right."

He didn't say anything. He'd already talked too much. Besides, since when was he such a bumbling idiot when it came to talking about tumbles? His words were all over the place. He blamed the cold.

They huddled close to each other on the sofa once the tea was ready. His hands thawed as he held the warm cup, and with the thawing came the pain of dozens of invisible needles pricking his skin. The flames sizzled and swayed when a particularly strong gust of wind struck the house.

The orange light of the fire reflected in her warm eyes, igniting them with gold. She had lovely eyes, expressive and captivating. Why he was noticing that detail now, he had no idea.

"Better?" he asked.

She nodded. "Every inch of my body hurts, but my fingers and feet aren't numb anymore. What's this place?"

"It's my mother's cottage." He wrapped a few blankets around them and pulled her closer. She gazed up at him but didn't protest. "She died years ago." The sting of pain whenever he talked about her stabbed him more fiercely than usual. "The duke bought it for her after she had me. Sometimes he comes here even now just to wander from room to room, remembering her."

"Do you come here often?"

"Not really. She died when I was eleven, and from that moment, Father found me one accommodation after another until I started going to Eton. Because of his visits, it's kept supplied with wood and food. I guess I can't complain about that."

"Without this place, I'm not sure we would have survived." She jolted when the wind caused a shutter to rattle. "I can't believe the weather changed so quickly."

Slowly, her warmth reached his body.

"I don't think the storm is going to pass any time soon," he said.

She sagged against him. "My parents must be worried."

He rubbed her arm under the blanket. "We'll see what happens in the morning. If we're lucky, this bloody wind will stop through the night."

She straightened, alarmed. "Do you want to spend the night here?"

"No, absolutely not." He feigned outrage. "I was thinking about trekking through the thick snow in the dark with the wind at one hundred miles per hour and the temperature dropping well below zero. Be my guest."

A little smile played on her lips. "No, thanks. I've had enough snow and cold for a lifetime. I meant ..." She shifted her position but didn't inch away from him. "Do you want to spend the night here on this sofa? Together? Alone?"

"We can try to invite someone. I'm not sure they'll come though."

She exhaled. "I'm serious, and you're being uncooperative." She looked adorable when she grew frustrated.

"I apologise." He held up a hand because she was right, but being an ass was the best way to reduce the tension and the worry of the moment and to distract himself from her presence. "This spot is the warmest in the house, and propriety is the last thing we should care about. As far as I'm concerned, this situation never happened. I didn't meet you on the path. You've never been here. You spent the night in another shelter, and I give you my word I'll be a gentleman, despite the fact I'm not a gentleman and I'll never be one."

"You're too harsh on yourself."

"It's not me. How do you think people react when they learn who I am?"

She shuddered against him, and he caught a whiff of her rose-wood scent. "How does the duke treat you?"

"You aren't going to repeat anything I say to anyone, are you?"

She lifted her large, trusting eyes to him. They made him uncomfortable in some way he couldn't describe. "I won't say a word. Besides, to whom? This conversation never happened."

The blanket slid down her shoulder, and he pulled it up to cover it.

"Good point." He took a deep breath. "My father took good care of my mother and me. He really loved my mother, and I can't say he mistreated me, quite the opposite. He's always wanted to be present in my life, always to be close to me. But our relationship isn't an easy one."

"Why?"

He hesitated before answering. He'd never talked about his father to anyone. Pearce didn't count. They mostly shouted at each other anyway and disagreed wholeheartedly on how their father should behave towards him.

"I think my father suffers from my unfortunate situation more than I do."

"What do you mean?" She sneezed and rubbed her bare feet. "Sorry."

"Bless you." After putting his mug on the low table, he took one of her cold feet and massaged it. "Your toes are still cold and red."

"You don't have to do this," she whispered, going still.

"I know." He checked there were no signs of frostbite. "Does it make you uncomfortable?" He stopped touching her.

She flushed, her eyes growing wider. "No. It's nice."

"And important for your toes. They're too red."

A moment of silence stretched between them, but he kept pressing his thumbs into the sole of her foot and rubbing her toes until they were warm.

"No one has ever done that to me," she said, watching his every move.

"Good. It means you've never risked dying in a snowstorm before." He smiled.

She smiled back. "What were you saying?"

"My father wants nothing more than to introduce me as his son to the whole world, take me to his house as an official member of the family, and tell everyone I'm his son, claim me, which is impossible. For starters, the duchess would never allow it, and to be honest, I'm not sure I want that, either. I came to accept who I am, to accept the fact I'll never have a proper family, and that I'll always carry the origin of my birth as a disease. I'm all right with that. I was lucky to have my mother. We were happy together. But Father can't find peace. I guess because he loved my mother so much."

"And you. He must love you very much as well."

"I don't know if it's love or a sense of duty combined with a good dose of guilt. But yes, he protects me fiercely, and I appreciate that. But after my mama died, I was shipped from one house to another because Father couldn't find a proper place for me. I told him I didn't care where I lived and that I could be on my own, but he wished to keep me close."

He moved her feet away from his lap to stoke the fire and not let her see the turmoil bothering him.

You're wonderful. His father often told him that, but he didn't believe it.

"Does your brother know the truth?" she asked.

"Pearce." He huffed, adding another log. "He does. Besides, the resemblance among us three is astonishing. Father tried more than once to get us close, unsuccessfully so. It's difficult to become friends with someone who calls you a disgrace and a waste of space. Pearce is convinced Father favours me in everything and that he loves me more than he loves him. Rubbish. Pearce is the duke's only heir. He has everything he wants and more."

She opened the blankets to welcome him when he sat on the sofa again, and the gesture felt somewhat too intimate. "But your brother likely wants something else from your father, not only the title."

"He can enjoy Father's company and attention whenever he wants. I have to be content with the scraps Father can offer and to see him in secret. No one would dare call Pearce names."

"I've met your brother several times, but I can't say I know him well. We didn't speak of personal matters. He might be jealous of the love your father feels for you."

"His problem, not mine. I don't understand what he wants. He has everything. He doesn't have to endure the scorn or the beatings—"

"The beatings?" She straightened. "What do you mean?"

He pondered if telling her the truth or not. In for a penny ..." Eton's headmaster has old-fashioned rules when it comes to disciplinary practices. He believes that physical punishments strengthen the will of a student."

She closed her hand around his, causing his heart to stutter. "Does your father know?"

"I've never told him. I want to deal with the situation myself without complaining about every little thing that happens to me."

"Christopher, this isn't a little thing. Your headmaster beat you. It's awful."

"Don't pity me. Please don't. I must learn to face problems on my own because Father can't always protect me. My life already causes him too much trouble."

"He seems happy to take care of you."

"I don't want him to worry about me."

"You don't want anyone to worry about you, but those who care for you will always worry." She rested her head on his shoulder in a familiar way that made him smile for some reason. "I'm sorry for the pain you have to endure."

He didn't know what to say. It was the first time someone had shown compassion and understanding towards him. Shocking.

"You deserve love, Christopher," she whispered, leaning against him.

Again, he didn't know what to say, so he only stroked her arm to keep her warm.

The gale howled and shook the house, sending a chill down his spine as the roof groaned. He wouldn't be surprised if it cracked open and collapsed.

Snow drifted inside the sitting room from underneath the

front door, but Elizabeth didn't seem to share his concerns; she curled up next to him and closed her eyes. He stroked her hair as her soft breath fanned on his neck. Her words echoed in his mind.

Pearce had no right to be jealous. Pearce had no idea what kind of hell Christopher lived in.

six

THE CONSTANT NOISE of the storm woke Elizabeth up.

The grey light of dawn crept along the floor, and the dying embers glowed in the fireplace, casting an orange halo on Christopher's hands. The cushion under her cheek smelt of mould and burnt wood, tickling her senses. His strong arms were wrapped around her in a protective hold, and her back touched his warm chest. She could feel its rhythmic rise and fall.

Finally, she wasn't cold or numb. Quite the opposite. With Christopher's body pressed against hers, she felt warm and safe, which was surprising, considering she barely knew him. No, that wasn't correct. After yesterday, she knew him a lot better. He was kind, honourable, and very lonely. He believed he didn't deserve anyone's compassion, and that worried her. He must have received only scorn to believe something so horrible.

The gale hadn't stopped through the night. It was like a monster pounding its way through the walls, shutters, and door. She removed his arm from around her waist as gently as possible, but he jolted awake.

"What is it?" he asked, pulling her closer again in a vice-like grip.

"I want to look outside. The wind is still blowing."

He slid out of the covers, and she missed his warmth immediately.

"Let's see." He pulled open the curtains.

But there wasn't much to see. The snowstorm raged at full capacity. Snowdrifts a few feet tall rose from every corner. Just looking at the snow-covered view and the grey sky caused her stomach to churn with worry.

The landscape was unrecognisable—an endless white expanse battered by the gale.

"Bloody hell." He drew the curtains closed. "We can't leave if the storm is blowing."

She sat upright, pulling up the blankets. "My parents. They must be sick with worry. I didn't even leave a message."

He knelt in front of the fireplace to add a new log and stoke the fire. "If the wind slows down, I'll try to go out to get help."

"I'm not sure that is a good idea." Her stomach gave a roar of hunger that broke the moment.

He showed a charming, lopsided smile framed by his dishevelled hair. "Hungry? I'm starving. There should be something in the pantry. Come."

When he took her hand, she couldn't ignore the little flutter in her chest. So silly of her.

Holding her hand, he led her to the small kitchen. Dust covered the countertop, and a cobweb hung over the stove like old laundry. But the room had a cosy, warm style she appreciated. Her breath turned into mist as she followed him.

He opened the pantry. "Honey. The only food that never expires."

"Really?"

"Archaeologists found jars of edible honey in ancient tombs. Then we have potted meat, dried apricots, and nuts."

"I'd eat anything." She put a hand on her rumbling stomach.

They set the low table in front of the fireplace next to their still-damp clothes. In the few minutes she'd spent in the kitchen, her fingertips had become numb. The wind kept pummelling the house as they shared their meal in silence, well aside from the howl of the wind.

He poured her a cup of tea. The leaves were a bit stale, and their aroma wasn't as strong as it should be, but the tea was hot and with a generous spoonful of honey, it was perfect.

She couldn't help but spy on his profile. The light of the fire lit his blond hair with golden hues, but the glow didn't make him look angelic. Quite the opposite. His strong jaw and sharp cheekbones were too male for that. He was handsome in a rough, harsh fashion, and his ice-blue eyes added a layer of menace to his looks.

He glanced at the completely frosted window. "This town is nearly empty in winter. Don't you feel lonely?"

She held the cup with both hands and sipped, tasting the honey on her tongue. "Now that my brothers and sisters are all married and live somewhere else, yes, Spencer Hall is lonely. And boring. I promise, sometimes I'm so bored that the grass watches me grow."

He burst out laughing. She liked the sound of his laugh. It was honest and full.

"But we don't spend the whole year here," she said. "We come to Spencer Hall only when my father has work to do on his estate, and we usually don't stay for longer than a month. In summer, the manors close to us are crowded with people. Mother and I always attend every event in the town hall."

"Are your neighbours your friends?" He stuffed his mouth with a generous dose of potted meat.

"They used to be." She stared at her cup of tea, not sure she wanted to talk about the disaster of a few summers ago.

"What happened?"

She chewed a corner of her mouth. "You'll think I'm an idiot."

He touched her hand, and the calluses on the pads of his fingers scratched her skin. "I'm not going to tell anyone or judge you. You know my biggest secret. So tell me everything."

She cleared her throat. "Well, a couple of years ago, in summer, there was a competition in the town hall on general knowledge. The judges would ask the competitors questions on history, geography, and literature, all subjects I notoriously don't excel in."

"And what happened?" he prompted when she didn't add anything.

"I won."

He nodded. "I see. The others became jealous of your success."

"No, not really." She took a deep breath. "Actually, I cheated," she said in a low voice.

He paused sipping his tea. "How?"

"It was a case of opportunity meets need. By chance, I happened to find the list of questions the judges were going to ask. I didn't want to make a fool out of myself during the competition, so I quickly copied a handful of them and spent an entire night researching the answers before the competition. I was lucky. The judges asked several questions I'd copied."

He whistled. "I'm impressed. You memorised all the answers."

"Er ... no. I mostly copied them in tiny pieces of papers I hid in my skirt. Not that I understood half of the answers, but I've never been good at history or geography. I prefer algebra and numbers to strings of facts and names to remember. But I cheated, and the other participants never forgave me although I was a child."

"Were you stripped of your victory?"

"No, there was no evidence of my cheating, but the others suspected the truth. Anyone who knows me is aware of my dislike for anything but mathematics." The memory of those heated conversations with her former friends haunted her. "The arguments with one of my friends in particular, Rebecca, became quite ugly. She said she knew I cheated because I was too ignorant to answer those questions. In a way, I guess she was right. Even my governess was sceptical. Especially my governess."

"Why did you cheat then?" He stopped eating and focused on her only.

She trapped her bottom lip between her teeth to stop it from quivering. "Because I was tired of hearing I was too vapid, daft, or distracted to understand history, geography, and literature. Cheating was a stupid thing to do. Isn't that ironic? I think I proved the rumour right."

"Who told you that you're too daft?"

"My parents aren't happy with my marks. Aside from mathematics, I don't excel in anything else, and they don't consider numbers particularly useful for an earl's daughter. Poetry and history are the subjects they want me to excel in. But I can't memorise something that has no logic. Yet, Mother insists."

"Your parents have plans for you." He stared at his cup of tea. "Surely they want to see you married to a toff."

"That's what happened to my elder sisters, but would the subjects I excel in be important? I'm sure my future husband won't care about my preference for numbers." She pulled the blanket around her shoulders. "Anyway, my parents were disappointed to learn I cheated. The rumours became straight accusations, and I confessed and renounced the winning title. It wasn't enough though. Many people stopped talking to me anyway. The ironic thing is that I confirmed what everyone thought about me, that I'm too stupid to learn history."

"Rubbish. You aren't stupid because you dislike something." He closed his hand around hers. "I think you're brilliant."

When she'd first seen him, she'd found his eyes unforgiving and cold. They still held a certain diamond-like quality that intimidated her, but there was a vulnerability behind them she couldn't dismiss. His touch held kindness and the compassion that marked him as one of those people who had suffered a lot.

"You aren't as hard and dangerous as you want everyone to believe," she said.

She laced her fingers through his. After they'd spent the night huddled together, she guessed she could hold his hand.

His long eyelashes fluttered down. "What other defence do I have? I have no protection. No one looks after me. My father does everything he can, but even he can't protect me from the people's hate or from who I am. He's a duke with an aristocratic family and a status to keep, and being a bastard in that family isn't an easy life." He chuckled bitterly. "I think that, had I been the bastard son of a baronet, my life would have been easier. But a bloody duke? A duke is too close to royalty, and Father is very close to the queen."

The coldness in his eyes crumbled, showing all his vulnerability and his fear of being hurt. A phantom pain reached her heart, too.

"I don't want to sound awful, but I don't think your life would have been easier. But I can tell you this." She stroked his fingers in a gesture that was more intimate than she'd foreseen and that caused more sensations than she could bear. "You have me now. It's not much. I understand that. But you don't have to face a storm alone."

He flashed that quick, lopsided smile she started to like. "It is a lot. But shall I remind you I'm the reason you're stuck here? If you hadn't followed me, you'd be dry and warm at home with your family."

"It was my decision to search for you, and if I hadn't sneaked into your room and started a fire, there wouldn't have been any reason for me to apologise."

"We can play this game all day."

"Do you have anything better to do?" she asked.

He barked out a deep laugh. "I don't know. A fight?" He stretched out his arm towards the cushion, arching his brow.

"Oh, no." She snatched the cushion before he did and hit his shoulder.

"Hey!" He protected his head with his arms as she hit him. "It was my idea."

"There's only one cushion!"

He tugged at the cushion, but she didn't release it. A tug-of-war started, although she suspected he wasn't employing all his strength. She laughed so hard her belly hurt. He yanked at the cushion, and she didn't oppose enough resistance to fight back, getting dragged forwards by the momentum.

She fell on top of him, and suddenly the game wasn't funny anymore.

They'd spent the night snuggled up together. Their closeness wasn't anything new, but as she stretched on top of him, feeling his hard muscles tense, her pulse thundered in her ears. The position felt wrong and right at the same time.

She dipped her gaze to his bobbing Adam's apple and a vein ticking in his neck. The odd urge to kiss it almost overwhelmed her. She wondered how a kiss would taste. Hard and cold like his eyes, or warm and safe like his touch?

He sucked in a breath that reverberated through her.

He caressed her cheek with a light touch and parted his lips, but no word came out. It didn't matter though. His gentle stroke was worth an entire conversation.

She'd never cared for boys, but Christopher was different. He made her feel different. She leant against his hand, and he drew in another breath. His chest heaved, pressing against hers.

Where did this desire to kiss him come from? Had it always been inside her from the moment they'd met, lurking before springing out? Yielding to it seemed the only reasonable action, and she trusted logic more than anything else.

"You're so beautiful," he whispered so low she barely heard it.

She'd received compliments on her looks before, mostly from her parents, but the breathy, shy way he'd said it sounded real and touched her deeply at a visceral level. He meant every word, and his honesty was the best compliment ever.

The noise of the rattling shutters diminished, and the gale died down in a moment, like a candle that had been snuffed out. The deafening silence broke the spell between them.

"It's stopped," she said, moving off him.

He stared at her for a long moment before standing up. "Let's take a look."

He pulled the curtains apart. The landscape showed complete stillness. No wind, no swaying trees, and no snowflakes. A small avalanche filled the entry hall when he opened the front door, and the scent of pine resin tickled her nostrils. Freezing air swept the cottage.

"Damn." He shoved the snow aside and stuck his head out. "The wind truly stopped."

Wrapped in the blanket, she rose on her tiptoes to check the sky. Tiny, innocent-looking flakes floated down like white petals. The clouds still had that pearly-grey colour that promised more snow, and the unforgiving temperature hinted at simply a moment of calm before another gale. In fact, the floor was so cold she put on a pair of boots lying around. They were too big for her, but it was better than chilling her feet.

"I'm not sure it's a good sign," she said. "I think it's going to start all over again in a moment."

"I'm going to take advantage of the break anyway." He put on a pair of sturdy, dusty boots and grabbed his coat.

"You can't be serious." She pointed at the snowdrifts. "The wind will come back and you'll be frozen in a minute."

"I'll be as fast as possible to get some help. It's worth a try."

"No, it's not."

"We'll think about a plausible story later, but for now, I'll get help."

"I don't care about a plausible story." She took his hand. "Christopher, please listen. I've spent enough winters here to understand the weather. I can interpret the sky if you will. The storm will come back soon, and you won't be quick at all, plod-ding through the snow. You'll be dead."

He patted her shoulders. "I believe you, but I must take the risk."

"Risk of what? Dying? You won't have enough time to trudge through several feet of snow and arrive at Spencer Hall alive."

"I'll get help. If I keep to the woods, the snow won't be as thick as the main path."

He wasn't listening.

"You'll risk having a tree discharge its snow load over your head. You might break your neck or fall unconscious and then freeze to death."

"Keep the fire going."

"Tarnation!"

He wrapped the scarf around his face and braved the snow, which meant climbing over the snowdrift before reaching the fully covered drive.

He paused in the middle of the path to wave at her. "Don't worry. It'll be fine."

seven

ELIZABETH DIDN'T WANT to shut the door.

She had to watch Christopher for as long as possible. Maybe she was too pessimistic, but leaving at that moment was wrong. Lethally so.

Every instinct inside her screamed for him to stay. As much as she was desperate to send word to her parents, she didn't believe that was the right moment.

He took a side path that seemed clearer from the snow compared to the others, but something bothered her. She didn't know the area around the cottage as well as the moorland around Spencer Hall, but the small lake lay in that direction. Christopher was going to walk right over its frozen surface. Was it safe? How deep was the lake?

She first calculated the value of the "fifteen freezing days" constant. The thickness of the ice increased at a rate of one inch for every "fifteen freezing degree days" in a twenty-four-hour period. Approximating the value of the temperature, the result wasn't encouraging. Merely a couple of inches. And Christopher weighed around one hundred and eighty pounds plus the clothes. Not good. And Miss Martin said maths was useless.

The temperature was low enough to have frozen the surface of the lake almost completely, granted the lake wasn't too deep. Surely the ice wouldn't crack, would it?

She had barely time to think about that before he vanished from view as if sucked into the ground.

"Christopher!"

She darted out of the cottage as fast as she could. The blanket impeded her movements, so she dropped it. Her breath came out in harsh pants through the freezing air as she pushed her legs to their limit. The oversized clothes didn't help trek forwards.

Snow filled her large boots while she tried to follow his deep footprints in the snow. She snatched a thick stick likely from a broken tree branch.

At the edge of the pond, she crawled over the ice on her belly, wincing at the contact with the cold snow.

He was down to his shoulders in the icy water. No shout came out of him. The cold must have shocked him into silence.

She shuddered, almost losing her grip on the stick. "Grab this."

She stretched out the stick towards him, aware that unless he crept out of the hole himself, there was little she could do. But she had to try something.

Teeth chattering, he grabbed the stick with both hands, and she pulled as much as she could, inching backwards. His face was ashen, and his lips were the same colour as his eyes.

"You need to help me," she said. "I can't pull you out on my own. You must get to a horizontal position and kick your legs towards the edge."

He did as told, and between her pulling and his kicking, he crawled out of the icy hole.

"Don't stand up." She took his arm and tugged him towards her. "Roll with me until we are on the path."

A roar like thunder shattered the eerie silence. The gale resumed howling with a vengeance, like a monster just woken up from its sleep. The cold gusts froze the water on her clothes, her muscles contracted to the point of spasming, and pain slashed through her like blades. He couldn't have been faring better. He shivered so hard his hands moved out of control.

"Quick." Holding him up as best as she could, she slogged through the snow towards the house.

The wind pushed her from behind, lifting the fresh snow on the ground and carrying new flakes. She could barely see through the thick sheets of angry snowflakes. Christopher leant against her too heavily. Her knees buckled.

"So-sorry," he stammered.

They scrambled up to their feet and went on, half-dragging each other.

Shutting the door took her a few attempts, both because her hands were stiff with cold and because the wind was too strong. Christopher's silence worried her.

"We must be quick," she said, blinking the snow away from her eyes.

She half-shoved and half-pulled him towards the fire while starting to strip him of his wet clothes.

He helped, but his movements were slow and clumsy. She yanked his coat and jacket off, muttering under her breath as the scarf got in her way. His boots didn't cooperate. Their soaked, frozen laces couldn't be untied.

From the kitchen, she snatched a pair of scissors and cut the darned laces. Then it was a matter of ripping the drenched shirt, trousers, and ... everything else. Goosebumps swelled on his naked skin as his teeth chattered so hard she feared he might bite his tongue off.

As he turned around, his back was exposed to her, and the shock made her forget about the cold for a moment. Scars marred his skin, thick and ugly as if an animal had clawed him. She couldn't hold back a gasp. Someone must have whipped him hard, and the bruises from the recent beating were still vivid.

But it wasn't the moment for questions. If he died, she wouldn't be able to ask him anything.

"On the sofa." She helped him lie down and covered him with a few dry quilts.

Her wet clothes froze her body, so she added a log to the fire before stripping as well.

There was no time to think about her modesty or propriety, about right and wrong. He needed to get warm fast. Fully naked, she lay next to him, shivering at the contact with his cold skin.

She covered his arms and shoulders. "Why didn't you listen? When this is over, I'm going to give you a piece of my mind."

His breathing came shallow when he tried to speak, and he seemed to have trouble keeping his eyes open.

"Shush. Any excuses you're thinking of, they aren't worth it. It was a stupid idea. Save your energy."

The more she rubbed him, the warmer she got. The exercise thawed her limbs, but his temperature didn't rise, and he kept shuddering. He hadn't stayed in the water for long. His chances of recovering were good. They had to be. Dash it, she didn't know the probability of surviving after a full immersion in the freezing water, but he was well-built and healthy. There was hope.

"I'll make some tea."

She wrapped a blanket around herself and brewed a fresh pot of tea, casting glances at him. His strong quivers made him look as if he suffered from convulsions.

She had to help him drink it, but after the second cup, he stopped shivering and his lips regained their pink colour.

"Thank you," he whispered. "I've never been so cold in all my life."

"I told you not to go. Did you listen? No." Now that the scare had passed, a flare of anger threatened to come out. "When the wind calms down, we must wait to see if the weather is turning again. The colour of the sky needs to change from grey to blue before we venture out. We're safe here for now."

He nodded. "I know. I wanted to get help for you."

"I'm fine." Her voice cracked with the fear of having almost lost him. "Don't scare me like that again."

She hugged him. He rested his head on her chest, and they remained like that until she fell asleep.

The sun lowered by the time she woke up. She touched him, worried he might have died while she was sleeping, but he was warm again. Sighing in relief, she crushed him into a hug that woke him up.

"Elizabeth." His voice came muffled as his mouth was squashed against her shoulder. "... need to breathe."

"Better?" she asked when she released him.

"Much better." His voice sounded strong again.

Oddly enough, not an ounce of embarrassment bothered her. They were naked, holding each other with only a blanket separating them. Yet a sense of trust and safety spread through her.

She stroked his back, feeling the bumps of the scars on the skin. Heavens, the whipping must have been incredibly painful. She traced every ridge, wondering how old the scars were.

His breathing quickened as she explored his past with her fingers.

"What did they do to you?" she whispered.

She didn't expect an answer, but he spoke, his face buried in the crook of her neck as if seeking comfort.

"A group of Eton students attacked me in an alley with a whip one afternoon when we were in Windsor. They didn't want a bastard in their school." His words were hesitant, but their meaning wasn't. "Officially, I was a distant relative of the Duke of Grafton, a cousin who was recently orphaned, but some students didn't believe the tale, and my mother was a famous prostitute among the lords before retiring to become Father's mistress."

"Those students knew who your mother was?"

"Their fathers mostly. Or worse, their mothers. They resented women like my mother, considering them the cause of problems between their parents. Or they simply find the idea of the son of a prostitute repulsive. If anything, I was glad they'd taken their resentment out on me rather than on my mother."

A sob remained trapped in her throat. She held him more tightly.

"So I was attacked."

"Even by Pearce?"

"No. That was the only time he defended me. The only time he took care of me." He swallowed. "He intervened, stopping the beating and taking a few blows himself. Then he helped me go to the physician. He didn't argue with me until I recovered."

"That was decent of him." She kept caressing the scars. "Did those students cause your expulsion?"

"No. It was Pearce. He got angry when he learnt that Father wanted to take me to Paris with him for a few weeks and leave Pearce in London. He accused me of poisoning Father's mind against him. I told him I had nothing to do with Father's decision. It was a surprise for me as well. The argument became heated, and we almost punched each other. He complained to the headmaster, saying I stole his pocket watch. The headmaster didn't even ask me if the accusation was true."

She squeezed him. Only the blanket around her separated their bodies, but their souls were fully in contact. "I'm so sorry."

"Don't be." His voice cracked with so much pain she felt a pang in her chest.

He wrapped his arms around her, and she held him closer as the storm pounded against the cottage. His breathing came out in a slow rhythm, and his muscles loosened.

They fell asleep again on the sofa, hugging each other against the world.

eight

CHRISTOPHER WOKE UP warm but exhausted.

His body must have consumed all its energy to keep him alive and heat him up again. If Elizabeth hadn't pulled him out, he was certain he would have died.

Elizabeth. Brave, beautiful Elizabeth.

He swallowed hard. She was asleep in his arms. The blanket she'd used to cover herself had bunched around her hips between them, so their naked bodies pressed against each other. No barrier. No space. Just skin against skin.

Her skin was smooth and soft; it smelled of burnt wood, which wasn't unpleasant, and had an exquisite shade of pink.

He shouldn't touch her. He shouldn't be so close to her. Hell, he shouldn't even think of her.

He caressed the tangled mop of her hair and the curve of her back before stopping lest she think he was taking advantage of the situation, which he didn't want. But he couldn't deny a certain stirring at the close contact with her lovely shapes.

Her naked, spectacular breasts were pressed against his chest, and her leg coiled around his waist almost in a possessive fashion.

He loved how her lower back arched to give way to her

rounded arse. He loved how fierce and brave she was. How compassionate and sweet. He loved how she felt in his arms, how *he* felt with her in his arms.

She shifted, torturing him with the friction of her hips against him. A rosy nipple made an appearance, hardening in the cold air, and he couldn't gaze away. The temptation to rub it with his thumb to hear her moan was so strong his mouth grew dry.

They looked like two lovers who had fallen asleep after an intense tumble. That made him pause and slapped him back to reality. Both because he didn't want his body to react to his pleasant thoughts—thank goodness he was exhausted—and because he had to think about her reputation.

No one would ever know they'd spent these days locked up together. He was considered a liar, a thief, and an arsonist on a good day. He didn't want to be considered a defiler as well.

He pulled the cover up to cover her properly. No more peeking at her pretty nipple. Her soft breath feathered his neck, tickling his skin.

Since there wasn't much space, he placed his arm around her waist again, not to touch any inappropriate parts of her body, which brought them even closer. Soon, when the storm stopped, she'd return home, and he would never have the opportunity to hold her again. She'd find a husband, who had never been whipped or called names, and would forget about the boy she'd shared a few days with in a cottage. The idea pierced his chest like a blade, but in a way, that future was the safest for her.

The eerie howl of the wind and the crackling of the flames were the only sounds but in a comforting way. He wished that moment would stretch forever, that he could watch her sleep and share her heat with him for hours on end.

She stirred and opened her deep eyes, staring at him with a hint of surprise. He was surprised himself. He barely knew her. They'd confessed each other's secrets, and the forced closeness had sparked a fast intimacy, but at the same time, he was aware he shouldn't be naked with her on a sofa, hold her, or caress her. Or even wishing to protect her so fiercely. There was too much desire to be with her in that wish.

"How are you?" She cupped his cheek, and the touch of her soft hand melted his heart. "Your skin is warm."

On fire.

He swallowed a couple of times. "Much better. Just tired. The cold is exhausting me."

"I feel tired, too." She didn't withdraw her hand, and he didn't mind.

He couldn't remember the last time someone had taken such good care of him. His mama had been the last person. The only one. When Pearce had helped him after the beating, he'd simply sent for a physician, which was a lot, anyway. But he certainly hadn't spent time next to him, making sure he was all right.

And the occasional tumbles he had with those women who didn't care about his illegitimate status never showed any tenderness towards him. The physical exchange was for mutual pleasure. Nothing more.

The lack of kindness and intimacy had never bothered him—in fact, he'd appreciated it—until now. Maybe it was the absurd situation he was in, but Elizabeth made him long for more, for a deeper connection, for lazy mornings while lying naked on a sofa, for slow caresses.

Her compassion made him realise what was missing in his life. Somehow, it hurt. Deeply. Intimately.

Ignorance is bliss. It was true.

He shouldn't have tasted her kindness. Now he wanted to get drunk with it. He was addicted to it.

She caressed his jaw, and he couldn't pretend the gesture was merely to ascertain his temperature.

"I've never been more scared in my whole life than when I saw you drop in that lake," she said, stroking his cheek again.

"That makes two of us." He tilted his head, brushing her inner wrist with his lips.

A rush of heated energy went through him, warming him in a moment. Something flickered in her gaze, igniting her brandy-coloured eyes.

"What will happen to us?" she asked.

Oh, he knew what she meant.

He stopped her wandering hand by covering it with his. "If they don't find us, which is likely, we'll go to Spencer Hall separately. You need a believable story, so no one will suspect we were together. Is there a nearby shelter you could have used close to your house?"

The tip of her tongue darted out to run over her bottom lip, and he couldn't refrain himself from noticing it. He wanted to taste her lips and see if they were as soft as they looked.

"There's a small hunting lodge at the edge of the forest. My father and his friends use it when hunting. It has a stove and chopped wood. The gamekeeper keeps it well stocked. I think my parents will believe me if I tell them I stayed there."

"We didn't see each other. You left the house to get some fresh air when the storm hit. That's it. You don't know where I am."

She nodded, resting her head on his other arm. "I'm sorry we have to lie though."

"Well, we certainly can't tell anyone we lay naked on the same sofa and slept together." His voice had a quiver of sheer sadness he didn't know he could produce.

A flush crept over her cheeks. "No, we can't. I don't think I can even tell myself without blushing."

"Listen." He held her face because he wanted her full attention. "You saved my life. I'll never forget that. If the truth comes out, you'll blame me. Say what you have to say to protect yourself. Tell your parents I forced you to stay here with me. Tell them I threatened you. Whatever you need to say."

Another flame flashed across her eyes. "No! I can lie about where I was, but I can't lie about you. That's wrong."

"Everyone already has an opinion on me anyway. My reputation would remain unchanged. Why ruin yours? If I were a gentleman your parents respected, they'd ask me to marry you. But a bastard? They would never allow that, and you'd be branded as a trollop. Your life will become a nightmare. I won't allow that."

He reluctantly released her face only for her to hold his cheeks in both her hands, and he wanted to close his eyes, sink in her kindness, and forget the world.

"Stop. Let's survive this storm first. Then we'll ..." She fell silent, staring at him with too much intensity. "Do you think your father will make you leave Spencer Hall? Where will he take you?"

"I don't know."

"Will I see you again? In London, perhaps? We might meet there."

"Elizabeth." He lowered her hands. "You'll have a lovely, happy life, find a good husband, and have a family. Be loved and respected. That's your future."

"It sounds dreadful."

He laughed and hugged her.

She snuggled closer and rested her cheek on his chest.

"You'll be happy, Elizabeth. I promise."

They held each other with desperation, and even though she triggered a hunger he'd never experienced inside him, he wanted to just hold her and make sure no one would hurt her.

He kissed the top of her head before falling asleep again.

THE GALE DIED during the night, not without a fierce fight. It kicked and screamed before admitting defeat and vanishing. Christopher could tell because of the silence. No more thumping against the windows, howling wind, or hissing.

He disentangled himself from Elizabeth's arms to walk to the window. A shiny blue sky shone for miles overhead. The sun burned with all its mightiness as if apologising for its absence. He was almost sorry the storm had passed.

Elizabeth stretched out her arms over her head, yawning. The movement uncovered her breasts, and he caught a welcome glimpse of her taut nipples.

He averted his gaze, focusing on the view. "The sky is clear." His voice sounded all wrong as if he'd swallowed sand.

Wrapped in a blanket, Elizabeth walked over to him at the window. Her chestnut curls fell down around her waist, and he wanted to run his fingers through them and see how they caught the sunlight.

"Yes, I think the storm won't be back." She sounded sad, or maybe he imagined things.

"We should go."

She nodded. "We should."

Neither of them moved. He had to remind himself of all the valid reasons why staying with her was bad. There were plenty— her reputation, her worried parents, her safety. As for why staying with her was good, there was only one reason—he loved being with her.

He collected his clothes. "I'll change in the kitchen."

"Does it matter?" She put a hand on the knot holding her blanket up as if threatening to get naked in front of him.

He swallowed past the lump in his throat. "Yes, it does."

Because they were about to leave the cottage and return to the harsh reality, and because forcing himself not to kiss her was already an arduous task without seeing her naked.

He strode to the kitchen and changed, tugging and pulling at the fabric with too much strength, not caring about the chill. Curse him for being a bastard. He'd never hated his own birth as he did now, which was unfair to his mother. She'd done her best to raise him, and Father had always been present. Still, Christopher was and always would be a bastard.

Elizabeth wore her own clothes when he returned to the sitting room. Her skirt and coat were crumpled and stiff with mud, but she couldn't return home in his old jacket and trousers.

"Are you ready?" he asked, putting his gloves on.

She smoothed down her skirt. "No."

Neither was he.

The sunshine couldn't hide the fact the temperature was still low, and the blinding glare from the snow bothered his eyes. Not to mention that it took them two hours of trekking through the fresh snow to simply reach the road. Sweat soaked him, and he panted, his muscles burning.

They paused on a sunny patch, both breathless.

"Hell," he said among pants. "At this pace, it'll take us all day to reach Spencer Hall."

"Christopher." She paled, pointing at something in the snow.

He craned his neck to take a look. It was a frozen hand, blue and frosted, poking out of the white mantle. He dug into the snow, partially uncovering the person underneath, but there was no point.

"Don't look," he said.

"Too late." Her eyes widened in horror.

"Let's go." He turned her around and led her on. "It won't be the only one. We must keep going."

The body only fuelled his determination to get Elizabeth home. Along the way, they met more people who had frozen to death, collapsed roofs, fallen trees, and upturned carts and carriages. The storm had left a trail of devastation and despair behind it.

He plodded on to open a path in the snow, ignoring his tired legs. It was like shoving boulders uphill. Getting Elizabeth safely at home was the only thing that mattered.

"We can take turns," she said. "I can walk in front and open the path, so you can rest."

"No, I'm all right." He wasn't, but the frantic urge to keep her safe was stronger than his exhaustion.

He exhaled when Spencer Hall swept into view after a curve. He was wheezing, sweaty, and bloody tired, but it was worth it.

"You go," he said, releasing her hand.

She didn't move, her cheeks red with the exertion. "When are you coming?"

"Don't worry about me. I'll wait here for a while, then join you."

"You'll freeze."

"I'll keep moving. Go."

"Christopher—"

"Go. We're getting cold and—"

He didn't finish the sentence. She kissed him hard, pulling him down by the lapels of his coat. He didn't hesitate and kissed her back with sadness because, surely, that was their first and last kiss. The fatigue that had plagued him in the past days was gone. The kiss shot energy through him while also scaring him to death because leaving her would hurt ten times more now.

The kiss felt too good, too right, and too impossible. It'd taunt him for the rest of his miserable life, reminding him of what he could never have.

When she darted out her tongue to caress his lips, he had to break the kiss before it was too late, before he kissed her deeply and delivered his whole heart in her hands, never to see it again.

"Go. I'll see you later," he said in a curt tone.

"Don't wait too long. Please."

She went down the path that led to Spencer Hall, stopping to wave at him.

When she became a tiny dot next to the estate's front gate, he headed towards the village.

His body would recover from the snowstorm. His heart wouldn't.

nine

THE MOMENT ELIZABETH entered her house, burning tears streamed down her cheeks in a combination of happiness, exhaustion, and worry.

She'd left Christopher behind, which was overwhelming, but she couldn't deny the relief of being home. A maid cried out upon seeing her. Another maid helped her to the dining room, asking questions she didn't understand.

Her mother held her, crying as well. Her father crushed them both in a fierce hug. Then it was a blur of activities with the maids helping her get a warm bath and change her clothes.

After she'd changed into a fresh gown and her hair was dry, Elizabeth sagged into an armchair in front of the fire in her warm sitting room. No draughts sneaked through the windows. The thick walls kept the cold outside, and her clothes were dry and smelling of soap. All little things she hadn't noticed before.

The only concern was Christopher. Where was he?

"What happened to you, darling?" Mother tucked a blanket around her in the armchair.

"Miss Martin told us you retired to your bedroom because of a headache," Father said. "Then you disappeared and the storm hit."

She sipped her hot tea; it was rich and strong. "I needed a walk, so I left the house and didn't tell anyone because it was supposed to be a quick affair. But the storm hit without warning, and I found refuge in the hunting lodge at Stormy Tor."

She ended her story there. If her father had checked the lodge, her lie would be short-lived.

"Good thinking." Father sat on the sofa. "We didn't know what to do. The storm was too strong. I tried to come out and search for you, but I didn't go far."

"I'm glad you didn't. You could have died." As all those people frozen to death she'd seen.

"It was a nightmare, darling." Mother held her hand.

"Is anyone else missing?" she asked casually, sipping her tea.

Her parents exchanged a glance.

Father lowered his voice. "We don't know where Christopher is."

She feigned surprise although she did wonder where he was. A few hours had passed since she'd returned. He should be here by now.

"He left to go to the village and never returned. No one saw him." Father rubbed his brow. "The trains have stopped working. The roads are impassable. Many houses have crumbled. It's chaos. I was lucky to send a wire to the duke before the whole network collapsed. I'm not sure William received my message to inform him the boy was missing, though."

"Quiet," Mother whispered, glancing around. "He probably found shelter in the village, and he'll come back when he can. No need to worry."

But Elizabeth did worry.

Dusk fell quickly, covering the white expanse with starlight. The view was beautiful, but she wouldn't enjoy a snowy landscape as she'd used to before the storm. The temperature was dropping again, and Christopher hadn't returned.

She paced in her bedroom, her incredibly warm, comfortable,

and dry bedroom, wondering if he was warm enough or conscious. Perhaps the fall into the icy water and the trek through the snow had tired him more than he'd admitted, and the added walk and wait in the snow had weakened him to the point of exhaustion. He might have collapsed somewhere and frozen to death. Why had she listened to him?

She grabbed her thick dressing gown and hurried out of the bedroom. "Mother?" She knocked on her mother's door.

"What is it?" Mother flung the door open and put a hand on Elizabeth's cheek. "Do you feel sick?"

"Any news about Christopher?"

Mother shook her head, narrowing her gaze. "Your father sent Vickers and George to the village to search for him."

"I'm worried."

Mother eyed her as if searching for an injury. "Do you care about him that much?"

"I nearly froze to death in a hunting lodge. I saw dead people in the snow. I've seen what the storm did. Of course, I care. He must have been scared as much as I was, being alone out there."

"Well, there's nothing we can do about it. Go to bed." Mother waved her away. "When they find Christopher, I'll let you know."

"I want to go out and search for him."

"Don't be ridiculous." Mother took her arm and dragged her to her bedroom. "You almost died out there, and you wouldn't know where to search anyway. Let Vickers and George do their work. If you get lost, we'll have to search for you instead of him."

That was a good point, but worry was eating her from the inside out.

She flinched when Mother slammed the door shut. Going out alone at night wasn't the sensible thing to do, and she was weak, but she couldn't sleep in her safe bedroom, knowing he was out there.

Christopher wouldn't survive the night if he'd been too weak to carry on and fallen unconscious on the path. The images of the frozen limbs of those dead people tormented her. What if he needed her?

Enough. She'd wear her warmest clothes and find a footman who agreed to escort her. She had to search for Christopher, do something. She would start from the point where they'd separated and search for him from there.

She opened her armoire when the sound of a door shutting came. Loud voices echoed from the corridor. Footsteps thudded.

Dash it all. She slipped out of her room. A maid rushed down the corridor, and Elizabeth followed her.

"In the blue room," Mother said from the ground floor. "Quickly."

"Mother?"

Elizabeth sped up but skidded to a halt upon seeing Vickers and George holding up an unconscious Christopher by his arms. His head hung over his chest, and he was so pale she feared he didn't have any warmth left. The tips of his boots hit the steps as he was dragged up the stairs like a ragdoll.

She clamped her hands over her mouth.

"What are you doing here?" Mother pushed her towards her bedroom. "You're in your dressing gown."

She craned her neck to keep looking at him, but Vickers and George disappeared behind a corner. Then Mother tugged her into her bedroom and shut the door behind them.

"How is he?" she asked.

"Not well. They found him staggering on the path on his way here. He's extremely weak because of the cold. Vickers fears he might die."

A sharp pang sliced Elizabeth's chest open.

"I want to see him." She started to brush past her mother but didn't go far.

Mother seized her arm with surprising strength. "Absolutely not."

"Let me go." She shrugged herself free.

"You aren't leaving this room."

"I must see him." She sidestepped her mother who seized her arm again.

"What is the meaning of this nonsensical behaviour? You barely know him, and you aren't supposed to talk to him." Mother pulled her towards the bed. "I don't know what happened or why you care, but you aren't going to see that man ever again."

"He nearly died!"

"So what? No one will miss him. Go to bed."

"Mother—"

"Listen to me." Mother pointed a finger at her. "Stop this fuss. You're tired and weak. Go to sleep. That boy doesn't matter. He's no one."

But he did matter, and he was everything. She tried to make a dash for the door, but Mother was quicker.

Before exiting, Mother took the key and locked the door. The click sounded like thunder.

"Mother!"

Elizabeth thumped the door, hurting her fist. Hot tears stung her eyes. How could her own mother be so cruel? She slammed her hand on the door and screamed, but no one came. Exhaustion caught her until her punches became weak slaps and her throat hurt too much for her to even whisper.

She sagged on the floor, crying.

The important thing was that Christopher was home and safe. Almost.

If Christopher died, they would tell her, wouldn't they?

THE CHILL never really left Elizabeth, despite the fact her bedroom was more than warm. A night spent worrying about Christopher had left her tired, cold, and defeated.

In the early morning, when the flame-keeper maid unlocked the door to light the fire, she sat bolt upright on the bed.

"Is he alive?" she asked.

The woman jolted. "Who, my lady?"

"Mr. Blackwood."

"I don't know, my lady."

"Where did they take him?"

"I have no idea, my lady. Sorry." The maid kept her gaze on the fireplace until she finished scooping up the ashes and lighting the fire.

With the help of her personal maid, Elizabeth changed into a thick, high-necked dress—both because of the cold and because she didn't want an argument with her mother about low-necked gowns—and marched down the corridor where Christopher had been taken. But the bedrooms in that part of the house were empty. She searched the other corridor, but nothing. More empty rooms.

She headed for the dining room. The day had barely started, but anger simmered strong and fierce in her chest.

Mother was having breakfast alone at the pristine table with the white tablecloth and a steaming cup of tea. Porridge, eggs, kippers, and bacon. For some reason, the sight of that feast irked Elizabeth further.

"I demand to see him," she said.

"Is that the way to address me? Not even a good morning?" Mother paused eating her porridge. "And no, you can't see him."

"Did he die?" The breath rushed out of her mouth in a painful exhale.

"Good gracious." Mother put down her cup of tea with enough energy to spill a few drops. "I'm so tired of having this conversation. Why are you so worried about him?"

"Because he's our guest and a ..." She glanced at the maid serving at the table.

The urge to tell her mother she'd been locked in a cottage with Christopher during the storm almost made her confess everything. The only reason she stopped herself was because she didn't want to cause Christopher further trouble.

If the truth came out, her parents would order him to go away at best, and send for the police at worst. As he'd said, they would blame him the most.

"Mother, please," she whispered. "He deserves some compassion and is our responsibility. If something happens to him, the d—"

"Quiet." Mother rubbed her forehead. "He's alive and recovering. That's all you need to know."

"I want to see him."

Mother rose from the chair in one smooth movement. "No."

"Where is he?"

The slap stung Elizabeth's cheek, but the surprise hurt her more. Mother had never, ever raised a hand to strike her children. Elizabeth had never been slapped by anyone.

Mother shook with rage. "I don't know what has got into you, but your reputation can't be associated with that young man for any reason. It's already too dangerous having him here. The fact he went missing attracted too much attention to us without you behaving so irresponsibly."

Elizabeth put a hand on her cheek. "How could you?"

"He isn't simply illegitimate but a thief as well and the son of a fallen woman. He's been expelled from the most prestigious school in the country for thievery. His reputation is akin to that of a criminal. The last thing you need is to get close to him."

"He isn't a thief."

Mother glared at her, likely understanding Elizabeth's interest in Christopher was more than compassion. She waved dismissively. "Go back to your bedroom. You'll have your breakfast there."

Elizabeth strode towards the door but paused on the threshold. "I'm ashamed of being your daughter." She left before her mother could reply.

ELIZABETH DIDN'T KNOW what hurt the most: her cheek her mother had slapped or her heart. At least Christopher was safe. That was the only good thing about the past two days.

Alone in her bedroom, she stared at her cup of tea slowly getting colder. Her plate with ham and eggs lay untouched on the table.

After the awful conversation with her mother, Elizabeth had avoided her, having her meals in her bedroom and roaming the house in search of Christopher when possible. The anger had been replaced by sadness and a deep sense of bewilderment at her mother's behaviour. She'd experienced how illegitimate sons were discriminated against for a matter of hours, and she was already exhausted and disappointed. She couldn't imagine how tiring and frustrating it had to be for Christopher.

When a knock at the door came, she didn't glance up from her cup.

"My lady," the maid said, "Miss Norton is here to see you."

That got her attention. At least a visit would distract her, possibly not in a good way since Rebecca, daughter of Viscount Keadew, was one of those people who had been furious with her for having cheated at that stupid competition. Although it was nice of Rebecca to come here and visit Elizabeth.

Rebecca stepped inside the room, staring at her as someone would stare at a dangerous beast. Her auburn hair was styled in a complicated chignon more suitable for a fancy dinner party than an afternoon call.

"Elizabeth, sorry to come unannounced, but I heard you went missing. How are you?"

"Thank you for coming. I'm well now." Not really.

"My family and I were locked in the house during the storm, and it was awful. I can't imagine being outside." Rebecca took the chair in front of her. "Goodness, is that a bruise on your forehead?"

"I'm all right. It's an old bruise."

"Your mother told me you found shelter close to Stormy Tor."

She cleared her throat. "I stayed in my father's hunting lodge. It's well supplied, thank goodness."

"It must have been terrifying for you." Rebecca eyed the untouched breakfast. "I think I saw you three days ago from my window after the storm. You were heading to Spencer Hall. It was about two in the afternoon."

She perked up. Rebecca might have seen Christopher as well. "It was probably me."

"But if you'd found shelter in your father's hunting lodge, you would have come from the opposite direction, and I wouldn't have been able to see you."

"I took the easiest path to reach home. The less snowy one. I'm not entirely sure which route I took."

"But you must have walked for miles around the estate to come to Spencer Hall from the northern path. With the snow, it would have been too hard for you. How is that possible? It sounds odd to me."

Oh, no. She didn't have time or patience for accusations. "I don't know what to say."

Rebecca insisted. "But you couldn't have been at Stormy Tor. I don't understand how you managed to trek through the snow for miles."

"And I don't understand what you're implying, Rebecca." Elizabeth wasn't in the mood for polite conversations, or worse, hypocrisy. "Your visit sounds like an interrogation."

Rebecca flushed. "I simply wanted to make sure you were all right."

"It seems you doubt my story." Which was understandable

because everything Rebecca had said made sense, but Elizabeth had to protect Christopher.

"I was concerned. And I saw your servants coming and going from Spencer Hall for days."

Elizabeth frowned. Rebecca spent a lot of time at her window. "And?"

"Well, I wondered who else in your family was missing since obviously your servants were looking for someone else, and with all those carriages arriving after the road was cleared, I thought something important had happened."

"What carriages?" Only the physician had arrived to visit her, but she hadn't paid attention to the visitors, and her bedroom window didn't overlook the driveway.

Rebecca's silence implied she found the sudden activity at Spencer Hill odd. So did Elizabeth.

Rebecca hesitated before speaking. "I think you had visitors. Someone did come here. I've seen at least one travelling coach arrive. Don't you know?"

Likely, Rebecca had asked the same questions to Mother, who hadn't answered. Hence Rebecca's impromptu visit to Elizabeth.

"No, I didn't," she said. "I've spent a lot of time in my bedroom."

"I see. But no one else is missing, right?"

"No one."

"Not even that mysterious guest of yours?"

Dash it. "I'm not sure whom you're referring to."

"A blond man? Tall and with a dark coat?"

She feigned lack of surprise. "One of Father's friends, perhaps."

Rebecca's expression seemed to say, 'yes, sure.'

Elizabeth didn't add anything.

"Well," Rebecca said, standing up. "I'm sorry if I bothered you. I'm simply concerned about you."

And curious to know who had come to Spencer Hall.

"Thank you, Rebecca."

"I wish you well. Really." Rebecca paused at the door. "Just so you know, a man came out of the coach that arrived an hour ago. I hope everything is all right."

Elizabeth rubbed her aching forehead when Rebecca left. She hoped everything was all right, too.

ten

IF SOMEONE TOLD Christopher that he'd been run over by a freight train, he would easily believe them.

His whole body ached. His head throbbed, and sheer fatigue weakened him. On top of that, he hadn't seen Elizabeth since he'd returned to Spencer Hall, and every time he asked about her, he was met with shrugs and blank expressions.

He propped himself up on the bed, looking at the moorland from the window. The servants had moved him twice to two different bedrooms, and now he was confined in a cottage detached from the main house.

The snow hadn't melted an inch, but the people of the town had worked hard to clean up the roads and remove the fallen trees. He'd watched the progress from his bed.

Over two hundred people had died in the storm from the cold, or because the roofs of their houses had collapsed under the weight of the snow. The newspapers called the storm the *Great Blizzard*. The name sounded like the title of an adventurous novel while the reality had been a nightmare. Not completely a nightmare, at least for him, if he had to be honest.

The days he'd spent with Elizabeth had been the most peaceful of his life. If only he could see her, make sure she was all right.

After they'd gone separate ways, he'd planned to simply take a short walk to keep himself warm before going to Spencer Hall. But he'd come across a desperate woman asking for help because her husband had remained trapped in the collapsed barn.

He'd helped as best as he could to remove the logs and pull the man out, but afterwards, he'd been so exhausted that he'd fainted on his way to Spencer Hall. It'd been by chance that the footman and the groundskeeper had found him before he'd frozen to death.

The door opened, and a maid came into view. "You have a visitor, sir."

Elizabeth.

His pulse pounded faster, but it plunged back to a slog when his father entered the room. He'd dispensed with his expensive, fine suits and swapped them with thick, travelling clothes. Aside from that, he was the same imposing man with a natural, commanding aura that demanded attention. His blond hair, so similar to Christopher's, was greying at the temples, and dark circles bruised his blue eyes. An ageing, tired lion, but a lion, nonetheless.

After bobbing a curtsy, the maid left the room.

Father raked a concerned gaze over him. "Christopher."

Before Christopher could say anything, his father crushed him in a powerful hug that tasted of fear. It wasn't the first time Father had hugged him, but it was the first time Christopher had seen him scared and desperate. A quiver went through Father.

Christopher returned the hug, inhaling the familiar scent of tobacco and the minted shaving cream his father used.

"I was worried." Father released him and sat on the edge of the bed, searching his face. "How are you?"

"You didn't need to come here."

His expression hardened. "Is that the first thing you have to say?"

"I'm surprised to see you here."

"I had to come. I had to see you. Tell me how you are," Father said.

"Tired. The physician said I only need rest and food, but otherwise, I'm all right."

Physically. Emotionally, it was a completely different matter.

Father touched Christopher's head, cheeks, and shoulders as if needing to make sure his son was all right. "Where did you find shelter during the storm?"

"Mama's cottage."

Father's expression changed again, softening. "She protects you even now."

Their love for Mama was the strongest thing they had in common.

"I was eager to come," Father said in a low voice he rarely used. "I had to see for myself if you were all right. Charles sent me a wire to tell me you were missing. To come here, I changed trains three times and hired a horse sleigh. Many roads are impassable, and many railways aren't clear yet. Hours of waiting without knowing if you were alive or dead."

"I'm all right, Father. Thank you for coming. I'm happy to see you."

Thick with emotion, his low tone matched Father's. Perhaps they had more things in common than he wanted to admit.

Father hugged him again. It was a gentle hug that caused an ache in Christopher's chest. The people he cared about weren't allowed to be with him. Father, like Elizabeth, couldn't show his affection for Christopher publicly.

"What happened in Eton?" The question didn't lack kindness. "I can't believe you stole from Pearce."

Damn. Christopher didn't want to lie to his father, nor did he want Father to punish Pearce and have an argument with him, and he was too damn tired to talk about Pearce.

"I'd rather forget the whole incident."

Father pressed his lips in a grim line. "Pearce lied, didn't he? And the headmaster believed him."

"It doesn't matter."

"It does." Father clenched a fist, the fatigue vanishing from his face. "You'll get back to Eton. I promise. And Pearce will receive the punishment he deserves."

"Father, don't." Christopher reclined back on the pillow, closing his eyes for a moment. "Please. It's pointless. To be honest, my life there has been nothing but a nightmare. The story we agreed to tell didn't cover the truth for long. No one believed I was your orphan distant cousin. I don't want to go back, and Pearce already hates me. Don't punish him because of me. It'll make things worse."

There. Now he and Pearce were even. Pearce had saved him from the whipping, and Christopher had returned the favour.

"Your marks are commendable. Your teachers say your tests are exemplary. I got word that you're one of the best students of your year. Your economics teacher wrote me that he disagreed with the headmaster on your expulsion. Pearce doesn't have your scores."

Yes, and that was another reason why Pearce hated Christopher.

"I can't go back, Father."

He wasn't going to mention the beatings, bullying, and abuse. There was a limit to what he was willing to confess. Besides, unless his father fully exposed himself, there wasn't much he could do about Christopher's mistreatment, not when at school, Pearce, the golden boy, had every student wrapped around his aristocratic finger. The sons of earls, viscounts, and marquesses were all against Christopher. And he wasn't going to mention what the students had said about Mother. Father would ask the queen to bring back public hangings.

"I appreciate you protecting your brother," Father said. "I wish you and Pearce could be friends and support each other like brothers." He squeezed Christopher's hand. "When I'm gone, knowing that you and Pearce are friends would be of great comfort."

Yes, well, and fairies would spread their glittering, magical powder, and every flower would blossom. Christopher made a noise that could mean anything.

"What do you want to do then?" Father asked. "Without a proper education, a gentleman's education, you won't achieve anything."

"I can work. I don't mind using my hands."

"I want to employ you at my estate in Yorkshire. You can start as an assistant manager and work your way up. Management and business are what interest you the most, aren't they?"

Yorkshire. Up in the north in an estate Father visited once a year if the weather conditions allowed the journey. Far away from scandals. Far away from London. Far away from Elizabeth.

But then again, that was the future awaiting him. If anything, he was grateful to be granted a good position and his economic independence. Elizabeth was a beautiful, untouchable dream. The first girl to ever care about him. The first kiss that mattered. The first true friend.

Those shared moments in the cottage would be their last.

"Thank you, Father."

He patted Christopher's hand. "I'll make arrangements to leave immediately. You're coming with me."

"Immediately? I don't think I can travel."

"I won't take you back to London. We'll stop at my estate near Exeter until you recover. I want a trusted physician to examine you and a good cook to take care of your meals." Father rose. "I'll ask the butler to pack up your things."

Christopher took a moment to think after his father left. He wouldn't have time to see Elizabeth, and the worst thing was he couldn't even complain about that.

eleven

ELIZABETH DIDN'T EVEN know in which room Christopher was.

After her conversation with Rebecca, she'd wandered through the house, exploring every nook and cranny without success. She doubted he was in Spencer Hall. Her parents might have sent him to the gamekeeper's cottage at the edge of the estate.

The fact she wasn't allowed to see him was ridiculous. And who was the man Rebecca had seen?

Since she was tired of this farce, she walked to her mother's parlour, determined to find out where Christopher was. A few days had passed since he'd been found, and no one told her anything. She'd confess to what had happened in the cottage if she had to. She'd spill the whole truth if it granted her a visit. Probably not. Confessing would make things worse, but she was desperate.

She knocked on the door but entered before Mother could answer. "Mother, I must speak my mind."

Mother was working on her embroidery in front of the warm hearth, the weather being still chilly. "I know what you want to ask me, but it's done. Thank heaven."

"What do you mean?"

Mother lowered the pretty handkerchief she was working on and stared at her with unforgiving brown eyes. There had been a time when Elizabeth had found her mother's eyes similar to hers.

"The duke has taken him away."

"What? When? The duke came?"

"It was a quick visit. He was in a hurry and incognito. He came here to see your father and me, then he visited Christopher, and they both left. The trains are running again, now that the railway has been cleared. So they'll take the first train, and we'll be free. I'm so relieved that young scoundrel isn't our burden any longer."

"Why didn't you tell me Christopher was leaving?" She was choking with anger.

"Because he is none of your concern!" Mother's voice rose. "Honestly. I don't understand your fascination with him."

"When did he leave?"

"Forget about him."

"Tell me!"

"An hour ago. Less. I don't know." Mother stood up, disregarding the embroidery that ended up on the floor. "Now go back to your room."

"I'm not a child!"

"Then don't behave like one," Mother said.

"I'll ride to the station then, since you don't want to help me." She spun towards the door, but her mother grabbed her arm.

"You aren't going anywhere."

Elizabeth shook with fury. "Try me."

"Don't you dare use that tone with me."

"Then hit me again. Go ahead and slap me." Her voice cracked as she shrugged free of her mother's strong grip.

Mother's lips parted in shock. "I don't recognise you anymore."

"Good, because I don't recognise you, either."

Elizabeth strode out of the parlour and towards the stables.

She didn't bother changing into her riding habit and just grabbed her coat.

"Which horse is ready?" she asked once in the stable.

"My lady?" The stable hand stopped throwing hay bales to the horses.

"I need a horse. Now."

He gazed around, the pitchfork in his hand. "Ghost is warm and ready. Just returned from his free turnout in the paddock. We took it slowly to warm him well in this cold weather. I was about to brush him."

"Saddle him, please."

"Yes." The stable hand did as told.

She jumped on the saddle of the chestnut and held the reins.

"My lady, let me fetch a footman."

"No need. I won't be long." She touched Ghost's flank, and the stallion trotted out of the stable.

She didn't spur him on since the air was too cold, but she led him to a nice canter, which was the most difficult thing she'd ever done. Every instinct urged her to ride as fast as she could.

Along the road boarded with tall snowdrifts, the recent marks of a carriage were visible, starting from Spencer Hall. A sickening lump swelled in her throat. Christopher had returned from a dire ordeal, fell ill, and then left, and she hadn't had the chance to say goodbye.

They'd taken care of each other in the cottage, shared food and heat, risked their lives together, and saved each other, and he'd left, likely believing she didn't care about him, wondering why she hadn't seen him.

She hated the fact he might believe her cold and snobbish, that she'd used him to survive the storm, only to discard him later when she didn't need him.

She wiped the tears blurring her sight. By the time she reached the small train station, she and Ghost were sweaty and hot. She jumped off him and ran to the only platform, where the train was pulling out.

In a large puff of steam, the train started to move, right when she stepped onto the platform. She ran along it, searching the windows of the carriages, but the train was picking up speed and the floor was slippery with mud and melted snow.

She pushed her legs harder. The weakness from the past few days slowed her down, though. Her heart jolted when Christopher's face swept into view behind a frosted glass.

She raised her hand, still running. "Christopher!"

He turned his head, his eyes flaring wide. He lowered the window, and the gusts ruffled his silver-blond hair. She came to a stop at the very edge of the platform as the train raced off into the mist.

"Christopher." She couldn't say anything else as emotion swelled in her throat.

"I'll never forget you," he shouted before vanishing with the train.

The sense of loss crushing her chest was ridiculously overwhelming, considering the small amount of time she'd spent with him. But the pain was so very real, so visceral that she couldn't help but feel it deeply, as little sense as it might have had.

She would never forget him either.

twelve
Five years later

E LIZABETH SMILED, FANNING herself, only to have something to do other than pretend she was enjoying the evening.

The ball at Viscount Keadew's townhouse was considered the event of the month because of the latest music being played by an orchestra of talented musicians, the most fashionable dances, the exquisite food, and the exclusive guests. The ballroom sparkled with the light from two crystal chandeliers, and the white marble floor gave the illusion the room was bigger than it was. The scent of fresh roses filled the air.

All lovely, but she couldn't focus on the conversation she was having with Rebecca and her two friends—Maude, Lady Bletchley and Irene, Lady Worthington.

Her old governess, Miss Martin, had been right when she'd complained about Elizabeth's lack of focus, but it wasn't Elizabeth's fault if she found the conversation rather dull. Maude didn't stop chatting about how happy she was to have returned to London after years abroad without seeing her friends, but Elizabeth didn't remember where the lady had gone. France, perhaps. Not that Elizabeth cared about that.

Her thoughts easily drifted away to more pleasant subjects, like the latest issue of the *American Journal of Mathematics*. Fascinating. An American mathematician developed a clever theory about the—

"Isn't that true, Elizabeth?" Rebecca asked.

"Yes, I love Paris," she said.

The ladies showed matching frowns.

"We weren't talking about Paris," Irene said.

"I beg your pardon. I was distracted." She waved a hand.

"We were recalling the awful Great Blizzard that hit Dartmoor years ago. Some of the houses that collapsed under the snow have still to be rebuilt. Isn't that terrible?" Irene said.

The houses weren't the only things that needed to be rebuilt.

Elizabeth had never recovered from the blizzard. Physically, she was in excellent health. Her body had flourished, developing nice curves. But her heart was still frozen in a small cottage battered by the wind.

She hadn't received a single word from Christopher or a piece of news about him. His name was forbidden in her house, even after the Duke of Grafton had died.

"You were there, weren't you?" Maude said. "Rebecca told me you survived the storm after getting lost along the way to the forest."

"How dreadful." Rebecca shook her head. "I remember visiting you. You were so pale and nervous."

Yes, because Rebecca had asked a lot of questions.

"How did you survive?" Irene asked.

"I found shelter in my father's hunting lodge close to the forest," she said without thinking. No one had asked her about the dreadful blizzard in a while.

Maude frowned, exchanging a glance with Rebecca. "The lodge south of Spencer Hall next to Stormy Tor?"

"So close, yet so distant. It takes me less than half an hour to walk there from Spencer Hall, but after the storm, it almost took me the entire day."

Rebecca narrowed her amber eyes. They reminded Elizabeth of those of a lion.

"And a detour, if I remember correctly," Rebecca said. "You told me you wandered a lot."

Dash it. Elizabeth didn't remember exactly what she'd said to Rebecca.

"I don't understand," Maude said. "I was there. I found shelter in that lodge with my parents after the storm surprised us while we were taking a walk. We were rescued by a party of our footmen three days later. My father resupplied the lodge as a thank you to the earl, your father."

Elizabeth fiddled with her fan. *Botheration.* She'd never cared to verify if someone had been there, and her father had never mentioned anything. How was she supposed to know someone had been there? Five years had passed, for Pete's sake.

"That's odd," Maude continued without mercy. "I didn't see you. You must be mistaken. You must have found shelter somewhere else."

She gazed around, searching for inspiration. "Well ..."

Irene closed her fan with a snap. "Were you in actual danger, Elizabeth? Or perhaps you fabricated a story just to draw attention to yourself. It wouldn't be the first time."

Maude nodded. "I believe you confessed to cheating to win a competition."

She released a breath. "I was a child, and I didn't lie to attract anyone's attention."

"But you weren't a child during the Great Blizzard," Irene said. "What truly happened? Where were you? Safely at home, making up stories?"

"No," Maude said. "I believe Elizabeth was indeed away from home during the blizzard. The question is where. Not her family's hunting lodge."

Three pairs of judgemental eyes set on her.

"I must have been confused," she said with an unconvincing shrug. "It was such an ordeal that I probably don't remember well. Perhaps it was another hunting lodge."

"There aren't any other hunting lodges for miles. Where were you?" Maude was like a bloodhound who caught a trail. "A friend's house? You can tell me who this friend was. I know everyone in the village."

Great. Elizabeth opened and closed her fan. "I don't recall."

"We can easily clear up this misunderstanding," Maude continued. "We'll just ask your father what he knows about his hunting lodge. Surely he remembers that my father thanked him."

Irene laughed. "Not if the earl has his daughter's memory."

Oh, no. If Father were aware of Elizabeth's lie, he'd never said anything, and she'd rather avoid any discussions with him.

Mother walking towards Elizabeth spared her from finding another excuse. "Sorry to interrupt, but the Duke of Grafton is here, fashionably late."

Rebecca let out a small, ladylike gasp, patting her curls. Maude finally averted her gaze from Elizabeth, and Irene smiled.

Elizabeth searched around the ballroom, her pulse speeding up for a silly moment. Of course, the duke wouldn't be Christopher but his half-brother, Pearce. And here he came, tall and elegant, bowing politely to the hostess, the viscountess.

The resemblance to Christopher was striking, though. Same peculiar silver-blond hair, same build, and same strong jaw. She'd been with Christopher for a short period, but she could tell the duke moved with the grace and elegance Christopher didn't have. Not that she preferred Pearce, for that matter. Christopher had a bumptious gait she found charming.

"Elizabeth, come with me and have a chat with the duke," Mother said, excited.

Elizabeth shared her mother's enthusiasm, despite herself, only because the duke reminded her of Christopher, and perhaps she might learn something about his whereabouts from his brother.

In the past years, she'd never managed to talk with him vis-à-vis, also because he'd travelled a lot, and the opportunities to see him had been rare. Then his father had died, and she'd seen him a handful of times and always with her mother present. Never a chance to ask about Christopher.

"We must, Mother."

Mother's face brightened at Elizabeth's agreement, likely misunderstanding her eagerness.

Rebecca tilted her chin up. "My father does business with the duke and they attend the same gentlemen's club. I shall come with you as well and make a formal introduction."

Mother's expression turned serious. "We need no introduction, my dear. My husband the earl and I were very close to the late duke, and we've met His Grace on several occasions. Unfortunately, the last time we saw him was at his father's funeral. So, thank you, Miss Norton, but no *formal* introduction is needed."

Rebecca was flustered. "Of course, I was aware of your mutual acquaintances. I meant simply that ... I was happy to go with you."

"Not necessary, my dear." Mother smiled coldly.

Elizabeth didn't care how the greeting would happen as long as she could get closer to Christopher. When the late duke died, Christopher must have lost any protection he had. She burned to know where he was.

Right then, the duke lifted his gaze and stared at her as if immediately captured by her. She stared back because those eyes had the same shape and colour as Christopher's, and she missed them. Sometimes, if she focused, she could taste on her tongue the honey they'd shared in the cottage.

Mother was gloating when she was close to the duke. "Your Grace, what a pleasure meeting you here."

"Lady Lincoln, Lady Elizabeth." He offered a perfect bow but kept his gaze on Elizabeth.

"It's been a while since you've seen my daughter." Mother beamed proudly. "Time flies, doesn't it?"

"Indeed." The new duke smiled at her, but the smile lacked the charm Christopher had.

"Your Grace." She bowed her head. "It's wonderful to see you again."

Not so wonderful the fact her longing for Christopher hadn't diminished a bit. She blamed it on the lack of news about his well-being. If she knew how he was faring, if she was certain his father's death hadn't caused him further suffering, she would bring the dramatic experience of meeting him to an end and move on. She needed a closure of sorts. The silence and secrecy around him drove her mad with uncertainty and made her curious, obsessed even.

"You've deprived us of your company for a long time," Mother said.

"Alas, ducal duties keep me busy." Pearce glanced at Elizabeth again.

She didn't know what to make of his attention.

A lively country music started.

"Oh, a galop," Mother said. "I'm afraid I'm too old to dance it. But you do go on, darling." She raised her eyebrows at Elizabeth.

He offered her his arm before she could say anything. "Would you give me the honour of dancing with me?"

Well, refusing a gentleman was rude, and dancing was her best opportunity to talk to him without her mother's control.

"I'd be delighted, Your Grace." Elizabeth could almost touch the wave of satisfaction coming off her mother.

The moment she took his arm, disappointment bothered her, which was silly of her.

His arm didn't feel like that of Christopher. The shape and the tension of the muscles were wrong. It broke the illusion she was actually seeing him, but the disappointment was her fault.

In a way, she despised the fact she kept hoping to meet him.

Five years had passed since the blizzard happened. She didn't blame him for not having sent word to her, and even if he had, Mother would have made sure Elizabeth never received it. But the lack of certainty in their brief but intense relationship was like a disease from which she hadn't recovered yet. Perhaps she was as proud and stubborn as her mother said.

The duke led her onto the dance floor gracefully. Not once did his leg brush her skirt or his elbow touch hers. He smiled when he positioned himself in front of her before the beginning of the dance. His hand on her waist was firm but light, but the contact didn't stoke any flame within her.

Whispers from other women reached her. Sideways glances were tossed in her direction. Likely, the gossip about an impending engagement between them was already circulating. If the ladies only knew. They had no reason to be jealous of Elizabeth.

"It's astonishing we haven't seen each other in such a long time, considering we're almost neighbours," she said, turning at the upbeat music.

"I spent a lot of time out of London after my father's untimely passing. I underestimated the amount of work that fell on my shoulders from one day to the next." A shadow crossed his face as he twirled her around. "I wasn't ready to take my father's place. He had a lot to teach me but left me too soon."

The pain sounded genuine, and some of the tension bothering her left.

"I'm so sorry."

He let her spin gently, careful not to tramp on her skirt. "I keep travelling throughout the country to manage my estates. I confess I long for some quiet time to enjoy the company of a beautiful lady." Another smile.

"I gather, in your many travels, you've never been to my father's estate in Dartmoor."

"Alas, I haven't."

"You must. Dartmoor is beautiful. Your father visited us after the Great Blizzard." Not very subtle, but it was the best she could do.

His smile vanished, and his hand gripped her waist more tightly. "I believe you're mistaken, my lady. Father didn't travel during that unfortunate time. Why would he?"

"But he met my parents."

"He didn't." His clipped tone held all the authority of a duke. That he'd learnt quite well.

She didn't press the matter further lest he avoid her at future encounters. But his denial meant he was aware of the reason for his father's visit to Dartmoor.

"It's a pity you don't have any siblings, a spare perhaps, who might help you with your work." She couldn't help herself.

His eyes turned positively hostile. "Yes, a real pity."

The worst thing wasn't that he was upset, but that, from his tone, she couldn't guess anything aside from his dislike for Christopher.

They performed the rest of the galop without talking, not even while performing the slow chassé steps during which the other couples chatted. Her fault. She was as subtle as an avalanche. On these occasions, she regretted not having paid attention to Miss Martin's lessons. She might have learnt something about political negotiations.

"I hope to see you again soon," the duke said when the dance ended. His tone was flat and neutral, and she couldn't understand if he meant it or not.

"So do I, sir."

He was about to leave when she said, "Your Grace, I apologise if I offended you. Please forgive me.

His expression didn't change. "It wasn't you who offended me," he said, walking away.

thirteen

W HAT A MAN could accomplish in a few years of dishonest work was astonishing.

Christopher strode with Finn along the pavement on the high street in Whitechapel, marvelling at how people tripped over their own feet to move out of his way without him having said or done anything. Not now, at least.

While he fully enjoyed the unlawful fruit of his smuggling and gambling work, he didn't relish in the fear his mere presence triggered in the hearts of everyone. But then again, it was better to be feared than loved, and he had a reputation to keep.

A boy stared at him, frozen in shock, and stopped playing with a worn ball. "The King?" he whispered.

Christopher didn't nod or shake his head, not sure if the child would be terrified or pleased by the answer.

"I'm sorry, Mr. Blackwood." The mother hurried to scoop the child up and carry him away. "It won't happen again."

Christopher gave her a quick nod. Telling her the child was welcome to play on the pavement wouldn't help with his business. Although he'd taken Finn with him to look less menacing for the particularly delicate negotiation he was about to have.

Finn was a lad, still wet behind the ears with a sweet-looking face and enough charm to make the scandalous poet and libertine Paul Verlaine look like an amateur. He couldn't possibly intimidate anyone.

Nods and tipping of the hats from passersby followed Christopher as he strutted down the street. He could commit murder right here, right now, in broad daylight, and no one would send for the coppers to arrest him, and even if they did, the coppers wouldn't touch him. That was a power only fear could buy, and he'd be lying if he said he didn't find it intoxicating.

"Our last victory on the gang of the Reapers has really marked you as the unspoken king," Finn said. "Them thugs are still groaning in pain after the beating."

Yes, but Christopher suspected that his general appearance—dark coat, sturdy boots, and the not-so-hidden daggers and gun at his side—helped with the sense of fear and was part of his persona. Half of the work of being a feared criminal lay in the looks and the attitude. A good sense for business didn't hurt.

Finn clicked his tongue. "I wish I'd seen the battle."

"No, you don't. It was brutal and bloody, and the Reapers are ruthless criminals who don't hesitate to murder unarmed people."

"That's why I wanted to see the battle."

"You're sixteen."

"Practically, a man." Cheeky sod.

"What's the woman's name again?" Christopher asked to distract the lad from bloody battles, taking a side alleyway.

"Sarah," Finn said. "She lives right there."

They stopped in front of a door that smelled of rotting wood and poverty. The broken glass of the window had been repaired with a couple of wooden planks, and part of the roof leant to the right as if tired.

Christopher went to knock but changed his mind. "You knock, Finn. We don't want to scare Sarah."

"Sure, Guv." Finn did as told.

"Hat off." Christopher snatched the lad's hat. "Where are your manners?"

Finn patted his jacket and trousers pockets. "I'm sure they're here somewhere."

"Ha-ha." Christopher shot him a glare.

The door inched inwards, revealing a dark-blonde woman with fearful blue eyes.

"Madam," Finn said. "We want a word."

She gasped upon seeing Christopher.

"The King," she said. "I don't have money. I barely have a few shillings for food. Please don't ask me for more. I have a baby to feed."

He arched his eyebrows. Fear was one thing, but blatant lies spreading about him were quite another. He'd never, ever harassed the people of Whitechapel for protection money or any other means of extortion. Young single mothers had nothing to fear from him or his organisation. He guessed the lies helped keep his reputation high and criminal competitors at bay, but he had some damn principles.

"We aren't here to ask for money." Quite the opposite, if the story about Sarah was true. He removed his hat and stepped closer, letting the woman take a good look at him to notice his resemblance to Pearce. "Do I look familiar to you?"

Her mouth hung open. "Goodness."

"Can we go inside and talk?"

She gave him an unconvincing nod.

He doubted she let him in because she trusted him. She trembled when they brushed past her into her flat. He had to swallow not to gag at the smell of mould and humidity. The single room that functioned as kitchen, dining room, sitting room, bedroom, and even the water closet could be an extension of Newgate Prison. One might catch consumption or the clap just by breathing.

In a corner, an infant slept in a makeshift crib made out of a wooden crate. He stepped closer to the baby, but Sarah blocked his path, a fierce light in her scrawny face.

"Don't you dare!"

Great. So he wasn't only a gangster who extorted money from impoverished, unwed mothers, but also a killer of children. His constructed persona was getting more outlandish by the minute.

He held up a hand. "I have no intention of hurting the child." Besides, the child was likely his nephew. "He's the reason I'm here."

"You can trust the King," Finn said. "He's a man with honour."

Not always, but anyway.

She moved aside reluctantly. "Arthur isn't well. He's been coughing since yesterday."

Not surprising, given the humidity.

Christopher needed only one glance. The child's silver-blond hair gave him away as a member of his not-so-happy family. "The Duke of Grafton is Arthur's father."

"He is," she whispered.

Something cracked in Christopher's chest at the sight of the scrawny sleeping baby. "I guess Pearce refused to take responsibility."

Sarah lowered her gaze. "I begged him more than once to help me, but he doesn't believe Arthur is his son."

"Bastard," Finn muttered.

Ironic, considering Christopher was the real bastard. Right now, he was looking at what his life would have been, had Father behaved like Pearce.

"How did you learn about me?" she said.

"Nothing happens in Whitechapel without me knowing it." Almost nothing. Exaggerating was part of his image, too. "You were Pearce's mistress."

"For two years until he was convinced I had a lover. A misunderstanding, because it wasn't true. Someone must have spread gossip about me. Pearce was my only one. He left me. A few weeks afterwards, I discovered I was with child. I talked to him, but he didn't hear reason. He believed that Arthur belonged to another man. I had to leave the flat he'd paid for me. I couldn't find a job once I was showing, and an unmarried mother isn't welcome in many places. So I ended up here."

Curse his brother.

Arthur started coughing, awful, raspy sounds that seemed too loud for a baby that small.

"It's all right." Sarah held him up, and Arthur clung to her with his tiny arms.

As the baby coughed, his large eyes widened, showing their sparkling blue colours. No doubts. The baby was the son of the Duke of Grafton.

He sucked in a breath to ease the worry within him. "You're going to leave this dump today. I'll send my men in less than an hour. Don't be alarmed when they come. They'll help you and Arthur move to a nice place. I'll find a physician for Arthur as well, and you'll get bags of fresh food every day."

She didn't look relieved. "In exchange for what?"

"Arthur is my nephew. I take care of my family."

She kept rocking the baby gently as Arthur stopped coughing. The fit had left the baby red and shaking, though.

"Arthur will get better, and you two won't lack anything," he said. "You'll receive a decent allowance and will always have my protection."

He didn't expect gratitude and didn't care for it, so he walked out of the house before his fury towards Pearce showed.

"Madam." Finn nodded at Sarah and sped up to keep up with Christopher's angry strides.

Pearce had always had everything from money to the title to Father's company, and yet he refused to take responsibility for his own blood. Father had never backed away from his duty. Hell, Christopher's mother had been a prostitute, turned mistress of a duke, and Father had loved her dearly. She and Christopher had never lived in poverty. The fact Christopher appreciated his father more now that he was dead was sad.

He tensed when a hand closed around his arm. "What?" He turned around only to exhale when Sarah's worried face came into view.

"Sir," she said. "Thank you."

He nodded, not trusting his voice to remain steady.

He'd do more than give her a house and food. He'd talk to his bloody brother and tell him how despicable he was. For a criminal, he had a strong sense of justice when it came to responsibilities and illegitimate children.

She released his arm and rushed back inside.

"What you did for that woman was right and fair," Finn said, punching the air.

"No, it wasn't. It was nothing."

He walked home in a foul mood, ignoring the terrified glances and the people scurrying away from him. Once he stepped into his *royal palace*, he headed upstairs to his personal rooms.

Since everyone in Whitechapel knew him as the King, it was only appropriate that the headquarters of his operation, the garrison, and his home were called royal palace.

"Finn, go to Smithy and tell him to prepare Sarah's new home, get her some money and a physician," he said. "Quick."

"Will do, Guv." Finn rushed to the other side of the garrison.

Darko wagged his tail and jumped on Christopher upon seeing him, putting his large paws on Christopher's chest. The dog's damp black nose bumped against his chin.

"Mate." Christopher patted the dog's flank.

Darko was so tall, when he stood up on his hind legs his amber eyes stared straight into Christopher's. Sometimes he found the dog's stare hard to hold, as if Darko knew secrets no man could fathom.

Darko followed him up the wooden stairs and to the gallery, grunting all the way as if complaining about something.

Christopher kicked the door to his bedroom open, remembering too late there was a woman asleep in his bed. She bolted upright, her hair dishevelled and her chemise wrinkled.

She yawned, rubbing her eyes. "Are you back?"

"I believe I am."

He sat on the bed and removed his boots with a yank. He needed a good boxing session to vent his frustration. It would cost little for a wealthy man like Pearce to take care of Sarah and Arthur. He had the means and the power to do so without sacrificing anything of his privileged life. No one expected him to marry Sarah, and mistresses were tolerated among the aristocrats as long as the affair was carried on with discretion. Hell, Sarah wasn't even a prostitute. Yet his brother had decided to let his son and the mother die of starvation. What a paragon of honour.

The woman ran a hand over Christopher's shoulder. "We can finally start."

"Actually, I've changed my mind. You can leave. Or stay here and sleep. I don't mind."

"But we didn't do anything."

"I'm not in the mood."

Which wasn't unusual. When one had to deal with smuggling whisky and tobacco, avoiding the non-corrupt peelers at every turn, keeping rival gangs out of his territory, and bribing as many police officers and judges as possible, there wasn't much time left for anything else.

A criminal business wasn't different from any other business. It required strategy, knowledge, and a good instinct for making and handling money. His business teacher at Eton would be proud of what Christopher had achieved in a few years. Or maybe not.

He hadn't slept for almost thirty hours straight, having to take care of a particularly delicate shipment to the Americas. Then he'd gone straight to Sarah, and now the combination of fatigue and sheer anger at his brother gave him a headache. The last thing he wanted was a tumble.

He lay in the bed, and the woman snuggled closer to him, warm and soft and smelling of flowers. Unbidden and uninvited, Elizabeth's sweet face came to his mind; it happened every time a woman huddled with him in bed. Sometimes at night, when he slept with a woman next to him, he would wake up believing Elizabeth was next to him. His mind played nasty tricks on him.

He'd spent only a few days with her, but the snowy days he'd shared with her had branded his soul with fire. If he'd known that moment, when he'd let her go ahead to Spencer Hall, would have been the last they would ever share, he would have behaved differently.

He would have held her in his arms one last time, thanked her for saving his miserable arse, and kissed her again but with more passion. But no. He had to live with a pale ghost and the memory of her waving at him from a wet platform as he left her.

After all, he'd told her he would never forget her.

fourteen

S INCE AFTER THE Great Blizzard, whenever something terrible was about to happen, the back of Elizabeth's neck tingled.

It was tingling now as she sipped a cup of tea in her sitting room with her mother and Pearce. Two weeks had passed from the day they'd danced together, and he'd insisted on her using his Christian name rather quickly and on seeing her as often as his ducal duties allowed him.

Aside from the particular intimacy of using their names, she couldn't say their acquaintance had grown deeper, nor did she understand why he kept wanting to see her.

The most annoying thing was that she hadn't learnt anything regarding Christopher. She hadn't learnt much about Pearce, either. What she knew about him could be surmised as thus: he loved cricket, fine clothes, and caviar; he disliked French poetry, beaches, and being alone. He loved talking about anything that popped up in his mind, changing the subject of a conversation constantly, and he could read a book in a day.

That was it. Nothing personal about who he was, what he

feared, or what he desired. She knew the baker down the road better.

Although the time they spent together wasn't a matter of quantity but quality. She'd spent a few days with Christopher and knew him rather intimately.

She took another sip while Mother and Pearce discussed the outrageous speed with which London was growing.

"... buildings sprout out from the ground almost overnight," Mother said. "And young ladies are rebelling everywhere! Young women are disparaging rules of etiquette in favour of studying science. Why would a lady need to be knowledgeable about science?"

"I agree. It's difficult to find a lady who cares about propriety these days," Pearce said.

"There's nothing wrong with wanting to study," Elizabeth said. "Education and knowledge are everything, and ladies are entitled to them. I for once love mathematics."

Mother gave her the slightest shake of her head.

Pearce didn't seem shocked. "Interesting. But you wouldn't teach mathematics at Oxford, would you?"

She jutted out her chin. "I would, actually, if they let me."

"Elizabeth has the oddest sense of humour." Mother forced a laugh. "Of course she wouldn't."

"I'd love to work as an accountant. Many times I have asked Father to let me help with his accounting books, but he refuses."

"Because your father is a sensible man." Mother's tone was final.

"But—"

"Quiet, darling. Mathematics is a boring subject." Mother turned towards Pearce. "Are you going to Lady Bletchley's upcoming ball?"

Pearce replied yes, and then the conversation steered towards ... she had no idea. She should be frustrated at how Mother dismissed her, but after all those years of hearing that what Elizabeth liked was boring, she didn't care. She preferred counting the tiny florets in the cores of the daisies in the vase in front of her. Their spiral distribution followed Fibonacci's sequence. How peculiar.

"Well then, I'll leave you two alone," Mother said, interrupting Elizabeth's musing.

What? Elizabeth lifted her gaze from the flowers, wondering which part of the conversation she'd missed. What was happening?

Mother glowed from within, smiling at Pearce. Then grinning at her, she shut the door behind her.

The door shut? A moment of panic took her.

"Elizabeth." Pearce put down his cup and angled towards her.

Sometimes, when he didn't show the fake smile he reserved for everyone, his resemblance to Christopher increased tenfold.

"I wanted … is something the matter?" he asked. "You look tense."

"I simply wonder what is happening."

He took her hand, and she suppressed the instinct to withdraw it. "I talked to your father."

Oh, no. She swallowed past the lump in her throat. Not that.

"He gave me his blessing to court you."

Something had to be wrong with her because she didn't feel anything. Nothing. No elation, interest, or even annoyance. A void of emotions. Her brain was stuck on counting the petals.

"These past two weeks have been very, very lovely," he said with an honesty she couldn't dismiss.

"But brief. Very, very brief."

"I don't want to hurry your decision, but we could see each other during our courtship and know each other better before announcing our engagement. We can have a long courtship if you like." He chuckled clumsily as if embarrassed. "You'd make me the luckiest man in the world if you'd become my duchess."

The very first thought in her head was about her parents.

No matter what she chose, her parents would push her into

marrying Pearce in a matter of months. A ducal marriage wasn't something a woman refused. Especially if the said woman didn't have other serious suitors. Her two older sisters had married into old noble families, an earl and a viscount. And a duke was a duke. Appearances and all that.

How frightening.

The only thing she could do was take time to think; rejecting his proposal immediately would be a mistake. Her parents would be upset. She might be at the centre of any sort of gossip. But perhaps if she allowed their courtship, she could find another way out ... like incompatibility. She'd make Pearce see they wouldn't get along after she proved to him they didn't have anything in common. Her parents wouldn't blame her if he was the one who didn't want to marry her.

"A courtship would be appropriate," she said. For lack of a better word. "We'll spend some time together and ... understand each other better. Then we'll see what happens."

He sagged his shoulders. "Thank you. That's wonderful. I was worried you were going to say no. And do not worry." He flashed a shy smile. "Of course, you can study whatever you like. You can even become my personal accountant if you wish so. I didn't say anything because I didn't want to upset your mother."

"Thank you."

He kissed her hand, and while she didn't dislike the polite gesture, it bothered her.

"May I ask you something personal?" she asked, gathering her courage.

"By all means." He kept holding her hand.

"The year of the Great Blizzard, we had a guest in Spencer Hall." There. She'd said it.

He stiffened immediately. "We discussed the matter before."

"No. I'm not talking about your father. I'm referring to something else." She gave him a pointed look. "To someone else."

He released her hand. "We don't need to discuss that."

"You've just asked me to court me." *After we've seen each other for two weeks.* "I think I have the right to ask questions about something I experienced, and that involves you. Something you've always refused to acknowledge or discuss."

"Fine." He worked his jaw. "I know whom you're referring to, of course. I swear on my honour he won't bother us. He won't be a problem or interfere with our lives. He won't have anything to do with us."

She released a breath. "Is Christopher still alive?"

"Yes." He drew his eyebrows together. "He's a problem in my family's history. My father shouldn't have been so close to him. Father gave him the wrong idea of who he really was. He didn't teach him what his right place was."

She wanted to say many things, but since Pearce had never talked about him, she listened.

"Father had a misplaced sense of duty towards that fallen woman and her child. Providing for them was one thing, but having two families was quite another. He should have thought about our reputation and my mother. Instead, by acknowledging Christopher's existence, he put my mother and me in a difficult position. I had to endure Christopher's presence even at school." He clenched a fist. "I've never been more humiliated in my life."

She had to sink her teeth into her bottom lip not to speak her mind. If he'd taken time to know Christopher, he would have never felt humiliated.

"But I promise." He took both her hands in a pleading gesture. "You will never, ever be the subject of gossip because of him. Your reputation will remain impeccable. Your name will never be associated with his. Please don't let his shadow ruin what we have. Don't refuse my courtship because of him."

Well, they didn't have much, to be honest. "Do you see him?"

He lowered his gaze. "Occasionally. The last time I saw him was over a year ago. We had a dispute about that dreadful cottage in Dartmoor. His mother was born in some village there. He claimed the cottage was his. I think it should be sold. Anyway." He waved a dismissive hand. "He's turned to criminality, unsurprisingly so. I won't see him again for your sake. Do not fear."

But she was afraid because she wanted to see Christopher again.

"I'm ashamed of what Father did in the year of the Great Blizzard. He shouldn't have asked your family to accommodate Christopher in your house. I understand if the experience bothers you to this day."

It did, but not in the way he thought.

"Do you hate him?" she asked.

"Hate is a strong sentiment I don't think I can embrace." He released her hands again. "Father favoured him. He always sang Christopher's praise about his marks at school, his intelligence, and his strong character, all things he found me lacking. He spent more time with his mistress than with my mother, ran to see her and Christopher whenever he could, and lamented the fact Christopher couldn't be the next Duke of Grafton. My mother was the daughter of one of Prince Albert's cousins, practically royalty. Father's shameful behaviour hurt her deeply and humiliated her. I spent many nights comforting her as she cried because Father was with that woman." A hard glint flickered in his gaze. "How do you think that made me feel?"

"But he's your brother, your family."

"He is not. We don't have anything in common. We live in two different worlds." His voice became sharp. "I don't want anything to do with him, and you won't even be aware he exists. We'll not speak of him ever again."

Oh, she had plenty of other subjects to talk about, especially after he disparaged Christopher.

She tilted her chin up. "Why do you want to court me?"

He gave her a puzzled look as if the question didn't make

sense. "You're beautiful and the daughter of an earl, who was one of my father's best friends, and I'm in need of a good wife."

It sounded as if he were buying a piece of furniture. "You don't know anything about me."

He laughed. "That's why we have courtships."

Well, there was no arguing with his logic.

fifteen

ELIZABETH DID HER best to smile as she and Pearce announced their courtship to her parents.

Pearce shook hands with Father, and Mother seemed about to cry of happiness.

"So have you chosen a date yet?" Mother said.

"We have invitations to print." Father checked the calendar on the table. "A summer wedding would be ideal. And your brothers travel often. They'll need to know when they should come to London."

Elizabeth slid her arm out of Pearce's. "Pearce and I agreed to a courtship. It's too early to choose a date."

"We'll have to book an appointment with Mrs. De Bellefort." Mother wasn't listening. "Heaven knows she's busy. She's sewing gowns for every bride in London."

Father chuckled. "I'm sure she'll find time for us."

Was she speaking English? She wasn't sure. "Mother, an appointment with the modiste would be premature."

"No harm in getting prepared, darling."

"Your mother is right," Pearce said. "Better be ready."

"But we aren't engaged." She gazed around, but her parents seemed too giddy to listen.

After another round of 'wonderful news' and jokes about not inviting Uncle Robert to the wedding because he had an odd laugh, Pearce left with Father to go to their club, and Elizabeth wondered what had just happened.

"He proposed. Isn't that wonderful?" Mother's eyes were shining with too much delight.

"It's a special courtship, Mother."

Mother hugged her. "My clever girl. I wasn't sure what you would do. You're so unpredictable. All those weeks spent negotiating with the duke were worth it."

"Excuse me?"

Mother didn't catch the tone in Elizabeth's voice. "Your father and I have been discussing with the duke a possible marriage to you."

She shouldn't be surprised. Now Pearce's interest with her at the ball made sense. It was all planned. "You should have told me."

"I'm so happy for you and for us! Perhaps next year, I'll call you Your Grace."

Elizabeth made an effort to stay calm. "We haven't talked about our engagement yet. Nothing is official. There's time."

"But a wedding is going to happen." Mother took her face, becoming serious. The merriment vanished. "You can't refuse a duke's proposal, and he's young and handsome. You can't ask for more."

"What about love, respect, and affection?"

Mother removed her hands. "What about your family? All your brothers and sisters married well, but a duke! We'll have a duchess in our family. Mary and Anne married when His Grace was too young, and I thought it was a shame, given how close your father and the late duke were. But you are His Grace's same age. Perfect."

Nothing of what Mother had said mentioned happiness or love.

"What if, after I get to know him, I really don't like him?"

She played with fire, but her family wasn't impoverished or on the brink of bankruptcy. She didn't need a good match to save her family's financial situation, and she was the last in the family to be married. Like her sisters, she had a sizeable dowry, but a marriage with a duke was all about prestige, wasn't it?

Mother pressed her lips. "You won't disgrace this family by refusing a duke who's also a family friend."

It was amazing how Mother's tone changed from thrilled to menacing in the span of a moment.

Elizabeth matched her mother's attitude. "If I dislike him, yes, I will."

Mother leant closer, tensing as she'd done that time she'd slapped Elizabeth. "Listen to me. I've put up with your odd behaviour too many times because you were the youngest. Your stubbornness about wanting to study mathematics instead of French, your horrible behaviour when you cheated during that contest, attracting all that attention on us—"

"I can't believe you're bringing that up!"

"And your obsession with that awful young man." Mother lowered her voice. "Enough. You aren't a child anymore. You'll do your duty and marry the duke."

Tension thickened the space between them so much that Elizabeth could feel its pressure on her chest.

"I don't want Pearce as my future husband," she said in a low tone. She hadn't planned to tell the truth so soon, but Mother knew exactly how to provoke her.

"You'll be a duchess. What you want doesn't matter." Mother showed her teeth.

"My lady," the maid said, breaking the moment. "Miss Norton wishes to see Lady Elizabeth."

Mother straightened with an air of triumph. "Show her in." She leant closer to Elizabeth. "Rebecca and her mother set their eyes on the duke. Too late."

As if it were a competition. Maybe it was.

Rebecca's strained smile made Elizabeth think she somehow knew about Pearce's visit. She dropped a quick curtsy. "Lady Lincoln, Elizabeth."

"Miss Norton, what a pleasure." Mother entered the sitting room where the scent of Pearce's cologne still lingered.

Elizabeth followed reluctantly. She had no intention of being paraded as a trophy. They sat on the sofa and armchairs in a swish of silk and rivalry.

"I hope you don't mind my calling on you," Rebecca said without sounding apologetic at all, "but I was walking by and wondering if you'll be present at the Duke of Grafton's ball. He sent a formal invitation to me."

Elizabeth was sorry for her because Mother was about to wipe any traces of gloating from Rebecca's face. Although she had no idea if Pearce had mentioned a ball.

"We will," Mother said. "His Grace came here *himself* to invite us. We've just had tea with him, haven't we, Elizabeth? I'm surprised you didn't meet him on your way here."

"Mother," she whispered. "Will you be present as well, Rebecca?"

Rebecca blinked a couple of times. "Of course. I'm thrilled to go."

Mother inched closer to Rebecca and whispered, "Don't tell anyone, but the duke proposed to Elizabeth."

"Mother!" Elizabeth closed a fist.

The colour drained from Rebecca's cheeks. "Oh."

Elizabeth had to endure a scorching glare from her mother and a desolate one from Rebecca.

"You must be happy," Rebecca said in a quivering voice.

"What about you, my dear?" Mother asked. "Are there any suitors who caught your eye?"

Rebecca flushed to the roots of her hair. Her red cheeks clashed with her glossy chestnut hair. "Baron Hatley seems to show interest."

Mother waved a hand. "A baron. It seems a good match for the daughter of a viscount. I wish you all the happiness."

Elizabeth rubbed her temple. If Mother continued, Rebecca would burst into tears. "I wish you well, too." She meant it.

"Thank you." Rebecca stood up. "Well, it was lovely seeing you. My lady, Elizabeth."

"Don't you want to stay for tea?" Mother asked, all innocence.

"I'd love to, but my mother is waiting for me at home. Another time." Rebecca walked out of the sitting room with her shoulders slumped.

Mother chuckled when they were alone. "A baron. Oh, goodness. She has no idea."

"Mother. Please. There was no need to humiliate Rebecca like that."

"You must be joking. She always tries to overshadow you." Mother huffed. "And I'm doing her a favour. She isn't prepared to be a duchess."

"Nor am I, and Rebecca is very pretty. She easily attracts gentlemen's attentions. She doesn't try to overshadow me."

"Tosh. I understand people better than you do, and let me tell you that Miss Norton isn't the shy, sweet lady you think she is. She's a chess player. She won't come to the ball, mark my word."

"Why not?"

"Because she was humiliated. She thought the duke was interested in her and came here to boast about her good fortune, only to discover she was utterly wrong. Trust me. She won't show herself."

"Poor Rebecca." Again, she meant it.

THE DUKE OF GRAFTON'S townhouse in Belgrave Square could be considered a palace. Elizabeth thought everything about it was excessive.

The cavernous rooms had domed ceilings she found unnecessarily high. The sweeping stairs were large enough to allow six people to walk abreast, and there wasn't a corner without a priceless porcelain vase, a painting by a master, or an expensive piece of furniture.

Generations of dukes and duchesses stared down at her with disapproval from their portraits as if they knew her heart better than she did.

Elegant guests poured into the ballroom, chatting and laughing. The ladies cast curious glances in her direction from behind their fans. The news of the Duke of Grafton's proposal had spread faster than the most scandalous gossip. She supposed her mother had something to do with that.

Mother opened her fan, surveying the ballroom as a general would a battlefield. "I was right. Miss Norton didn't come. She's at home licking her wounds. Serves her right."

Elizabeth admitted defeat. "Mother, honestly. This vindictive behaviour of yours is unappealing."

Wasted breath. Mother didn't acknowledge her.

"Little coward, she is. She'll learn to stay quiet before spouting nonsense. And look, everyone envies you." She said that as if it were something to be proud of.

"The duke and I only agreed to a courtship. Elizabeth hid behind her own fan, tired of having to repeat that.

"Nonsense. The moment you and he dance together everyone will understand how perfect you are together."

Speaking of the devil. Elegant in a dark tailcoat and a white silk bow tie, Pearce weaved his way through the crowd, bowing and smiling, to stop in front of her. She had to admit his excitement seemed genuine.

"Elizabeth." He bowed, never averting his gaze from hers. "Lady Lincoln, would you mind terribly if I borrow Elizabeth?"

"Not at all, sir." Mother bowed her head.

Pearce offered Elizabeth his arm. "Please, my dear."

She slid her arm over his, sensing the gazes of all the guests on her. "Everyone is looking at us."

"Yes, isn't that wonderful?" He bowed his head at a passing lady.

Not really.

"I met Miss Norton yesterday afternoon," he said. "I believe she's your friend."

"We've known each other since childhood."

"I've met her at Garrad's—"

"Garrad's?" The jeweller.

"She seemed rather out of sorts. I guess that's why she didn't come tonight. She did congratulate me on our engagement though."

"Courtship."

"Yes." He led her out of the ballroom and up the stairs.

"Where are we going?" She wished her voice didn't sound panicked.

"I want to show you something. Something that will make you understand about us." He showed her to a room that was as excessive as the rest of the house.

Marble everywhere, heavy walnut furniture, and embroidered brocade curtains. She jolted a little when he shut the door.

"Just a moment of patience." He opened a safe and pulled out a velvet box.

It couldn't be … They hadn't been out together yet. Pearce couldn't possibly offer her an engagement ring so quickly.

He lifted the lid of the box, revealing the brightest diamond mounted on a gold band she'd ever seen.

"What …" Her mouth grew dry.

"When the Koh-i-Noor was found, it was cut by a master jeweller before it became the diamond our queen wears on her brooch. The diamond on this ring comes from a piece of the Koh-i-Noor, the Mountain of Light itself." He slid the ring on her finger. "You'll wear the same diamond as the queen."

Excessive, of course.

Her first instinct was to shrug her hand and remove the ring. A choking sensation crept over her as the walls seemed to close in on her. She was trapped. Everyone was pushing her to do something she didn't want to do.

"Pearce, our courtship barely started." She was growing tired of saying it.

His eyes narrowed to slits. "I just wanted to show you what will be yours if you become my duchess." He removed the ring and put it back in the box. "You don't have to remind me we're just courting every other minute."

"And you don't have to push me towards a definite marriage every other minute."

He shut the safe door with a snappy gesture. "Your parents expect us to be together. We're the best match in London."

"Is that a good reason to get married?"

He exhaled as if suddenly tired. "No, of course not. But I wanted to impress you, all right? I saw the ring and thought it'd be perfect on your finger."

She leant against the wall. Great. Between Rebecca and Mother, everyone believed she was to be engaged to the Duke of Grafton. And Rebecca had seen Pearce buying an engagement ring.

Meanwhile, she had no idea what to do. Her plan to buy time had backfired in a spectacularly terrible fashion.

"The ring is beautiful." Excessive, but beautiful. "But I don't want to be rushed."

Pressing his lips together, he nodded. "Forgive me. I thought you would have loved it and agreed to marry me upon seeing it."

"I didn't agree to becoming your duchess, and it takes more than a diamond ring to woo me into marriage."

"You don't have to pretend you aren't interested in the title and my money." He inched closer, flashing a confident smile. "Or me."

"I'm not pretending."

"My opinion of you won't change if you yield to me now. My marriage proposal will still stand." He caressed her cheeks, and maybe she was melodramatic, but the sensation was like that of spiders crawling over her skin.

And what did he exactly mean by *yielding*? A tumble?

She stepped out of his reach, shaking with a combination of frustration and desperation. "You aren't listening to me. I really am not interested in your title, money, or ... being your duchess." She regretted the bitterness in her voice. It wasn't needed, and it poisoned the air between them.

Anger glinted in his icy-blue eyes. "Then why did you agree to be courted?"

Dash it all, that was a good question. "I didn't want ... I thought I needed time."

It was a short version of her thoughts, but she didn't want to make her situation worse by admitting to having agreed only to reject him more softly later.

"Again," he said through clenched teeth, "that's what a courtship is for. You must like me more than you care to admit if you agreed to be courted by me, or you would have rejected me immediately. You like me. Admit it."

She liked his brother more. "But all of a sudden the courtship has become a sure engagement."

He flung the door open. "I'll take you back to the ballroom."

Where the guests would make more speculation about their absence.

"No, thank you. I need the ladies' room." She hurried out of the room and chose a direction.

Perhaps she was just too bitter, as Mother said.

No, the problem wasn't her. Or maybe she was. She should have refused the courtship right from the beginning.

sixteen

CHRISTOPHER DIDN'T BOTHER to change into fine clothes to pay a visit to his brother. No one, aside from Pearce and a couple of servants, would see him, and the meeting wouldn't be long. His black coat and flat hat were more than enough. He was even wearing a waistcoat for the occasion.

The visit was overdue, but smuggling liquor and tobacco was a job that had no respect for a man's private life.

He paused in a dark corner of Belgrave Square, watching Grafton House shine in all its glory. Carriages stopped at the front door to let out the aristocracy wearing their finest. A ball, perhaps. Who cared? If there was a ball, then Pearce had to be home.

He walked around the house towards the rear entrance. A short flight of stone stairs led him to the passageway where the servants put the containers of waste, as the smell of rotting vegetables suggested.

He knocked on the door and waited, gazing around.

"Who's there?" A footman came out.

Christopher shoved his way inside. "I need to see the duke."

The man was flustered. "Blackwood. It's not possible. His Grace has guests tonight."

"Then don't waste his time. Go to tell him to see me now."

"I have instructions not to let you—"

The rest of the sentence was cut off by Christopher closing his hand around the footman's neck. The man was tall and strongly built, but Christopher sparred and boxed with vicious criminals every other day. A prim footman eager to do his duty was a piece of piss.

He didn't need to squeeze. In fact, his grip was rather gentle. The move was all about attitude with a generous dose of bad reputation.

"Now," he said calmly.

Face reddening, the man left the anteroom and disappeared into the kitchen. Christopher propped an elbow on a barrel of apples, silently daring the man to send for the police. The sound of distant voices came from upstairs. Pearce would be furious about the fact Christopher had chosen that night to see him. Good.

The footman returned pale and shaking. "This way." He led Christopher to the servants' stairs. "First floor, second door to the right."

"Good job. You deserve a raise." He clapped the man's shoulder and went up.

The temperature and the smells changed as he entered the upper floor. Warm air and the scent of wood polish reminded him of those times his father had visited him. He'd always carried a present for Mother—perfume, a new hat, a necklace—and something for Christopher—toy wooden horses or sugar sticks.

Grand memories.

The room also reminded him of the few times he'd been here. None of the visits pleasant.

He slid into a small study, which looked like a sitting room. Chintz armchairs, a large fireplace, and a glass cabinet competed for space. Pearce's mother had been a Prussian princess, or something similar. They said she'd wanted Grafton House to look as regal as possible. She'd failed. The place looked overwhelmed with riches like a pirate cave.

Pearce arrived like a storm cloud. "What the hell are you doing here? How dare you demand to see me?"

"Stop this fuss. I won't stay long." He put the piece of paper with Sarah's address on the desk. "Your son, Arthur, and his mother, Sarah, need you. This is their address. Take your responsibility and do right by them."

Pearce glanced at the paper. "What responsibility? I'm sure the child isn't mine."

"All you need is a glance at him to understand he is."

Pearce crumpled the piece of paper in his fist and tossed it in the cold hearth. "They aren't my responsibility. And even if Arthur were mine, I wouldn't behave as Father did, sharing his time between two families."

"Taking his responsibility was the only decent thing Father could do."

"Leave, Christopher. Sarah is a cunning woman, and she tricked you, too." Pearce started to open the door, but Christopher slammed a hand against it, blocking it.

"Arthur was sick for days because he lived in a damp house. Sarah was struggling. You don't want to spend money on them? Fine. I can provide for them, but I can't be the child's father. He needs you. You must be present in his life."

"No."

"Sarah was your mistress before you discarded her."

"I broke our arrangement because she was meeting with someone else," Pearce said. "I wasn't her only one. Then three months after I broke the affair, she claimed she was carrying my child. How convenient."

"She says you were her only one."

"She's lying. She didn't favour me."

"Bollocks. Arthur is your child."

"Just leave, Christopher, and don't come back." He paused as if exhausted, before rushing out of the room.

Bloody fool.

Christopher took the piece of paper from the hearth and headed for Pearce's bedroom. The noble duke needed a reminder of the not-so-noble deed he'd done.

A maid gasped when he walked past her, dropping the pile of towels she carried. "Good Lord!" she cried out.

"Oh, stop it. I'm leaving."

Pearce's bedroom had belonged to Father and hadn't changed a bit. Christopher had been there only once when he'd said goodbye to his dying father.

Not so grand memories.

He put the address on the escritoire and left. Perhaps when Pearce was alone, he'd look at the address and decide to do the right thing. Christopher's presence always triggered the worst responses from his brother.

Now, time for a pint and—he came to a grinding halt. His heart gave a stuttering kick, threatening to stop. Staring out of a bay window stood the last person he'd ever imagined seeing there that night. Or ever.

"Elizabeth." He wasn't sure if he'd whispered or said it out loud, but she turned towards him.

Her glossy chestnut hair framed her heart-shaped face, exalting her deep eyes that held him captive. He wasn't ready for the physical pain seeing her again caused him; it was like a punch in the chest. But it wasn't only pain.

There was a longing so powerful he staggered on his feet, a visceral desire to hold her, and a burning need to hear her laugh.

When he'd imagined seeing her again, he'd thought he'd be happy, grateful, or excited. But not that he would be in sheer pain.

Her lips parted, the only movement she made. "Christopher."

She raked a glance over him, reminding him of how he looked. Long hair, black clothes like a highwayman, and a gun.

He took a step towards her, almost without realising it. "It's been so long."

She walked closer, her chest rising and falling quickly in her tight silk bodice. The ivory-coloured gown she wore made her look like a princess shrouded in light and gold, like a star and just as unreachable.

"I was worried about you," she said. "All these years, I searched for you, but no one knew anything. You weren't present at your father's funeral. I hoped to see you there. I wanted to see you so much. I had so many things to tell you."

"I..."

A rush of energy shuddered through him, ordering him to move.

He closed the distance between them with one stride and hugged her with desperation. For a moment, he feared she'd shove him away or scream bloody murder, but she wrapped her arms around him, and right then, he was transported back to the cottage when it was only the two of them and he wasn't the bastard son of a duke but only Christopher. A boy who liked a girl.

Her scent hadn't changed; it was the same delicate rosewood fragrance. But her body had changed. She had more curves, and her gaze had hardened. Despite that, she felt the same in his arms—beautiful and perfect.

He gently cupped her cheeks, needing to see her eyes. "I didn't expect to see you here."

She put a hand on his chest, sending frissons of excitement through him. The diamond earrings swinging from her earlobes caught the light.

"What happened to you? Are you all right?" she asked.

"Yes. How are you?" He couldn't take his gaze off her.

She let out a sloppy laugh halfway between a snort and a gasp. "I've missed you so much. My mother didn't let me see you after they found you." Her voice grew high-pitched, and she shuddered.

"I wanted to. You have to believe me, but she locked me up in my room, and I was worried you thought I didn't want to see you—"

"Shush. It's all right."

He stroked her cheeks with his thumbs. Her skin was as silky as he remembered.

Her eyes flared wide at the gun. "Why are you carrying a gun?"

Reality was a slap to his face. Five years ago, he hadn't had any right to be close to her. Now, he shouldn't even share the same air she breathed.

He released her. "My life has changed." He was a criminal now, a gangster. More than a gangster. The head of a very successful criminal organisation. "It's better if no one sees you here with me. You should leave."

"Now that I've found you? No."

He stepped back, but she followed him, stopping an inch from him.

She breathed hard. "I tried to find you. I wanted to talk to you. It wasn't me who decided to stay away from you."

"I know. I've never thought it was you."

"Then you left without saying goodbye."

"I wanted to see you. My father didn't let me." His hand moved of its own accord and found her cheek again. "Not a day has passed without me thinking of you."

She pressed her cheek to his palm. "Promise me we'll see each other from now on."

"Elizabeth!" The sharp, feminine voice ripped through the quiet corner of happiness. "Come here immediately."

Elizabeth turned around. "Mother."

He stepped back from her, despite every instinct in him saying otherwise.

"What are you doing?" Lady Lincoln strode towards them with the determination of an executioner.

She grabbed Elizabeth's arm and gave it a hard yank, forcing Elizabeth to stagger towards her.

"Mother, you're hurting me," she said.

"Release her." He didn't care about courtesies. Not anymore.

Lady Lincoln pointed a finger at him. "You stay away from my daughter, or I'll send for the police." Her stern expression faltered when she saw the gun.

"I want to talk to him." Elizabeth shrugged herself free.

"No. You must leave," Lady Lincoln said.

As much as he wanted to spend more time with Elizabeth, he didn't want a scene or cause her trouble.

"We'll talk another time, Elizabeth," he said.

"There won't be another time." Lady Lincoln gave a light push to Elizabeth, shoving her towards the other side of the corridor. "Go. Everyone is searching for you. I need a word with Blackwood."

Elizabeth didn't move, her hands clenched. "I want to talk to him."

Lady Lincoln lowered her voice to a hiss. "Do you want the duke to come here and see this? Go!"

Christopher frowned. "The duke?"

Right then, Pearce's voice echoed from the other side of the corridor. "Elizabeth? Where are you?"

"Go, for heaven's sake." Her mother urged her. "Before he comes here. It's better for Blackwood as well."

True. He nodded. "Go."

"Elizabeth?" Pearce called again.

"We'll meet again, Christopher, I promise." Elizabeth raised a hand in farewell before vanishing down the corridor towards Pearce.

Christopher jutted out his chin as the countess came closer.

"Do you care about her?" she asked.

"Yes."

"Then you don't want to ruin her, do you? She's engaged to be married to His Grace. It's a matter of weeks before we give the formal announcement."

The news was like falling into the frozen lake all over again. Pearce, his brother, who detested him, would marry Elizabeth, would hold her at night, would give her a child, and would grow old with her. All the cockiness leached out of him.

"You aren't going to ruin their future." Lady Lincoln shook with anger. "You're nothing but a disgrace to this family, and if you have a shred of conscience or good sense, you'll leave the duke and my daughter alone. You have nothing to offer her but pain and humiliation, and I won't allow it. Leave her alone. She's going to be a duchess soon. Her reputation can't be tarnished by you."

There was some truth in that.

He couldn't say anything. The pain that had struck him when he'd seen Elizabeth overwhelmed him because it was now ten times stronger.

Her expression softened. "I don't hate you, Blackwood, and I don't have anything against you, but you must understand my position. I'm protecting my daughter, and you're a danger to her. She's an earl's daughter. You're an illegitimate son. You two don't belong together. Now leave." She didn't wait for a reply before hurrying down the corridor.

He stood there, staring at the spot where Elizabeth had been a moment ago. Fate had a wicked sense of humour. He'd found Elizabeth but only for a brief moment, a cruel reminder of how much he desired her and how he would never have her.

seventeen

ELIZABETH HAD TO blink away hot tears as she left Christopher behind. As much as she disliked agreeing with her mother, if Pearce found her with Christopher, he would be upset and most importantly, she didn't want to cause Christopher trouble.

She had barely time to turn a corner before bumping into Pearce.

"Elizabeth." He put his hands on her shoulders. "I was looking for you. Are you all right?"

"Yes."

"You're flustered. Were you crying?"

"No, I ..." Couldn't she have a moment alone?

Christopher's intoxicating smell lingered on her skin, reminding her of how close they'd been a moment ago.

"Something upset you." Pearce took her hand and led her to a small sitting room.

When he shut the door behind him, a flare of worry pinched her chest.

"What are you doing?" she asked.

"Nothing. I just want to know what happened to you. Why are you upset? Was it me?"

"I had an argument with my mother. Nothing important." That was true. At least the part about the argument.

"She wants a quick engagement, doesn't she? She wants us married in six months. She's quite insistent. When I discussed the possibility of marrying you with your parents, they were both eager for a quick engagement."

She rubbed her forehead. "If you'll excuse me, I need the ladies' room ... again."

She went to open the door, but he took her wrist. The grip was gentle, but it was also a reminder of how strong and powerful he was.

"I'm sorry if I put pressure on you. I know you feel overwhelmed," he said. "Marrying a duke usually is. But it's the most logical decision for you."

Most logical. How awful. She loved logic and mathematics, but not when it came to matters of the heart. And if she heard one more comment on her phantomatic wedding, she was going to scream.

She tugged at her hand, and he let her go without hesitation.

"We can be happy together. You'll have all the things you want," he said.

Things. She didn't want things. She wanted love, passion, companionship.

"Thank you for your understanding." She left the parlour, wondering if he'd caught the sadness in her voice.

Since he didn't follow her, she walked back to the corridor where she'd met Christopher, but it was empty.

She returned to the ballroom and waited for her mother. Smiling and nodding her head politely at the other guests required a ridiculous amount of control. She paused in front of the window overlooking the street, hoping to catch a glimpse of Christopher.

Her heart stuttered when she spotted him watching the house. The glow from a street lamp lit his blond hair.

She had to admit that, for those who weren't aware of the days she and Christopher had shared in the cottage, her concern for his well-being had to sound absurd.

Officially, she had no reason to care about him, having seen him only once. Pearce wouldn't understand the bond between them—she didn't fully understand it, either—but he would also do his best to keep Christopher at bay.

On a cold, rational level, she couldn't deny her stubbornness; wanting to see him was impractical, to say the least. Dangerous at the most.

The combination of care and tenderness she felt for him had no future. She would never have the opportunity to explore those feelings because, unless she abandoned her status, position, and family, they wouldn't be together.

And what her future would be? She wasn't ready for such a drastic change of her life. There wouldn't be any going back. Was she ready to leave her house and family? No, unless Christopher shared her same wish to be together.

But he might not want to be involved with her in that fashion. Perhaps he didn't care about a wife. Perhaps he already had one.

She pressed a gloved hand on the glass. He lifted his head up and raised a hand although she wasn't sure he was staring at her. If she opened the window—

"I can't believe you didn't learn your lesson," Mother half-hissed, half-whispered, somehow managing to sneak up on Elizabeth unseen. "You're still thinking about him."

"He's a good man, despite what you say." Although she wondered why he carried a gun. Pearce had mentioned something about Christopher being a criminal, but a gun?

Mother forced a smile at a passing lady before speaking again. "You're about to become a duchess. You can't and mustn't associate yourself with someone like him. Whatever childish fantasy you indulge yourself in about him, it must stop now."

"I'm not about to become a duchess, and I don't indulge myself in any fantasy. I only think we behaved horribly with him."

"Of course, His Grace is going to marry you. He bought you an engagement ring. Everyone knows that."

"Oh, please. I've never agreed to marry Pearce." How many times could she repeat that without going mad?

"Tell me the truth," Mother said after another lady had passed. "Have you seen that man in secret all these years?"

"That's ridiculous."

"Think very carefully about what you want. Mistakes aren't always forgiven in society. Your father and I can't protect you from everything, and you'll excuse me if we don't want to be disgraced because of you. Because that's what will happen if you ruin yourself with that man. And that's it. I don't want to discuss this subject ever again."

Elizabeth glanced at the spot under the street lamp, but it was empty. Without his presence after their brief encounter, it was as if a cage were closing in on her, trapping her. The familiar choking sensation made her hitch a breath.

Pearce was dancing with an old lady, looking elegant and handsome in the glittering, excessive golden ballroom.

He was such a contrast with Christopher, who was all darkness and shadows, but somehow she wasn't sure she'd be warm in Pearce's light.

eighteen

AFTER THE BALL, a day spent walking Hyde Park's busy paths, shopping, and drinking tea in the teahouses had done nothing to cheer Elizabeth up.

She'd left home early that morning, barely eating her breakfast, and decided to stay away from home for as long as possible to think.

Her heart was torn in two. A part of her understood why a connection with Christopher was dangerous for her family. But another part didn't listen to reason. The prejudice against Christopher was unfair. He was a better man than many others she knew.

Perhaps the best thing she could do was marry Pearce to have the opportunity to protect Christopher. With time, she might convince Pearce to help his brother out of whatever dubious situation he was in. Or maybe she was simply trying to convince herself she didn't want to leave her house, face the world alone, and do whatever she pleased with all the dangers that decision would bring.

No, if anything, she was sure of one thing—she didn't want to marry Pearce. And the more everyone pushed her towards him, the more she grew convinced that marrying him would be the biggest mistake of her life.

The only possible solution was to have an honest conversation with him and make him understand she didn't want to become his duchess, courtship or not, diamond ring or not.

Dusk had fallen by the time she walked towards the carriage to go home. Her body was sore from the walk, and the beginning of a headache throbbed. She'd send a message to Pearce as soon as she arrived home, asking him to see her the very next day. Mother would have to accept her decision. Just thinking about breaking her almost engagement made her chest lighter.

The footman opened the door to the carriage for her, and she was about to climb in when a passing landau sprayed mud on her skirt.

"Botheration." She frowned at the offending stain.

"Elizabeth." Maude with her inseparable friend Irene stopped next to her on the pavement. She glanced at Elizabeth's stained skirt. "Oh, mud."

Elizabeth arched her brow, giving a curt nod as a quick greeting.

"Finally, you got what you deserved," Irene said.

The mud?

The two ladies laughed.

"How does it feel?" Irene asked.

"I don't understand." Elizabeth shifted her gaze from one woman to the other.

"The moment when a rumour becomes a certainty is always a shock," Maude said. "At least for the person at the centre of the gossip."

Oh no. The blasted wedding again. She put a foot on the step to climb into the carriage. "The Duke of Grafton and I haven't decided to get married."

Maude nodded. "Oh, we know."

"Have a lovely evening, Elizabeth." Irene smiled, walking away with her friend.

The two ladies paused to glance over their shoulders at her before speeding up and leaving her puzzled.

She wondered what Maude meant. Not that she would complain if Pearce had finally started to tell everyone that their wedding wasn't certain, but the lady's tone hinted at something else.

A flutter of activity animated the entry hall when she arrived home. Maids and footmen rushed by, casting her sideways glances and barely pausing to greet her.

She didn't have time to remove her coat before the butler approached her.

"Lady Elizabeth." He dabbed his forehead with a handkerchief. "Your parents and His Grace, the Duke of Grafton, are waiting for you in the drawing room."

Odd. "Thank you, Haughton."

A maid took her coat but didn't meet her gaze.

She might be imagining things, but she could swear the butler and the maid were scared. She entered the drawing room where the atmosphere was so tense the hairs on the back of her neck tickled her skin. If Pearce had come here to propose officially and announce their wedding, she'd take another walk.

He stood in front of the fireplace, an elbow propped on the mantelpiece. He shot her an incendiary glare that stole her breath. Father's jaw was clenched so tightly she worried he would hurt himself, and Mother's face was bloodless.

"What is it?" she asked no one in particular.

Father nodded at the footman to leave. He didn't speak until the doors were shut. "His Grace needs to talk to you."

She angled towards Pearce who looked like he didn't want to see her at all. "Is something the matter?"

"Do you think I'm stupid?" he asked in all seriousness.

Mother shivered, folding her hands on her lap.

Elizabeth gazed around at a loss. "I don't understand."

"Please," Father said. "No lies. He knows everything."

"About what?"

"Where have you been?" Pearce walked over to her, his eyebrows forming a deep V.

"I went shopping and took a walk. Why, what happened?"

He gripped her chin in a firm hold. "You're lying."

A wave of outrage shocked her. She stepped out of his reach, feeling his fingers still on her chin.

"I'm not. How dare you?" She glanced at her parents for support, but they shook their heads. "Why would I lie?"

Pearce's face had none of its usual beauty. "You were with your lover."

She let out a quick chuckle at the ridiculous accusation. "Absurd. What lover? You don't make any sense."

"My half-brother!" he said with contempt.

Mother clamped a hand over her mouth. Father stared at Elizabeth as if she were a stranger.

She clenched her fists. "I don't know what caused you to believe such a lie, but I'm not Christopher's lover."

"There is a trusted witness who saw you and Blackwood alone at the ball last night," Father said, "in a rather intimate attitude, talking about your next meeting. A meeting that would have happened today. You told him you would have left the house with an excuse and been with him all day."

"Poppycock. I didn't plan to stay out for the whole day. It was a sudden decision." She whipped her head towards her mother. "Mother, you saw me. You know that nothing happened."

"So you did meet Christopher last night," Pearce said.

"Yes, by chance, but nothing happened. Mother, please. Why did you tell Pearce I'm Christopher's lover?"

Mother swallowed a couple of times. "I'm not the witness, and I don't know who the witness is. Only His Grace knows. I had no choice but to confess to having seen you and that man alone in a corridor, but there was someone else watching the scene. Someone who was there before me."

"Who?"

Pearce shook his head. "That's none of your concern."

"Yes, because that person is lying. Who is lying?"

"I won't tell you. I know how Christopher behaves. I know *who* he is. He won't hesitate to harm the witness for revenge. And the witness isn't the point." He raised his voice again. "The point is that you lied to me and used me because you're in love with Christopher, because you want to elope with him, because you favour him over me."

"This is nonsense. Last night was the first time I'd seen Christopher in years. I didn't have any contact with him, as I don't have any now."

"The witness—"

"The witness is lying!" she said. "Is it Rebecca?"

Annoyed scoffs filled the air, but aside from that, Pearce denied it or confirmed it. She didn't want to marry him, but she wouldn't be accused of something she didn't do.

"You couldn't have disgraced this family more." Father rubbed his forehead. "You've always had the tendency to cheat and lie."

Not that again! "If you're talking about that stupid competition, you don't know me."

"Perhaps I don't," Father said. "But I was referring to the blizzard. I didn't say anything because I didn't want to embarrass you and because Blackwood was who knew where, but I know you didn't find shelter in our hunting lodge. I discovered it when I met Lord Bletchley who thanked me profusely for the hospitality in a moment of need."

Tarnation. Elizabeth licked her dry lips.

"You're a liar," Father said. "At first, I thought you were confused. I didn't suspect the truth, but now I believe you were with Blackwood during the storm, likely in that cottage that belonged to his mother."

"I wasn't with Christopher." She was aware to be a terrible liar, but if there was a single chance to protect Christopher, she would try.

Pearce shook his head. "Goodness, you slept with him, didn't you?"

Yes, but not in the way he meant. "No." Her voice didn't sound steady.

Mother sniffled.

Father had more to say though. "You must tell the whole truth to His Grace, and maybe, if he feels so inclined, he'll forgive you."

"Oh, that's so generous of him. Pity that I have nothing to confess." Her throat burned from her effort to control her temper.

"Then you can leave this house." Father straightened.

She took a step back. "You don't mean that."

Mother turned her head away from Elizabeth.

"Mother. You know I'm not Christopher's mistress."

"You've always been interested in him despite my repeated warnings," Mother said without looking at her. "How could you?"

"I didn't do anything. Nothing ever happened with Christopher. You all just hate him!"

She swept the room with her gaze, hoping to find a friendly face, but there was none. She was alone against three executioners.

Pearce turned around as well as if disgusted with her. "You should be grateful I'm giving you the chance to confess and redeem yourself. I believe that deep down, you didn't want to be unfaithful. Perhaps Christopher forced you. Did he force you? Did he threaten you?"

Every pair of eyes fixed on her in a silent warning.

"If he forced you," Mother said, "you have nothing to fear. Everyone would understand. He's such a despicable man—"

"He didn't force me." Her breathing came out in quick pants. She would never, ever blame Christopher for something he hadn't done, only to save herself. "Christopher isn't a despicable man. He's kind and honourable."

"Think carefully, Elizabeth." Mother glowered. "We're talking about our reputation."

"For the last time," she gritted out. "Nothing happened, and Christopher would never force me."

Pearce scoffed. "If you spend some time on your own, without the comforts you're used to enjoying, you'll come around and tell me the truth to redeem yourself."

Redeem herself? The more she thought about that, the more frustrated she became. "I'm telling you the truth now. You're too focused on yourself to see it."

"Elizabeth!" Mother said.

"Enough!" Father opened the door. "Out. A bag with a few of your things has already been prepared. Inside, you'll find a small amount of money. Do what you want. Don't come back unless you mean to tell us the truth and you're ready to redeem yourself."

Again that awful word.

"No." The room tilted. She didn't know if it was anger or exhaustion. "I didn't do anything wrong. I don't deserve this punishment."

"This is my house," Father said, "and you will leave. I'm sparing you the humiliation of having George escort you out kicking and screaming."

"Leave," Mother said. "Before you disgrace us further."

Elizabeth was so enraged she couldn't speak. Breathing was difficult, and a funny, pulsating dark spot filled her field of vision.

Desperation pushed her legs onwards, but Pearce held her back before she could cross the threshold.

"I respect your father. He was my father's most trusted friend, and I don't want to start a scandal that will destroy him and your siblings, but you'll never see me again unless you're ready to tell me the truth and beg for my forgiveness."

"Good." She marched out without glancing back at her parents.

If by 'truth' he meant her accusing Christopher of having forced her, then she didn't have anything else to add.

A maid waited for her in the entry hall, standing next to a carpetbag. "Your bag, my lady. You'll find five pounds in it." She bobbed a quick curtsy before leaving.

Hot tears stung Elizabeth's eyes, but she snatched the bag and walked out, wincing as the footman shut the door behind her. She strode along the pavement until the tears blurred her vision to the point she didn't see anything.

Five pounds and a bag of clothes.

She had only to find a place to sleep that night. Tomorrow, she'd talk to her parents again and clear up the misunderstanding without accusing Christopher of forcing her.

After hailing a cab, she composed herself. Her parents had to see reason. She cared little about Pearce. His accusations hurt too deeply, but she would never beg him for forgiveness for something she hadn't done. But she wanted to clear her name.

After that, she'd probably leave anyway because her parents' lack of trust was unforgivable. She might spend some time in the country with her sister until she figured out what to do.

The cab stopped in front of Rebecca's house. Elizabeth knocked on the door, aware it was night and she was unannounced. But Rebecca might be involved in this affair, and Elizabeth needed to talk to her.

A cold shiver crawled down her back as her anger-fuelled energy dwindled. She shifted her weight, her breath turning into mist.

"Keadew Residence." A maid stared at her with concern.

"I'm Lady Elizabeth. I'd like to see Miss Norton." She moved to enter, but the maid didn't let her pass.

"Wait here." The maid shut the door in her face.

The shock caused Elizabeth to remain still. It wasn't the first time she'd visited Rebecca, not at this hour, but the servants knew who she was.

The door inched open again, and Rebecca appeared on the threshold, glancing behind her shoulder. "Why did you come here?"

"You know what happened."

"Not really. I know enough to understand I shouldn't talk to you."

"How?"

"I met your mother when she was returning home while I was promenading with Maude and Irene. She was distraught. She didn't tell us all the details, but she told us you were leaving London for a while because something sudden had occurred. We found it strange. But since you're here with a carpetbag ..." Rebecca gave her a slow once-over. "Well, I guess that what your mother meant to say is that you disgraced your family and your parents threw you out. And servants talk." She started to shut the door. "Leave."

Elizabeth blocked the door with a hand. "Was it you? Did you spread lies about me?"

"How dare you! You're ready to blame anyone for something you did. You're the only one at fault here."

"I didn't do anything."

Rebecca's gaze was hard and cold. "I don't know what you did, but it must be something horrible. Otherwise, your mother wouldn't be so distraught. I have nothing to do with what happened to you, and I don't want to get involved. In fact, I don't even want to know what you did."

"Rebecca—"

"You must leave. I don't want anyone to see you here."

"Yes, because gossip can be brutal. You know something about that. You told Pearce you saw me with a man at the ball the other night."

"What are you talking about? I wasn't even there!"

True. That made Elizabeth pause. Not even Maude and Irene had been there. Taken by frustration, she'd rushed to come here when, in fact, she didn't have any evidence of Rebecca's guilt. If the witness wasn't Rebecca, then who?

"Leave." Rebecca shut the door.

Confusion quickened Elizabeth's pulse, but the shock froze her. She stood there, staring at the closed, shiny black door and feeling like a feather dragged this way and that, as the wind pleased. She was about to leave when the door opened once again.

She turned around, but it wasn't Rebecca.

"My lady," the maid whispered. "I'm sorry for what happened. Do you have a place to go?"

"No."

The maid glanced behind her. "Nottingham Street, Whitechapel. There's a cheap, safe boarding house. The landlady is a friend of mine. Tell her Nell sent you. She'll find you a place to work as well if you ask her."

"I only need a room for a night. Tomorrow, I'll come back home."

The woman's eyebrows lowered. "My lady, go to Nottingham Street. That's all I can do for you. But be careful in Whitechapel at night. Some say the Ripper is still out there, and the gang of the King is bloodthirsty and ruthless. The streets aren't safe at night. I must go now." She shut the door.

Elizabeth stood on the pavement for a long moment.

She didn't need to find a job, did she? Her parents would take her back soon. The misunderstanding with Pearce would be cleared, and she'd sleep in her bedroom tomorrow night and then she'd plan what to do next.

Yes, that was what would happen.

BEING A CRIMINAL was easy. One needed only a lot of imagination and not many scruples. The difficult part was to pay attention not to get caught.

From the moment Christopher had seen Elizabeth again, he'd lost some of his focus on the job and become sloppy, which meant risking a brush with the peelers. Also, the fact he spent every waking hour working or boxing didn't help sharpen his mind.

The intense activity did nothing to remove Elizabeth from his daily thoughts and nocturnal nightmares. She would be Pearce's bride.

Maybe that was for the best. No, sod it. It was for the worst. Pearce would never make her happy. The bloody duke was so worried about his own arse that he couldn't make himself happy, least of all someone else.

Just to complete that pile of shite, Christopher had sent Finn to the Earl of Lincoln's house to quietly contact Elizabeth. The lad was so charming and young that people easily talked to him.

Christopher had promised he wouldn't bother her since his being a criminal and her being a lady complicated the situation.

But after having seen her and because he was a selfish bastard, he'd wanted to see her again, be with her, and he was tired of denying it.

Sod Pearce. Sod the whole world. He wanted to be with her in whatever way she would allow.

Or so he'd thought.

His research had been wasted time. Apparently, she was visiting her sister in the country, supposed to return after a few months. She and Pearce might celebrate their wedding there.

Bloody fantastic. He guessed Pearce would visit her often, take long walks with her, kiss her ... the thought was sheer torture, and his mind enjoyed inflicting him pain.

Maybe Elizabeth had realised that seeing each other would be a mistake, and she'd decided to leave London to stay away from him. If that was the case, she'd done the right thing, and he wouldn't bother her. But he didn't have to like the situation.

Christopher yawned loudly as he returned home from the piers. Bloody smuggling was getting increasingly difficult, and the coppers were greedy bastards. Always asking for more bribes while his rivals kept trying to dethrone him.

The moment he entered the palace, Jane—the woman who was the housekeeper, cook, secretary, and everything in between—ran towards him, holding up her apron. Darko trotted next to her but reached him first.

"Mate." Christopher gave his dog a hug as usual. Regardless of how tired he was, he always had time and energy for Darko.

Black fur rained around. It didn't matter how many times Christopher groomed the hound, more fur would come off.

"Guv, Guv." Jane shifted her weight from one foot to the other.

"What is it?"

"Someone came here today, looking for you."

"Coppers?"

"No. A man in a shiny suit." She handed him a piece of paper. "He said this message was for you, private for you."

He unfolded the piece of paper and snorted. Pearce had sent his footman to the royal palace because he demanded to see him *immediately* at a nearby address.

Yes, of course, immediately. He would fly there. He'd run there at breakneck speed. No worries. Just wait and see.

"Did the man say anything else?" he asked.

"Only that it was very urgent. He came three times to see if you'd returned. He was quite insistent."

"Great. It must be important." He crumpled the piece of paper and lobbed it, missing a pot of geranium by an inch. Bad luck.

Jane snatched the paper ball from the floor. "With due respect, Guv, but you should go."

"I've just returned from the piers."

"We don't want to attract attention, do we?" She unfolded the piece of paper and folded it again neatly to stash it into his coat pocket. "We don't want a ducal footman—"

"You read the message."

"—coming here asking questions. That would lead to more questions, and we don't want that."

"Damn."

"Good lad," Jane said, although he wasn't sure if she was referring to him or Darko since the dog licked her hand.

Bloody Pearce.

Christopher marched out again, cursing under his breath.

If anything, he wanted to ask Pearce how he'd found him. Not that Christopher's address was a secret, but a duke didn't dwell in an area like Whitechapel.

He grunted and scoffed all the way. At least the place Pearce had chosen wasn't far. The house was a decent building, likely one of Pearce's many properties. Perhaps that was the house where Pearce had used to meet Sarah.

Christopher barely knocked before the footman he'd seen months ago in Grafton House opened the door.

"Blackwood. This way." The footman kept his distance, casting him a wary glance.

"Our last encounter has left its mark," he said.

But the chap lacked any sense of humour and didn't reply.

The footman opened the door to a sitting room. "Your Grace, Blackwood."

"Finally," Pearce said.

The footman held the door open for Christopher, shooting him a glare Christopher returned. The door was shut with a thud behind him.

Pearce had dispensed with his usual expensive clothes for a more practical suit, something Father would have done when visiting Christopher and his mother.

"What took you so long?" Pearce asked.

"Goodbye, Pearce. Wish you the best. Actually, no, I don't." He moved towards the door, but Pearce stepped in front of him. His expression genuinely pained.

"Why do you want to destroy me?" Again, honesty rang out in Pearce's voice.

Of all the questions Christopher expected, that one didn't make any sense. "What the hell are you talking about?"

"You took her from me just to prove what? That everyone favours you, and no one would choose me."

"You're barking mad." He brushed past Pearce. "Why did you tell me to come here?"

Pearce closed a hand on Christopher's arm, showing a strong grip that warranted some concern. "I'm here for Elizabeth."

That caught his full attention. "What does Elizabeth have to do with anything? And weren't you talking about me proving something? You don't make any sense."

"She's your lover, and together, you decided to humiliate me."

Christopher barked out a laugh. The idea was too ridiculous. "What type of opium have you been smoking? I tell you, opium is not a good choice. It turns your brain into a pulp and makes it bleed."

Pearce got uncomfortably close. "Having Father's affection wasn't enough for you. You had to steal Elizabeth from me."

Christopher scowled. "That's enough. This joke isn't funny. I haven't seen Elizabeth in a long time."

"Liar. Someone saw you two together."

He shrugged, not wanting to confirm anything and put Elizabeth in danger.

Pearce seemed undecided between anger and pain. "Where's she? I need to talk to her."

"What do you mean by that?" He put a hand on the knob but paused. He was about to say that Elizabeth was visiting her sister in the country, but he wasn't supposed to know that. "What have you done to Elizabeth?"

"I didn't do anything. Her father kicked her out six months ago after we discovered she was your mistress."

"What?" Christopher roared. He came face-to-face with Pearce without even realising it. In his haste, he didn't mention that Elizabeth wasn't his mistress. "Did you hurt her?"

Pearce's harsh mask fell for a moment, revealing only a sad, lonely man. "She hurt *me*. After her parents and I confronted her, she denied being your mistress. Her father disowned her and threw her out. I gave her a chance to redeem herself. If she told me the truth, I would have forgiven her, but she chose to leave her house to be with you."

"Bollocks. Where is she?"

"I have no bloody idea," Pearce gritted out. "That's why I asked you." The deep worry-lines on his forehead smoothed. "I thought she would have come to me after a couple of weeks of living on her own, but she didn't. I wanted her punished, yes, but now I wonder where she is. Her mother told me she'd received a few letters from Elizabeth, but she'd burned all of them without opening them. Silly woman. Now I can't find her. I'm worried."

So was Christopher. "Hell." He paced. "I haven't seen her. I'm not lying."

Pearce rubbed the back of his neck. "I don't know what to believe anymore. She lied to me. She tricked me. And I fell for it like an idiot."

"She isn't my mistress, you bloody twat."

"But you and Elizabeth were together during the Great Blizzard, weren't you?" Pearce recovered his ducal composure. "You were in your mother's cottage."

Well, lying was pointless. "Yes, we were together." He expected a new outburst from Pearce, a shout, a crass word, but nothing.

Pearce paled like a man bleeding from a lethal wound. He lowered his gaze, which was a first. The duke never looked away from his opponent. There was something eerie in his silence. "I'd hoped it wasn't true."

"Pearce ..." Christopher didn't know what to say. He'd never been in the position of comforting his brother, but the pain was palpable.

"Go," Pearce whispered.

Saying he was sorry was only a waste of time.

Time that he should employ to search for Elizabeth.

twenty

SIX MONTHS OF working as a waitress in different taverns across London had taught Elizabeth to steer clear of drunk patrons, lecherous hands, brothel madams, vendors who sold miracle drugs, and men who offered her money for dubious activities. A fast course on real life.

Still, even though she was careful, now and then she attracted unwanted attention.

"Where are you going, pretty lass?" A man slapped his meaty hand on Elizabeth's rear.

She scurried out of reach, managing not to drop the tray of mugs of ale she was carrying. "Get off me, cur."

Another thing she'd learnt was how to swear. Swearing got her some degree of respect from the patrons. Politeness didn't work in a place like the Hog's Head, a small tavern in Whitechapel. She'd been working there for only a couple of weeks, but she could already tell it wasn't different from the other dubious places where she'd found employment.

"Another ale!" a man shouted from a corner.

"Where's my dinner?" another one asked. "I ordered it an hour ago!"

Tobacco smoke formed a thick fog that singed her nostrils. The loud, rowdy conversations buzzed in her ears, and the floor was so greasy she could skate on it. A song started from a corner. Out-of-tune voices sang about a very specific, anatomical part of a beautiful woman. She thought she'd heard it all.

"Come here." Another patron tried to snatch her wrist, and she slapped his hand away without thinking. Habits.

After she delivered the mugs of ale to the patrons, she took a breather behind the counter. Her back hurt, and the skin of her hands was covered in cuts, calluses, and red spots where it wasn't peeling off from using scullery lye soap.

Unless she became faster at serving around the tables, she wouldn't find employment in a better restaurant or a teahouse. At least in a reputable establishment, the customers didn't paw the waitresses in public. They did it somewhere private, but it was an improvement.

"Lizzie," the cook called from the kitchen. "The bins need to be emptied."

"Again?"

"Get your lazy arse in the back and be quick!"

She weaved through other waitresses carrying more trays of mugs of ale or dirty plates. The kitchen was an inferno of steam and shouts. Everything smelled of garlic, even the apples. She smelled of garlic, too.

The bin overflowed with leftover vegetables and other unidentified rotting things.

She brushed a curl of hair from her sweaty face before grabbing the bin by the handles. Heavens, it was heavy.

"Can somebody help me with the rubbish?" she asked no one in particular.

"Just do it!" Natalie waved her off. "We're all busy. Stop whining."

Fine.

She dragged the bin towards the back door. The alleyway

behind the tavern was lit by a lonely lantern, but it was enough to see the rats feasting on the rubbish.

A muscle in her back got pulled, and she winced. On the threshold of the door, she carefully inched the bin down to the cobbles, lest it topple. Sweat trickled down her back.

A moment of fatigue caught her once outside. The cold air was a stark contrast with the heat in the kitchen, but at least it didn't smell of tobacco, just rubbish and coal dust.

She wiped the sweat from her forehead. A cut on her palm started bleeding again, staining her apron. Botheration.

She'd need to ask for a clean apron, which meant the manager would retain a full shilling from her pay, which meant she couldn't pay the rent. Her landlord would kick her out.

She leant against the brick wall behind her, wondering if she could hide the stain or wash it. Except that, the last time she'd tried to clean a stain from her apron, she'd made a mess, and the manager had kept two shillings.

Footsteps came from the other side of the narrow alleyway. She tensed, glancing in that direction. Passersby didn't usually walk in that secluded alleyway, and the narrow exit opened to another alleyway. The rubbish bins took up almost the entire space.

She held her breath as a man walked in. A flat hat hid his features. He was dressed in black clothes, which didn't allow her to understand how large and tall he was. At his side stood the biggest, scariest black dog she'd ever seen. The hound's yellow eyes fixed on her.

"You, girl," the man said.

She swallowed hard.

"We're looking for a woman called Elizabeth. She's a lady, the daughter of an earl. Do you know her?"

The dog growled, exposing long, sharp teeth.

All the air rushed out of her lungs. She'd heard stories of the most powerful gang in Whitechapel. Its leader was called the King. Those thugs didn't hesitate to kill and maim at will. Rumour had it the King kidnapped babies from their crates, forced himself on women, and beat those who didn't pay protection money. Not to mention that the Ripper was said to be still prowling Whitechapel. Plenty of reasons to be scared.

"Well?" the man prompted. "Do you know where I can find Elizabeth?"

"No," she whispered.

"What did you say?" The man came closer.

She stepped back. "Leave me alone."

"I only want to ask you a few questions." He spread his arms, revealing a dagger at his side.

The dog straightened its ears. The man moved in closer. He was younger than she'd thought, but she wouldn't make the mistake of considering him less dangerous.

Elizabeth grabbed a fistful of her skirts and made a dash for the other side of the alleyway.

"Where are you going?" The man followed her.

The dog chased her too, barking and baring its fangs.

She sped up, but her boots slipped on the wet cobbles and she fell over. A muffled groan left her when she slammed her head against the wall and pain turned everything white and then black.

Her last thought was that being killed in a dark alley was the proper ending to her six months of misery.

AN ACHE POUNDED in Elizabeth's head when she fluttered her eyes open.

She lay on something soft and smelling of soap. Definitely not the alley. Her first instinct was to scream, but she forced herself to remain quiet. If that thug had kidnapped her, she had to be careful and pretend not to be awake yet.

She remained as still as possible, trying to catch any sounds or signs she wasn't alone. Muffled male voices came from somewhere, and she focused on them.

"... not my fault, Guv." That sounded like the young man from the alley. "She fell. I didn't touch her."

"She's unconscious and with a bruise on her head." Was that Christopher?

"She ran," the man said. "She did everything by herself. I said, 'Hullo,' and she ran."

"You scared her. I told you not to hurt her." Yes, it was Christopher.

"But it's her, isn't it?" the man said. "I wasn't sure it was her. I asked one of the waitresses at the restaurant, and she said there was a woman called Lizzie working there."

"It's her, but you didn't handle the situation as I told you to do."

"That's unfair!" the man said. "She was terrified of Darko as well."

"Rubbish. How could anyone be scared of my pup?"

"Seriously, Guv?"

"Anyway," Christopher said. "Call the search off. She's here."

There were mutters, a bark, and feet shuffling. Then the door inched inwards, and a beam of yellow light lit the bedroom, a wide room in rich brown wood and patchwork quilts.

She slowly propped herself up, blinking in the semidarkness. "Christopher?"

He turned on a few lamps. "Elizabeth. How are you?" He was next to her in a moment in a flutter of black fabric.

She couldn't help but recoil at his speed.

He frowned, moving back. "I'm sorry if Darko and Finn scared you. I thought the presence of my pup would have reassured you in case Finn had found you."

"Pup?"

"Darko is my dog. His name means gift in Slavic. He's very sweet once you know him."

A more appropriate word for that beast would be hellhound. "Were you looking for me?"

"I divided my men into small groups to search for you. I was searching for you in another restaurant when Finn found you." He huffed. "You have no idea how many bloody Elizabeth, Elise, Beth, or Lizzie there are. It took me weeks to find you." He flashed a smile as he stared at her.

"So you know everything, that my family kicked me out."

He sat on a stuffed stool next to the bed and hunched his shoulders, failing to look less menacing. "Pearce took care of informing me. From the moment I knew what had happened, I searched for you. Actually, I tried to contact you a few days after the ball. I sent Finn to your house, but the maid told him you were in the country with your sister."

"Not exactly." She rubbed her aching forehead. "I had no idea you sent someone to my house." Not her house anymore, but anyway.

"I just wanted to see you again." He parted his lips as if he wanted to say something else, but he remained silent, his eyes unblinking.

They stared at each other, becoming for a moment two strangers. Or maybe she was too nervous.

"I'm happy to see you," she said.

His smile widened. "Hell, so am I. So relieved as well." He tilted his head after another long pause as if he didn't know how to talk to her anymore. "What happened to you?"

"A good dose of real life, I guess." She grimaced when she put her injured hand down.

"What is it?"

"I sliced my palm a while ago."

"Let me see." He gently took her hand and examined it in the glow of a lamp. "Nasty cut. It's infected. And the bruise on your forehead must be painful."

"Oh, this." She touched her forehead. "When I saw your man,

I got scared. Stories of those poor women found dead in the alleyways of Whitechapel made me wary. Some say the Ripper is still hunting."

"No, not anymore. We took care of him." He rose and rummaged through a cabinet to fish out a leather bag.

"What … what do you exactly do in Whitechapel?"

"Smuggling, illegal gambling, illegal bare-knuckle fights, that sort of thing." The honesty with which he stated that was disarming. "After my father died, Pearce made clear that he didn't want to support or help me in any way. Father had given me a job on his estate in Yorkshire, and Pearce unceremoniously gave me the sack. So here I am. I built my own kingdom." He spread his arms. "That's why they call me the King."

Dash it. Mother had been right. A little quiver crawled down her back. She was gobsmacked. Christopher was the infamous King she'd heard about.

"So it's true. You're a … criminal."

"Semantics. I prefer the expression 'tycoon with his own set of rules'." He sat next to her. "Does that bother you? You're free to leave whenever you want. The plan wasn't to kidnap you, but to talk to you."

"I'm surprised. But I'm not going to judge you. After having experienced extreme poverty, I understand why people resort to criminality. Surviving without help or support is a real struggle." But she'd be lying if she said she wasn't a little afraid.

"Don't be scared of me," he whispered, seemingly reading her mind. "You have nothing to fear."

"I know." She meant it. He might be the King of Whitechapel, but he would never hurt her.

He opened the leather bag to reveal a set of bottles, rolls of bandage, and other medical tools. "Give me your hand." His tone became low and serious.

She did as told and couldn't deny a quick shiver of excitement at the contact with his fingers.

"This is going to sting." He dabbed the cut with a cloth and disinfectant.

She gnashed her teeth. "It really hurts."

"They say the more it hurts, the more effective it is." He bandaged her palm with a clean strip of fabric, handling her hand with infinite care. "What would you like to do?"

"What do you mean?"

He didn't release her hand but held it gently between his. "Do you need money, a place to stay, or a new job? A cottage by the sea? All of those?"

The whole situation was so new she didn't know what to say. "I don't know."

He released her hand, trailing his fingers over her knuckles. "I understand if you're hesitant to accept the help of a criminal, but these are exceptional circumstances, and I didn't forget you saved my life." He raised his blue eyes to her. "I didn't forget you."

She touched her forehead again, her thoughts confused, and the throb in her head didn't help.

"Also, you might want to clear your name," he said. "I can help. I can talk to your parents and Pearce again, make clear we've never been lovers."

She chuckled bitterly. "No offence, but they won't listen to a word you say. They made up their minds about me, about us." She stared at her bandaged hand, the first sign of someone caring for her in months. "My parents had many opportunities to change their minds. I sent them letters to inform them where I was. They never replied. Nor did my brothers, sisters, and friends. Not even when I finished the money Father had given me and I had to beg in the streets before I found a job, not when I slept in an alleyway, covered by newspapers."

A muscle in his jaw ticked, and a hard glint flashed in his gaze. "Hell. Had I known, I would have helped you."

"I tried to search for you, but I had no idea where you were."

"You'll have a place here if you want. If you feel better, I'll show you around the palace to help you decide."

"The palace?"

He grinned. "I'm the King."

"I heard rumours about the King." She licked her dry lips. "But now that I know it's you, I can't believe you kidnap babies and attack women."

He couldn't be that heartless, could he?

He chuckled bitterly. "Just rumours. They're part of my persona as the King. I swear on my honour that I've never done any of those things. Please don't believe them. You're the only one who truly knows my heart. No one else."

Goodness. Now she felt guilty for having doubted him even for a moment. She lowered her gaze and fiddled with the bandage. "I do believe you, Christopher. I know you. I trust you."

His new smile was pure joy as if she'd given him the best of presents. "I'm sorry your parents threw you out. You should have blamed me—"

"No!" She raised her gaze to him. "Please don't. Pearce and my parents wanted me to blame you. They said everything would be all right if I said you forced me. I would never do that. So don't ask me."

He nodded. "I wouldn't have blamed you if you had. I mean, I'm a gangster. What could be worse?"

"Being accused of something you're not. I won't let anyone believe you attack women."

He exhaled and offered her his hand. "Do you want to take a tour of my palace?"

"Yes." She slid her hand into his, and the familiar thrill of energy didn't disappoint.

A little gasp escaped her. They remained holding hands and staring at each other. The intensity in his blue eyes should make her feel embarrassed. Instead, she felt treasured, beautiful, and adored as she had never felt.

He helped her up, and for a moment, as he dipped his head, she expected him to kiss her. Her chest rose with an inhale that brought a whiff of his clean scent, but he merely paused an inch from her lips, his breath fanning on her skin.

"Let me show you around," he said in a low, husky voice.

The palace was a renovated and glorified barrack with two-storey buildings set in a quadrangle around a courtyard. A front gate that looked like a castle's drawbridge closed the access to the street.

She leant over the handrail in the walkway. In the courtyard below, the hellhound was resting on a large cushion, chomping on a giant bone. Finn was sitting on a wooden bench at the side of the courtyard, eating a sandwich with gusto. Lanterns lit the walkway and the stairs, but her head bothered her, and she gripped the handrail for balance as she got dizzy.

"Careful." He slid an arm around her waist and held her up. "Maybe you need to rest more."

"No, I'm fine." She leant against him and didn't want to let go, finally feeling safe for the first time in weeks.

He hugged her. What had started as a simple touch to steady her had turned into a desperate embrace. He shivered as he held her closer and she rested her head on his chest. The steady beat of his heart thumped against her cheek. She sagged against him, letting his strength hold her up.

"You're safe here," he whispered, caressing the top of her head. "I promise nothing will hurt you here, and I hope you decide to stay."

She took his hand. "Show me your palace."

He led her down the stairs slowly, careful to watch her every step.

"This is where we gather or spend time," he said when they arrived in the courtyard.

The dog sprang up and rushed to him, his tail drawing circles in the air.

"This is my beautiful Darko." He ruffled the dog's head. "You won't find a sweeter dog, really. Don't be shy. Pet him."

"It's not a matter of shyness but a wish to keep all my fingers intact."

Darko closed his amber eyes as Christopher rubbed him behind the ears. Gentle cooing sounds came out of the hellhound.

She stretched out a tentative hand to pat the hound's head, but he curled up his upper lip, and she didn't trust him.

"Yes, very sweet," she said, snapping her hand back.

"Darko, be nice." He kissed the dog's head. "Don't be fooled. It's all a show. He puts up a tough façade to hide his vulnerable soul."

"I really doubt that."

They kept walking, Darko at Christopher's feet. "This is Finn, whom you already know."

The young man stood up, wiping his mouth with a napkin.

"Lady Elizabeth." Finn removed his flat hat, showing a mop of brown curls. "I'm sorry for the incident. I didn't mean to scare you although I'm pleased my tough attitude is finally coming out."

"Shut it." Christopher waved dismissively.

"I'm not Lady Elizabeth anymore. Just Elizabeth will suffice, thank you. And do not worry. I was scared, but you didn't do anything wrong."

"I did. Not with you, but there was a time when—"

"Maybe another time." Christopher patted Finn's shoulder. "That's Jane." He pointed to a woman with deep black eyes and black hair striped with white. "She runs the place. Whatever you need, ask her."

"Miss," Jane said, giving her a long, assessing glance. "I'm sure you'll find your stay here interesting."

"Are you staying, miss?" Finn asked.

Was she? The choice was between working in a restaurant where the drunk customers groped her, the pay was scarce, and the work hours were obscene, or staying with the head of a criminal organisation in his headquarters with a hellhound who growled at her.

Christopher angled towards her. She trusted him more than anyone.

She would stay not because she was desperate—although she was—but because she felt safe with him.

"Yes, I'm staying."

twenty-one

A WEIGHT LIFTED from Christopher's chest when Elizabeth said she would stay.

If she'd said no, he would have found another way to keep her safe. Although he hadn't started with the right foot in his job to protect her.

The bruise on her forehead reminded him of the night she'd come to his bedroom and tripped on the ottoman. If that bruise was the beginning of his second chance with her, then he hoped it was a good omen.

The months of hardship had taken their toll on her. She was thin and pale with dark circles around her eyes, but mostly she showed the signs of a defeated, crushed soul. For the daughter of an earl, who had grown up sheltered and pampered, she'd done well, fending for herself. But her time alone had been a struggle if her gaunt cheeks were any indication.

Finn smiled after Elizabeth said she wanted to stay, Darko bared his teeth, and Jane narrowed her eyes. Not the warm welcome he'd hoped for.

"But I want to work," Elizabeth said. "The days when I just read and did embroidery are well behind me."

"I've never had those," Jane said, folding her arms over her chest.

"You didn't miss much."

Jane didn't soften. "I'm sure embroidery is better than burning your hands with boiling water and lye soap while doing laundry for hours on end."

Elizabeth showed her hands; cuts and calluses covered them. "I understand what you mean. My hands are red and swollen from the laundry. I hate it."

Jane was about to say something else, but Christopher cut her off before another 'I suffered more than you did' contest would start.

"Let's finish the tour. Follow me." He crossed the yard, greeting other men entering the palace and staring at her with curiosity. He held the door to his workroom on the ground floor open for her. "Madam."

She flashed a little smile that seemed forced as if she hadn't smiled in a while, and now she didn't know how to do it.

"I've learnt many things in the past months, not only about myself," she said. "I can do the housework, other chores, and anything you need. I can help in the kitchen as well. I'm stronger than I look."

"I'm sure of that, but we're well organised with the housework. Everyone has their duty, and Jane makes sure people follow the rules. What I need help with is accounting." He touched the cover of a large register. "I have help, but I need more. I need someone I can trust."

"Accounting?" Her face brightened as if he gave her a present. "I'd love to do accounting for you, but you told me your activities are illegal."

"The illegal aspect doesn't matter when it comes to keeping track of our expenses. Not everyone here can do maths. Some of my men can't even read, and I know how much you love numbers."

Her first genuine smile stretched her lips. "Numbers. Of course. I'll be happy to help." She flipped through the pages of the register. "Goodness. You're busy. Tobacco, whisky, steel ... I had no idea."

"Taxes and bad decisions from the government are crushing small traders. Many of the men, who work for me, lost everything, lost their honest work because of bankruptcy, and to feed their families, they joined me. I have principles, though." He wanted her to understand he wasn't a complete thug. He wasn't Robin Hood but not a ruthless gangster either. "We don't traffic weapons or people."

"I'm happy to hear that because your numbers are impressive." She ran a finger down a long column of numbers. "I'd like to calculate the percentage of taxes you're evading just out of curiosity."

He laughed. "After you're fully recovered. You need rest."

She handed him the hefty volume.

He shoved the register aside and propped himself on the edge of the overcrowded desk. "Who spread the rumour about us?"

She walked around the room, and he couldn't help but notice that her elegance hadn't changed. She had the same proud bearing as before, walking as if she were dancing.

"I've been thinking about that for months. It wasn't my mother. She wasn't happy to see us together, but she would never risk my family's reputation or ruin my relationship with a duke."

Speaking of which. "I was surprised to know you and Pearce were close. Do you love him?" The question shot out of his mouth almost without him wanting to, but he had to ask that. He'd been wondering about her feelings for Pearce for a while.

She paused, a hand on the typewriter. "Pearce? I never did." There was regret in her voice, though.

"You were engaged to be married to him. Your mother told me."

"No, I wasn't engaged to him." She rubbed her forehead. "My mother hoped for an engagement, and there were rumours about it. Pearce proposed a courtship, which would have led to an engagement, possibly. I wasn't convinced, but you don't refuse a duke. I agreed to the courtship only to take time. Then everything changed. He bought me a ridiculously expensive diamond engagement ring and started to talk about me becoming his duchess. All of a sudden everyone was talking about my imminent wedding, and I didn't know what to think."

"Hmm." He tried to hide his relief. She wasn't in love with his brother. "Do you have any enemies?"

"Not that I know of, but I don't care at this point. I don't care about who spread the rumour. I don't care about what they want to achieve. They won."

"They ruined your life."

"I miss my old life. I can't deny that, but learning what my parents are capable of made me wonder if staying with them would have been right. They didn't let me talk. They didn't give me the opportunity to speak. They decided I was guilty and cast me out of my house with one carpetbag and five pounds. What kind of parents do that?" Her voice cracked, and her shoulders quivered. "I could have died, been attacked, or killed, and they didn't care."

He strode to her and hugged her, wishing he could protect her from the heartbreak. She leant against him, and he closed his eyes for a moment, aware that, this time, no one would come to take her away from him. If anything, the only good thing about her situation was that she was free to do as she pleased. Even stay with him if she wished so. That didn't erase the fact he was a criminal.

He caressed the top of her head gently while she shivered. "I'm sorry you're hurting," he said, inhaling her sweet scent.

She took a deep breath. "I don't want to cry. I've shed my tears. Six months' worth of them. My family and Pearce don't deserve them."

"I agree." He was about to let her go, but she rested her head on his chest, and he held her more tightly.

The more he caressed her head and back, the more she

slackened in his arms. The thoughts of what could have happened to her while she'd lived on the streets would torment him forever. If he'd known about her situation, he would have helped her.

She disentangled herself from him and wiped her eyes quickly. "I'm sorry."

He stroked her cheek, catching a precious tear. "Don't be. Look around. Everyone here is unwanted for one reason or another. Finn was abandoned by his mother and left in a workhouse. Jane worked as a maid in a house until the lady kicked her out because she was convinced that Jane was trying to seduce her husband. All rubbish. It was the other way around. But after that, Jane couldn't find any jobs until she met me."

"I've heard horrible stories of maids and governesses being attacked by their employers. It's awful." She wrapped her arms around herself. "What angers me the most is being accused of something I didn't do. I don't care about the broken engagement, but I was punished for a crime I didn't commit, and no one believed me. And I ..." She breathed hard, her cheeks reddening. "It happened to you as well."

"Yes. I know exactly how you feel. Take deep breaths."

She did as told, leaning against him again. She had to be exhausted.

"I'll show you to your room," he said.

He led her upstairs while thinking about which room was the best for her. He didn't want her close to the weaponry, nor close to the room where his men often gathered to drink. They wouldn't let her sleep with their loud voices, and sometimes they brought girls in.

The room in the corner of the first floor was draughty, and the sun didn't warm it until the afternoon, which left the room next to his. Warm, decently big, and quiet. And accidentally close to him. The furniture was sparse, merely a bed, a table, and a wardrobe. But there was a nice cast-iron stove, and the floor was clean.

"Here we are." He pushed the door open. "We'll fetch your belongings from the room you rented and bring them here. This is all for you."

She stepped inside tentatively, gazing around.

"If you don't like it, I can find something else," he said, already thinking about another room.

"No, it's perfect. In the past months, I slept in a room that was the size of a closet, sharing it with a family of rats. This is luxurious." She smiled. "Thank you."

"Wait to thank me." He folded his arms over his chest. "You realise what kind of life we lead here, don't you?"

She glanced at the gun at his side.

"I'm not going to lie," he said. "It's a dangerous life. If you live here, you'll deal with all sorts of criminals. I don't want you to accept my help, only out of desperation. If you don't feel comfortable here, I'll find another accommodation for you, a safer one."

She tucked a curl behind her ear. "I trust you, Christopher. You'd never hurt me. We faced death together, and I can't think of a better person to have shared that experience with than you. I'm sure you'll keep me safe."

A shock of stillness went through him. He hadn't realised how important her trust was until she paid him the most important compliment he'd ever received. Words failed him.

She tilted her head. "You look shocked. Perhaps you didn't expect me to agree to stay here. I can leave."

Her words shook him out of his stupor.

"Bloody hell, no. Stay. Please. I want you to stay here."

She sat on the edge of the bed as if tired. He sat next to her tentatively.

"I'm happy I found you," he said.

"So am I." She rested her head on his shoulder, and he felt as if he were the king of Britain. "Don't leave me again."

Ouch. That hurt. Because the way they'd been separated had

been a wound that had never healed properly. Even now, it hurt when the weather changed.

He laced his fingers through hers. "I've never wanted to."

Her cheeks flushed crimson. "I'm sorry. I didn't mean it in that way. It came out wrong."

But it showed how she felt, and he felt the same.

She hid a yawn behind her hand. "I think I need to sleep. I make no sense."

No, she made a lot of sense.

He brought her hand up and kissed it with reverence. "I have no intention of leaving you."

If his criminal life didn't scare her away from him.

twenty-two

BRIGHT SUNLIGHT STREAKED across the room when Elizabeth opened her eyes.

Someone had covered her with a thick quilt, but she didn't remember falling asleep in her new bed. The last thing she remembered was Christopher telling her he wouldn't leave her after she'd nearly accused him of having abandoned her on purpose. Heaven, she'd been too tired.

She must have slept for a day and a night because it was dawn. It was the first time in years she'd slept more than five hours in a row.

She gasped when she found her meagre belongings in the middle of the room. Her carpetbag and trunk sat on the hessian carpet, but she hadn't heard anyone entering her room and bringing them in.

Since she still wore the bloodstained clothes from her work at the tavern, she selected a fresh gown and washed herself slowly. The cut on her palm didn't sting anymore, not even when she used the soap, but, goodness, the water was icy cold, and goose pimples covered her skin.

She opened the door and peeked outside.

Loud, indistinct voices came from downstairs. The walkway was empty, though, and she didn't remember if Christopher had told her where the water closet was. A hot bath would be wonderful.

She left her bedroom, holding the bunch of dirty clothes, and stopped in the middle of the walkway. Christopher hadn't told her where his bedroom was, had he? She had no idea where he could be. Never mind. She'd ask Finn or Jane.

A low growl came from behind her, causing her to freeze. Her pulse turned into a fast pounding in a moment. Without moving her body, she craned her neck slowly to take a look over her shoulder.

Darko stood behind her, his fur on end and his upper lip curled up to remind her of how powerful his fangs were.

"I live here," she said in the gentlest tone possible. "You have to get used to my presence."

His amber eyes narrowed to slits. He growled again, this time with more passion.

They said that running away from an angry dog was counter-productive because a dog enjoyed the chase and would consider the runner as prey. But at that moment, she didn't care about what people said.

She made a dash for the room next to hers, since Darko was blocking the way to her door. He chased her, barking bloody murder. His paws scratched the wooden planks of the floor. A cry escaped her as she rushed into the room and slammed the door behind her.

The eerie sound of the dog's nails scraping the door made her shiver. He kept barking. Great. She had only to wait for him to calm down, get bored, and leave.

"It's a habit then," Christopher said from behind her.

"Bah!" She turned around, dropping her dirty gown and pressing her back against the door.

He was fully immersed in a large brass bathtub. Steam curled up in the air, filling the room with the fragrance of bergamot. He propped his elbows on the rim of the bathtub, showing his well-defined biceps and shoulder muscles. With his wet hair pulled back, his beautiful eyes attracted all the attention.

"What is it?" he asked as if it were perfectly normal for her to stand in his bedroom while he was taking a bath.

She swallowed hard. "Darko."

The dog intensified his barking in reply.

Christopher tilted his head up. "Darko, quiet."

His tone wasn't even commanding, but Darko stopped barking immediately.

"He scared me," she said. "I ran here."

"Never run in front of a dog. It makes them think you're prey."

"So have I heard."

He reclined, wringing a sponge. "I'm sorry about him. He can be an ass when he wants. I'll keep him away from you." The muscles in his arm became all sharp ridges as he squeezed the sponge. "Where did you want to go before Darko frightened you?"

"I was looking for the water closet to take a bath."

"What a coincidence!" He smiled, regarding her from underneath his spiked eyelashes. "Plenty of room here."

She chuckled. "I interrupted you. Sorry." She really wasn't.

"I don't look sorry, do I?" He gave her a smouldering look that raised the room temperature.

Her gaze locked with his, and a warmth she hadn't had the luxury to experience in a while spread through her.

"I should leave." She picked up her clothes and opened the door an inch.

Darko went mad with barking again.

"Botheration." She shut the door again. "Your dog is a menace."

"He doesn't trust you and is scared of you."

"I'm sure he isn't."

"He reacts to fear with aggressive behaviour." He went to rise but paused. "You might want to turn around. I don't mind, but you do."

"Yes, well, of course." She averted her gaze although she wasn't a lady anymore, so she didn't have to follow the strict rules of society, and she was a little curious.

The sound of water splashing and then of fabric came. She took a tiny peek in time to see him wrap a towel around his hips. Droplets trickled down the sharp edges of his muscles. When he turned around, the scars on his back glistened in all their horrors, a reminder of what he'd gone through. Her chest tightened for him. If Pearce had shown some compassion for him, he wouldn't have ended up in Whitechapel. Not that Christopher wasn't responsible for his choices, but she could understand the drive that desperation gave him.

"I'll have a new bath drawn for you." He walked over to her, all predatory menace, and once again, she remained frozen but not out of fear.

She was caught between an angry dog and a naked criminal, and she had no doubts about which one she preferred.

"Let me open the door," he said, never keeping his eyes off her.

"No!" She winced at her high-pitched voice. "I mean, of course, you can open the door of your bedroom. But it's dangerous." She stepped aside, clenching her clothes against her chest.

"Don't worry." He flashed a lopsided smile. "He won't hurt you."

"I feel rather pessimistic today."

As he inched the door open, she held her breath.

"Mate." Christopher let the hellhound in.

Darko barked and yapped, lowering his belly to the floor. His tail twirled like a windmill, going around in circles. He didn't look like the growling beast she'd seen a moment ago. He dropped on his back and exposed his belly, his hips moving right and left.

Christopher crouched to give him a belly rub. "He can be a little scary, but he's just a big puppy."

"I'm sure of that. It's the long, sharp teeth that worry me. And the growling. And the murderous attitude."

"He'll become your best friend soon, once he knows you." He rose and crossed the room to his wardrobe, and she couldn't help but stare at his naked back again.

The past years had shaped his body into a machine of muscles and harsh ridges, and she couldn't deny a hint of curiosity about his gangster persona. He had to be terrifying when he wanted to.

Darko followed him, completely captured by his master.

"I trust you feel better," he said, slipping behind a screen.

"Well rested. The bruise doesn't bother me, and the cut on my palm isn't even itchy."

"I'll take a look at it after you get a bath." He came out in a fresh set of dark clothes that added a new layer of danger to him.

"Why do you always wear black?"

"Black doesn't show the blood. If people don't see the blood, they'll think a stab or a bullet does nothing to you."

"Oh."

He straightened his jacket. "My water closet is the closest. Over there." He pointed to a door on the other side of the room. "It's not large enough for this bathtub, though. But I have a modern water boiler there. It won't take long to fill the bathtub again. Wait here."

Darko followed him out of the room, not paying her the slightest bit of attention. She unclenched her arms from her clothes, exhaling. The room was just like Christopher—no frills but only sturdy furniture, and it radiated safety. Everything smelled like him. It was as if he were holding her. She stiffened again when Jane entered the room and walked straight to the water closet.

"The Guv told me you need a bath."

"Yes."

Without looking at her, Jane connected a large tube to the base of the bathtub. The water in the bathtub was sucked away through the attached tube with a gurgling noise that made her giggle. Then it was a matter of filling it with hot water from the boiler, using the buckets. She helped carry the hot water although Jane scoffed and shot her sideways glances.

Jane wiped her hands on her apron once the job was done. "There. Hot water to the rim for the princess."

Elizabeth scowled. Being kind was one thing, but letting someone bully her was another.

"There's no need to be so bitter towards me," she said. "I'm no princess. I work at a restaurant."

"A few months of hard work won't change the fact you're an earl's daughter."

"We can't choose our parents, can we?"

"I'm not your servant."

"I've never thought you were."

"Every toff thinks that people below them are servants." Jane strode to the door. "When you finish, go to the kitchen. It'll shock you, but you're going to break your fast there." She left the bedroom and shut the door with a thud.

"I'm not shocked!" she said to Jane's back.

Unfair. She might have had a sheltered life but not an easy one. With a high social status came expectations, rules, and an astonishing lack of freedom. She hadn't been free to choose her own path, and it was easy to judge someone else's life. Oh, well.

The tension left her body when she sank into the hot water. She kept an eye on the door, half wishing Christopher would come, but he didn't. She shouldn't be disappointed by him being a gentleman.

"Elizabeth?" His voice came from the other side of the door.

She'd talked too soon, and she wasn't sorry. "Come in." Wait. Did she just tell him to come in while she was naked in the bath?

She didn't have time to add anything else.

The door was flung open. "Sorry, I was—" He entered, his jaw hanging open. "I ..." The heated, intense gaze he gave her was like a velvety caress on her skin.

Not that he could see much, just her naked shoulders, arms, and the top of her breasts.

Her cheeks flamed. "I forgot I was in the bath." Oh, what a great thing to say.

He kept staring at her. "Do you want me to leave?"

"No, it's fine." She cleared her throat, careful not to do abrupt moves, lest she show too much. "What did you want to tell me?"

He slid inside and shut the door. The room became small when he walked over to her. "I have to go to the docks and check on a shipment. I'll be away for a few hours."

She nodded. "All right."

From his position next to the bathtub, he had a good view of her body in the water, and judging by how his eyes darkened, he was fully focused on her. Although, since she was hugging her bent knees, there wasn't much to see ... unless ... She slowly straightened her legs as much as the bathtub allowed and unfolded her arms. He let out a deep sound of appreciation, which was funny. She was scrawny, and her skin had lost its healthy glow. She was as attractive as a scarecrow, but he didn't seem to mind.

He knelt next to her, letting out a breath. She thought he was about to say something, but instead, he trailed a finger over her jaw, leaving behind a path of goose bumps on her skin. She felt that light touch on her most sensitive parts. He was delicate and gentle, yet there was nothing delicate or gentle in the riot of sensations bursting within her.

He drove his finger down her neck and over her shoulder but stopped before reaching her aching breasts. She tried not to look disappointed, but she didn't have to worry.

He rolled up his shirtsleeve. His gaze dipped as his hand did. She let out a moan when he brushed her nipple under the water.

Her toes curled, and a throb pulsated between her legs. He rubbed and pinched her nipples lightly until she was breathing hard.

"I have to go," he whispered, his voice rimming with regret. Before withdrawing his hand, he dipped it further, brushing her thighs. "I wish I could stay."

She couldn't speak. Feeling cared for and desired was so good. He kissed her, a chaste, sweet kiss on her bruised brow, but she sighed, nevertheless.

"Rest," he whispered against her skin. "I'll be back as soon as possible."

She blew out a breath when he left. She had no idea why she'd behaved so boldly; she blamed it on the struggles she'd faced, on the fact that a lot of rules didn't matter anymore, but she didn't regret it.

twenty-three

THE PALACE WAS quiet when Elizabeth finished bathing. Thank goodness the hellhound wasn't anywhere to be seen. Checking the walkway for Darko just in case, she sneaked out of Christopher's bedroom, smelling of bergamot, as he did, and went downstairs, her stomach grumbling.

"Hello?" she called, entering the ground-floor room functioning as a kitchen and dining room.

A long, scarred table took up half of the space. Mismatched chairs and benches were scattered around.

"There you are." Jane dropped a tray with scones and tea on the table in front of her. "The Guv asked me to make you breakfast, but don't get used to this special treatment. I don't have time for this."

"I can prepare my own breakfast. I've done it for the past months."

"Good. You'll make your own meals then. I'm busy. I have to prepare breakfast for all the others." Jane kept cooking bacon in a large frying pan and sausages in another.

The sound of the oil sizzling was the only one in the wide room.

The moment Elizabeth took a bite of the buttered scone, her stomach roared in appreciation. The tea was strong and rich. She hadn't enjoyed such a good meal since she'd left home. Two men she'd never seen entered the room, nodding at her.

"There." Jane gave them two plates filled with eggs, bacon, and sausages with a smile.

"Thank you, Jane," they chorused.

They ate and chatted among themselves, sitting as far away from her as possible. Well, she was an outsider.

Finn walked in, waving around. "Good morning, Jane, Andy, Peter. Good morning, miss." He removed his hat and beamed. "Feeling better?"

"Much better, thank you."

"Any plans for today?"

"I hoped to start working on the register, but I need to wait for Christopher."

"Why don't you come with me? I have to buy groceries for Jane."

"Gladly."

After Finn wolfed down the largest portion of bacon, eggs, and mushrooms she'd ever seen, they left the kitchen.

It took Finn a bit to unlock and open the heavy door. Safety was something Christopher treated seriously.

She left with Finn, wrapped in her worn cloak, searching for Christopher in every corner.

People greeted Finn as he walked down the street with a strut, and he returned the greetings with a curt nods. The street vendors glanced at her with curiosity, but no one said a word. People moved out of their way to let them pass. Or rather, to let Finn pass.

"Thank you," she said to a woman who stepped aside. "Thank you," she said to a man, pushing a wheelbarrow, who paused to give them space.

"You don't need to thank them," Finn said. "You'll say 'thank you' all day."

"It seems polite."

"They fear the King. That's all."

She nodded at another passerby. "But Christopher would never hurt anyone."

Finn exhaled. "Unfortunately. It's all a pretence. For example, the Guv insists that we pay for what we eat. We could take whatever we want without spending a shilling, but he says we aren't that type of criminals. He says we have bonbons."

She laughed. "You mean *bon ton*, good manners."

"Yes. We're classy criminals."

"Classy?"

"With principles and rules. We don't just care about money. We care about the people of Whitechapel because they're struggling, and we aren't better than them. That's what he says."

A wave of fondness for Christopher made her smile.

They stopped at a store that sold spices, dried fruits, and even drugs. A bell rang when they pushed the door open.

"Finn, welcome. Miss." The man behind the counter regarded her for a long moment. "What do you need today?"

Finn read from a piece of paper he took out of his pocket. "A pound of brown lentils, half a pound of dried peas, and a cup of cinnamon."

"Right-o."

Elizabeth inhaled the fresh scent of cardamom and ginger. They reminded her of when Cook had baked her favourite biscuits just for her. Now Cook wouldn't greet Elizabeth if she met her in the street.

From the little she knew reading the newspapers, her family was faring well. The scandal had been contained somehow. It hadn't touched them. She hadn't found a single article or gossip on the scandal sheet about the Earl of Lincoln or Pearce, for that matter. She wondered what her parents had told their friends. For how long could they pretend she was staying in the country without raising questions?

"That's it." The man handed Finn the brown bags. "Fifteen shillings."

Finn handed him a handful of the coins.

The man gave him a farthing. "Here's your change."

"Thank you." Finn put a hand on the farthing, but Elizabeth stopped him, checking again the price of the brown lentils, cinnamon, and dried peas per ounce.

She calculated the total again.

"Wait. We need two shillings more," she said to the man. "You gave him the wrong change."

"Really?" Finn glowered.

"An honest mistake, miss." With a strained smile, the man handed the correct change. "There. It's all good."

Finn's expression hardened, making him look older. "You steal from the King?"

"As I said, an honest mistake," the man said.

Grabbing the bags, Finn marched out of the shop.

"Honest mistake, my arse. Excuse my French." He walked towards the palace, scowling all the way. "I can't believe he tried to trick me. He had no idea what we could do to him."

"What do you mean? Would Christopher kill him? You said you were classy criminals."

"The Guv doesn't kill unless it's necessary, and never a civilian. Now Whitechapel is peaceful, but two years ago, when the Guv was getting powerful, every day was a war. Brutal, miss. People got stabbed and beaten at every corner. The Reapers, the gangsters who controlled Whitechapel before us, were beasts. They set fire to the shops and houses of those people who didn't pay and killed on a whim. The Guv hated how they treated the locals. Them coppers didn't mind, too busy trying to catch the Ripper."

She shivered. "It sounds terrible."

He lowered his voice. His cheeks reddened, making his freckles more evident. "Please don't tell the Guv I almost lost his money.

Bloody hell, who knows how many times vendors took advantage of me?"

"I won't say a word, but do you know how to do maths?"

Finn blushed to the roots of his hair and paused in front of the heavy door to the palace. "A little. I can do simple things like counting to ten very fast and do sums, but no one has ever taught me."

"Would you like to learn? I can teach you."

"I would, but what for? I don't need it."

"I think you do, so no one will take advantage of you again."

"I'm too stupid to learn," he whispered, shaking his head.

She'd heard that before about her.

"Nonsense. You'll learn in no time," she said.

"I'm not sure, miss." He pushed the door open.

"You aren't stupid, Finn. Trust me."

His tense expression softened. "But what if you realise I really am as thick as a log? What if I make a fool out of myself? You'll regret having offered me your help."

"I won't. Do you want to learn?"

He gave her a shy nod. "Would love to."

She patted his shoulder. "Don't let fear stop you. As famous Mr. George Adair said, 'Everything you've ever wanted sits on the other side of fear.'"

"Was he a poet or a philosopher?"

"Neither. A real estate developer."

He nodded. "It makes sense."

twenty-four

CHRISTOPHER HATED RECEIVING bad news on an empty stomach.

When he'd left his bedroom that morning after a rather pleasant encounter with Elizabeth and an even more pleasant bath, he hadn't had time to break his fast.

He probably had shocked her. Years had passed since their time in the cottage. All the intimacy they'd shared didn't exist anymore. But he couldn't deny he'd kept thinking about her taking a bath in his bedroom. And after all, she'd given him a spectacular view of her beauty and allowed him to touch her.

He'd taken all his discipline not to kiss her hard and jump into the bath with her. But he feared his eagerness might be mistaken for an attempt at taking advantage of her. She was tired, shocked, and lonely.

He'd wait for her to be fully recovered before touching her again. No, before courting her. Properly. If she wanted him to.

He gnashed his teeth and focused on what Smithy had to say. The warehouse near the dock was so noisy with the sailors' yells and the ships' horns that his nerves were tense with frustration.

"The cargo of the last ship has been taken." Smithy waved a

hand around towards the half-empty warehouse. "The coppers have been thorough in their search. Didn't leave a toothpick."

He slammed a hand on the wall, staring at the crowded dock. "Who were the coppers?"

Smithy scratched his stubble. "Not our boys. New coppers. Guv, some of them were former members of the Reapers."

"What? Are they coppers now?"

Smithy nodded. "Hired as collaborators by the police. The Reapers know a few things about our routine. That's why they were so successful. The others were outsiders, but they said their gaffer is a toff, a powerful one. I heard them talking about having to report to the duke. Who the hell is that duke? A rival to the King?"

Christopher had a hunch. "Anything else?"

"The coppers' gaffer mentioned Gryphon House?"

"Grafton?"

"Maybe."

He muttered a curse under his breath. Damn Pearce. He must have used his political influence to send a new unit of peelers to Whitechapel.

So today's attack on his shipment was payback for something Christopher hadn't done, which was ironic, considering he'd done a lot of things. But Pearce's interference wasn't the main problem.

"How much did we lose?"

Smithy threw a meaty hand up. "Two thousand pounds, give or take. But the loss is more crushing for our partners. A few pounds make the difference for a family in Whitechapel. Lots of people are going to starve this week."

Not if he could avoid it.

His smuggling business was based on cooperation among small investors. Everyone put in the amount of money they could afford to gamble, and so far, the return had been favourable. But a detained shipment meant that several families had lost their income.

"Should we proceed with the next shipment?" Smithy asked. "Speed things up?"

"Yes, but change the date and time without telling anyone until the last moment. No more surprises."

"Aye, Guv." Smithy nodded and disappeared into the dark warehouse.

Christopher walked back to the palace in a foul mood. Pearce had declared war on him, and Christopher wouldn't let his brother ruin what he'd built.

That bloody, greedy, self-centred duke! He was also stupid because if he took the time to watch the real world, he'd realise Christopher had done nothing to take Elizabeth from him.

Before going to the palace, he stopped at Sarah's house. She lived in a flat in the driest part of Whitechapel where the humid air from the Thames didn't blow.

He calmed down before knocking, lest she get scared.

"Mr. Blackwood." She opened the door, offering a smile that, while small, didn't hold any fear.

"Call me Christopher. We're practically family. How is Arthur?"

Her smile brightened her whole face. A rosy, plump face, that is. No more gauntness.

"Heavy, hungry, and loud." She laughed, and he laughed as well. "Come and see him."

He was in a hurry, but he didn't mind staying. The warm air in the flat was rich with the scent of baked biscuits and fresh flowers. Sunlight flooded the sitting room, and pretty, frilly curtains adorned the windows.

At least he'd done something good by helping Sarah. Arthur was playing with a wooden train on the rug. His hair reached his chubby cheeks as he made little noises that might sound like words if one used a lot of imagination.

"No more coughing." Sarah picked him up and gave him a kiss with a smacking sound. "Do you want to hold him?"

He stopped smiling. "No, I've never held a baby."

"Time to start."

"I'm not sure—" Too late.

Sarah handed him the soft bundle of joy. Arthur watched him with those large blue eyes so similar to his own, except for the light of pure innocence shining in them. Innocence that Christopher would do his level best to protect.

He wished Arthur's eyes stayed shining and curious forever, that his nephew would never get hurt or resent anyone.

"Nephew," he said, inhaling Arthur's sweet scent.

With a little noise, Arthur placed a sticky hand on Christopher's cheek and said more gibberish with the confidence of someone making a proper speech. As he patiently listened to everything Arthur had to say, he wondered what Father had felt when he'd held him. Had he been regretful, worried, or happy? Had he truly loved him or only felt guilt?

Arthur returned the stare in a solemn way as if he could read Christopher's mind. A silent understanding passed between them as he promised to take care of Arthur, no matter what Pearce did. Arthur nodded as if telling him not to worry.

Then Arthur stretched out his arms towards his mama, giggling for who knew what reason.

"Thank you, Christopher." Sarah took Arthur back. "I owe you—"

"Nothing. As I said, we're family."

She turned serious. "I loved Pearce. I really did. He treated me with respect and took good care of me." She rocked Arthur, shifting her weight. "I still care about him, even though he didn't believe me when I told him I wasn't unfaithful."

"He doesn't deserve your affection." He stopped there, not to let out a string of curses in front of Sarah and Arthur.

"He loves deeply and completely. That's why he gets hurt so easily."

"He loves only himself."

She shook her head. The woman was stubborn and under Pearce's spell. "Please don't hate him. Not because of what he did to me."

"I have plenty of reasons to choose from."

"Ta!" Arthur waved his little hand, smiling so brightly Christopher's chest cracked.

He cleared his throat. The last thing he wanted was to argue about Pearce's soul with Sarah. "I have to go."

"Thank you, Christopher, for everything." She touched his arm with too much compassion.

He didn't deserve her affection, either.

As emotion swelled in his throat, he left the house, muttering a quick goodbye.

No matter what Sarah said, Pearce was responsible for the unhappiness of Sarah, Arthur, Elizabeth, and Christopher himself, but he didn't take responsibility for any of that. What a great example of a bloody duke. 'Loves too deeply' his arse. Pearce was a spoiled brat with too much free time on his hands.

Once at the palace, he went straight to his office. Darko asked for a pat on the head, and Christopher obliged. He opened the safe and took out a stash of banknotes.

"Christopher?" Elizabeth stepped inside, carrying the sunshine with her.

He smiled, tension leaving his shoulders although a different type of tension shuddered through him. She was the most beautiful woman he'd ever seen. He blocked visions of her in the bathtub from flashing across his mind because he didn't want to give her the impression he had only wild thoughts about her, which was somewhat true, but she didn't need to know.

"Do you have a moment?" she asked, blushing in an adorable way.

"Always for you." He slid the money into his satchel, doing a quick sum on how much he needed.

"I wanted to talk to you about Finn."

He paused. "Did he do something?"

"No, he's a nice young man, but he can't do maths."

"Half of the people in the palace can't." He shrugged.

"Yes, but he's a clever boy, and I think that an education would benefit him. I'd like to teach him if you agree."

He strapped the satchel across his shoulders. "Does he want to learn?"

"He does."

"All right. I've never thought he'd care. I'll have some books delivered here." He stopped on the threshold next to her, ignoring his blood boiling for her. "But Elizabeth?"

"Yes." She fiddled with her hands.

"You don't have to ask for my permission." He took her chin and stroked her jaw with a thumb, just to touch her silky skin. The feel of her skin was intoxicating. "You can do what you want."

"I know. It's that ..." She chuckled. "I don't know."

Bloody hell, she was adorable.

"You're free here to do as you please." And since he was a bastard indeed, he whispered, "as you did this morning in the bathtub."

She blushed more fiercely but laughed as well, and he loved the sound. "I ... well ... I acted on impulse."

"You should do that more often." He brushed his lips against her cheek just to hear her sigh. He ought to stop before he trapped her lovely face in his hands and kissed her, breaking his promise to be gentle to her. "Would you like to come with me? I have to do a round."

"A round?" Her expression turned wary.

"My brother had one of my shipments nicked by the coppers out of spite. Now I have to reimburse the people who trusted me with their money." He patted the satchel. "You said you trusted me, too."

Her smile was the first good thing of that day. "Let's go."

He threw glances at her as they walked through the coal-dust-covered streets of Whitechapel. Not that he looked for something in particular about her delicate profile, but he found fascinating the way her eyebrows pulled together when she was thinking about something that bothered her, or how she rolled her bottom lip between her pearly teeth when someone said something she didn't like.

He'd been deprived of her company for so long that he couldn't stop staring at her. If it hadn't been for his brother's stupidity, Elizabeth wouldn't be free to take a walk with him. So he guessed he had to thank Pearce for being such an ass.

"I think we should discover who's behind the rumours about us," he said, taking a shortcut through an alleyway.

"Why is it so important?"

"Because Pearce has become a thorn in my side. If he keeps blocking my shipments because he wants revenge, I'll be out of business in a matter of months. It's not just about me. Many families count on my business to put food on their tables. If I can provide him with evidence that we didn't do anything wrong, he'll leave me alone."

"I wouldn't know where to start. I have no idea why someone would be so malicious. I suspected someone, Rebecca, the daughter of Viscount Keadew, but she wasn't present at the ball the night we met. I didn't think about who the gossipmonger might be in the past months."

"There are two options. The person who accused us was genuinely mistaken. They saw something they misinterpreted and believed they were doing the right thing by talking to Pearce. Or they saw us, knew the affair between us would be an effective lie, and went on with their plan with the purpose of hurting you or Pearce. Personally, I think the first option is bollocks."

She nodded. "I agree. So the person could be one of Pearce's enemies or ours?"

"Let's start with making a list of the people who were at the ball that night."

"Whoever it is knows you as well. They knew Pearce would be furious if his own brother had an affair with me."

"Indeed. That should help shorten the list." He stopped at the door to Mrs. Jones's house.

The wail of a child sounded from the other side.

"The King." Mrs. Jones opened the door, holding a baby in one arm while another two children cried behind her, tugging at her skirt. "My husband isn't here." Her voice held a note of fear he didn't like.

"It doesn't matter." He didn't waste time and handed her the money. "For the lost shipment."

She didn't take it. He wasn't sure if her hesitation was due to fear of getting into trouble with him, or because she didn't think compensation was necessary.

"I won't use this compensation as leverage against your family," he said. "You invested your money in my enterprise. It's only fair."

Mrs. Jones glanced at Elizabeth who smiled. "Thank you." She accepted the money with a trembling hand.

"Good evening," he said, tipping his hat up.

They left Mrs. Jones and proceeded to the next one.

"What you're doing is very decent of you," Elizabeth said. "You don't need to reimburse these people, but you're doing it anyway. Why?"

"It's good business. My enterprise is based on repeat and solid partnerships. If the news spreads that I lose money and don't care about my partners, no one will want to do business with me."

"I don't believe that is the only reason." She put a hand on his arm. "You have a good heart, Christopher, no matter how hard you try to hide it."

"You see only kindness in people. I've been surviving for so long, thinking only about staying alive, I'm not sure I can't be selfish. When your focus is about surviving and finding the next meal, you don't have time to care about others."

"You're wrong." She hooked her arm through his. "When we were in the cottage …" She paused, and he tensed. It was the first time they'd talked about the cottage. "We were focusing on surviving, yet we took care of each other. Taking care of each other is what kept us alive. Caring is a strength, and we proved it."

"I was happy I could be myself with you without being judged or branded as the bastard son of a duke." He brushed her cheek with a finger but forced himself not to do more and withdrew his hand.

She took it, her lips parting. He waited for her to say something, but she simply laced her fingers through his. A moment of charged silence thickened between them, like one of those moments in the cottage when he hadn't been sure if he could kiss her or not. Not an uncomfortable silence, but there were things he wished to say, like that he wanted her to stay with him forever, which was selfish of him. She deserved more than his headquarters filled with criminals, and if her name could be cleared, she'd have a second chance at living her aristocratic life.

"Let's finish the round," he said in a raspy voice.

She didn't let go of his hand.

twenty-five

DARKNESS PAINTED THE windows of Christopher's room a deep black, but the bright glow from the lamp illuminated Elizabeth's hair as she sat in front of him at his desk. Darko slept soundly on his bed, now and then flipping his paws in one of his vivid dreams.

After the rounds, they'd been sitting at the escritoire in his bedroom to draw the list of guests at the ball. A very short list, that is. No one could possibly remember the over one hundred guests Pearce had invited.

"Barely forty guests," he said, reading the short list again.

She rubbed her temples. "I don't remember any more names. During that period, I attended several balls, and they're all blended together into one long night."

He reclined on the chair. "If we exclude your parents and those people who don't know me and who barely know you, we're left with nothing. A servant, perhaps?"

"I don't think so. Pearce mentioned a very trusted source. No, it has to be a guest, or more than one. Aside from Rebecca, I can't think of anyone else." She stretched out her arms over her head, and he wasn't enough of a gentleman not to notice the way her breasts strained the fabric of her shirt.

"We should talk to one of Pearce's servants," she said. "Ask them for a complete list of the guests."

"Finn can get information from anyone."

She frowned. "Don't involve the boy. He's too young."

He laughed. "Finn? Don't let his sweet manners and good looks fool you. He grew up in the rookery, stole wallets before he could speak, and he's an expert with a blade. He's no child. He grew up quickly."

"He should go to school and find a proper job instead of … ." She raised her gaze then lowered it. "I mean …"

"I understand. I plan to turn my business into a legal one. It's just a matter of doing a lot of paperwork and bribing the right people. Just so I don't have to bleed money to bribe every damn copper or to fight every thug in town. Finn won't need to be a criminal. But I prefer having him here with me than with another gang where he'd be forced to kill, or he'd be beaten."

She put her hand over his. "As I said, you have a good heart."

He glanced at her slender hand over his. "I'm the King of Whitechapel. Never forget."

"You're more honourable than Pearce, a duke."

She laced her fingers through his as she'd done earlier that day, and the same shot of energy coursed through him. He'd give her the world if it didn't mean involving her in his criminal life. She might care about him, but she didn't get a taste of his underworld life yet.

The light from the lamp ignited her eyes with a golden glow that started a flutter in his chest. And he couldn't stop himself. He'd promised he wouldn't touch her but … He cupped her lovely cheek and drew her closer. He paused an inch from her mouth, waiting for her to push him away. But she drew in a breath and parted her lips in an invitation he couldn't refuse.

He pressed his lips against hers with both fear and relief. The kiss was like going home after a long journey. Trembling with the effort of controlling himself, he traced the seam of her lips with the tip of his tongue as she breathed harder. He ought to go slowly because he didn't want to scare her away.

When she opened her mouth, he didn't hesitate to explore it with his tongue. He'd waited years to kiss her; he'd dreamt about kissing her; he'd filled his days with the memories of that one kiss they'd shared.

His body snapped with tension and anticipation. He slid his hand up to run his fingers through her hair, but her chignon stopped his progress. He wanted to see her curls fall over her breasts.

He broke the kiss only to remove her hairpins and undo her bun. Her glossy curls fell in a silky cascade over her shoulders. She looked beautiful with her hair down and her lips reddened by his rough kiss. He stroked her hair, caressing her shoulder, breasts, and waist. So much time had passed, so many lonely nights had tormented him since he'd touched her last. All the need and desire he had to lock away were now being released with a passion.

He held her by the waist and dragged her to his lap. Feeling her warm weight on him was the closest thing to finding peace he could get. Because when she was with him, he forgot about Pearce hating him, society mocking him, and his fellow Eton students beating him. The turmoil always stirring within his soul remained quiet, like a tamed beast.

Then he kissed her again, tasting her with more determination, tangling his tongue with hers until they were both panting with the need to be naked.

"Sleep with me," he said, kissing her neck. "Just sleep as we did in the cottage."

"Yes." She wrapped her arms around his neck.

For a long moment, he didn't move, enjoying her embrace and her breath on his skin. He had no idea how he'd lived the past years without holding her. She had the power to lift the worries and the tension from him. Maybe because in the cottage, he knew that everything was all right as long as she was next to him, as long as they were both alive.

He stood up and carried her to his bed. Darko stirred when he lay down with Elizabeth. She rested her head on his chest as he covered her. He'd dreamt of lying with her so many times, but the reality was better than any dreams.

Yes, he wanted to rip her gown apart and taste her skin everywhere, but his soul needed her quiet presence more.

~

ELIZABETH STILL FELT Christopher's strong arms around her the next morning as she washed the dishes she'd used for breakfast, lest Jane complain. The cut on her palm was healing well, reduced to a thin red line. Christopher had taken good care of it. So she could wash the dishes without discomfort.

He'd left early after kissing her long and hard, with Darko following him, and afterwards, she'd left his bedroom as well.

The sensation of being next to him was the same as when they'd been in the cottage. She'd felt safe and protected there; she felt safe and protected now.

"What are you doing?" Jane strode across the kitchen, tying her apron.

"You told me I had to work like everyone else." She rinsed the plate and put it on the rack.

Jane didn't seem pleased. "Don't expect me to thank you." She took out a bag of flour and one of sugar from the pantry.

"I don't expect anything from you."

"Good, because I'm busy. I have to bake a honey and acorn cake for the party."

"What party?"

Jane poured a few cups of flour into a bowl, frowning. "The Guv gives a party every two months when a full circle of shipping is closed. Although the last shipping didn't go well. Thanks to your betrothed."

"He isn't and never was my betrothed." Elizabeth wiped her hands on her apron.

"Anyway. I need the kitchen."

If there was one thing she was grateful for during her homeless experience it was that she'd learnt to stand up for herself more than she'd used to.

She tossed the kitchen towel on the counter. "I didn't do anything to you. I'm sorry for what happened to you, for the bad experience you had with rich people, but I'm not responsible."

"You aren't one of us." Jane added the eggs to the mixture without looking at her. "A few months spent on your own don't make you one of us. I'm talking in your interest as well. This life is going to crush you, and when you cry, wanting to go back to your rich house, you'll see what I mean."

"Living here can't be worse than being kicked out of my house by my own parents for something I didn't do."

"You got a taste of what your people can do. There's some justice in that."

"Just because you aren't born into an aristocratic family, it doesn't mean you have the monopoly of pain and humiliation. I'm going to stay here whether you like it or not."

She strode out of the room, almost bumping into Finn.

"Good morning! Miss, are you ready for my lessons? The books have arrived." He sounded more excited than she'd expected.

"Of course." She forced a smile, not wanting him to realise there was tension between her and Jane. "Let's go to the office. Or maybe not." She remained still when Darko padded into the dining room to drink from a large bowl in the corner.

Drops were splashed around as he took lazy, slobbering sips.

"What's wrong?" Finn snatched an oat biscuit from a plate on the table.

"Darko hates me."

"Claptrap. He's a big boy, but he doesn't hate anyone."

"I've heard that before." She chanced a step towards the door.

Darko lifted his head from the bowl to narrow his eyes. A low rumble reverberated from him.

"See?" she said. "He'll jump at my throat at the first chance."

"Give him some bacon." Finn nodded at the plate with strips of bacon on the table. "He'll become your best friend."

Without moving too much, Elizabeth took a piece of bacon and offered it to the wary hound. Darko sniffed the air, his eyes narrowing suspiciously as if he knew what she was trying to do.

Gathering her courage, she inched her hand forth. He licked his black nose and sniffed again.

"I don't bite," she said.

He slid a paw an inch towards her. She held her breath when he stretched out his neck to sniff her hand.

"Don't be shy," Finn said. "Dogs can smell fear."

"Great. Why didn't you tell me that earlier?"

Elizabeth suppressed a shout when Darko snatched the bacon with a movement too fast for her to follow. The bacon vanished in a slurp and a snap of his jaw as if it'd never existed. She selected another slice of bacon. He didn't waste time and wolfed it down with confidence. She went to take more bacon, but Finn pulled the plate away.

"Too much, and I want to eat the bacon for lunch," he said.

"I know, but I'm trying to become his friend."

"Let him lick your fingers."

"I don't think it's a good idea."

Darko sat in front of her, head tilted back as he waited for more bacon. A drop of drool trickled down from a corner of his mouth.

"He won't leave you alone until he understands you finished the treats," he said.

"Fine." Shivering, she opened her hand to him, hoping she wouldn't lose a finger.

Darko hesitated before pressing his cold, wet nose on her palm. Satisfied that she didn't have anything dangerous in her hand, he ran his long, raspy tongue over her fingers in a surprisingly gentle manner. She remained as still as possible while he removed every trace of grease from her fingers. Once finished, he yawned and stretched before leaving the kitchen, bored now.

"See?" Finn took a strip of bacon. "A few more of these exchanges, and he'll be your best friend."

At least she was making progress with one of those people who didn't like her presence in the palace.

The rest of the day went by explaining to Finn the basics of mathematics and the value of each coin. Finn proved to be a great student and listener.

"... so if the total is two pounds, how much change should I get?" she asked.

Finn chewed his bottom lip, creasing his forehead. He reviewed his notes. "A farthing."

"Yes! You learn fast."

"Phew." Finn sagged in the chair. "Thank you, miss."

"This is but the beginning. We'll go through the whole book. If you keep learning so quickly, you'll be quite knowledgeable in a matter of months."

"It's more interesting than I remembered."

"Did you go to school?"

"My mother taught me something before my father died, then she left me in a workhouse when we were starving and she couldn't take care of me." He spoke in a flat tone as if what had happened to him didn't matter. "Horrible place, miss, especially for children. If the Guv hadn't taken me in, I'd be dead from one of those nasty diseases the children in the workhouse catch or from the brutal work." He swallowed a few times. "I don't even know what happened to my mother. I searched for her after the Guv took me in, but the house where we lived was empty, and no one knew where she was."

"May I ask you something personal?"

"Of course."

She pondered her words carefully. "I resent my parents for what they did to me. Do you resent your mother?" She was surprised he'd searched for his mother after having been abandoned.

"No." His voice cracked. "If she'd kept me, we would have both died. Life is hard for a normal family as poor as we were, but for a widow with a child, it's gruelling."

Not that their situations were comparable, but she wished she could be so forgiving.

"If anything," he said, "I think your parents behaved more cruelly than my mama. They kicked you out not because they had no choice, but because they believed their reputation was more important than your safety. My mama was dying. That's a good reason to let a child go, I guess."

She wasn't sure what she would have done in his mother's place. But then again, Finn's situation had been more tragic than hers. "I'm sorry."

Finn lifted a shoulder. "It could have been worse. At least I have a place to stay, and the Guv takes good care of me." He leant closer. "Don't let what he does fool you. He's the King, but he's also a good man."

"Did I give you the impression of having a bad opinion of Christopher?"

"It's that ... you came here only because you had no choice. You didn't search for him before. Maybe because you don't trust him."

The boy was observant. "I searched for him, but I couldn't find any information. He and I are from two different worlds, or at least we were."

He shook his head. "I don't believe that. You and the Guv are more similar than you think."

"Am I interrupting the lesson?" Christopher entered the office in a flutter of dark clothes and golden hair.

She couldn't stop a sigh as he flashed his crooked smile.

"Guv." Finn stood up. "We've just finished."

"Did you have another problem with the shipment?" she said.

His smile vanished. "Pearce's coppers tried again to seize my cargo, but we fooled them, loading it on another ship. The shipment has sailed without problems."

"Great news," Finn said.

"Yes, a celebration is in order soon." Christopher leant against the doorframe, his hungry gaze on her. "I need to talk to Elizabeth."

"Yes, Guv." Finn collected the books and pencils. "See you tomorrow, miss."

"What is it?" she asked when Finn left.

Christopher shut the door and strode to her. Before she could ask again what the matter was, he took her face in his hands and kissed her hard. The way he cradled her head and angled it to kiss her more deeply started a fire in her belly. A fire that was always ready to burn for him.

He hauled her up and sat her on the desk before nestling between her legs without breaking the kiss.

She closed her legs around him, getting lost in the savage lashes of his tongue. She closed her eyes as he kissed her cheeks, jaw, and neck. A storm of sensations swept through her. It was amazing how a kiss from him sparked infinite pleasure in her body.

"I couldn't stop thinking about you for the whole day," he whispered against her skin. "And I was worried."

"Worried?" She brushed his hair from his face.

"I have this fear tormenting me, that someone might take you away from me, that I come back here and you're gone."

"No, it won't happen again." She searched his eyes. "I'm not going anywhere."

She must have said something that upset him because he frowned. Wasn't that what he wanted to hear?

He hugged her without saying anything; only his heart beat faster and louder.

"How did you join this life?" she asked, caressing his gorgeous hair.

He sat down on his chair, carrying her with him. "As I told you, Father assigned me a job in his estate in Yorkshire. It was a good job. I started as an assistant to the steward. Then I managed the estate myself for a short time until Father died. Pearce made it clear he had no intention of letting me anywhere close to any of the family's properties. He ordered me to leave and made sure no one in Yorkshire would give me a job. I moved around until my money ran out. When I didn't find any job and was starving, I joined a small gang in London. It was nothing too scary or dangerous, but after I witnessed the Reapers abusing and terrifying people, I decided to intervene and beat those bullies at their own game. I won. The rest is history."

"So you became the King to protect the people of Whitechapel."

He gave a dismissive wave of his hand. "I'm no saint, Elizabeth. The Reapers were competition, but yes, they were too violent not to do anything."

"As I said, you're a good man." She kissed his cheek. "I was worried about you after your father died."

He coiled an arm around her waist. "I wanted to see you. Before Pearce gave me the sack, I planned to visit you once my position as the steward granted me some respectability. I hoped to leave my illegitimate status behind."

"I never thought you cared about respectability."

"But your family did." His eyelashes fluttered down. "I wanted to present myself as a successful estate steward. Once that became impossible, I couldn't search for you as a criminal."

She tilted her head to stare at him. "You wanted a proper job for my sake? To see me?"

"Yes." There was a fierce determination in the way he said that and not an ounce of hesitation. "You're an earl's daughter."

Emotion swelled in her chest. He'd been ready to work hard only to see her. "Thank you."

A muscle in his jaw ticked. "Once your father realises his mistake, he'll want you back, and you'll be gone again. You'll leave me again. But it'll be right. You deserve to be happy."

"What makes you think I want to return to that house? No matter how deeply and sincerely my parents apologise, I'll never forgive them for having thrown me out. They didn't believe me. They listened to gossip and didn't trust me." Her voice broke with frustration. "I mean, they learnt I'd lied about the Great Blizzard, but they didn't believe me when I said that nothing had happened between us. I shall never forgive them."

His arms were around her, protective and soothing. She rested her head on his shoulders, fighting bitter tears. She didn't want to cry. She'd spent nights crying until her eyes had burnt, and she was tired of being sad.

Christopher brushed his lips over her heated cheek. The touch was feather-like and gentle, but it satisfied the hunger for sensations in her chest.

"You may change your mind after you experience my life for a while."

She shook her head, hiding her face in the crook of his neck. Why did everyone keep saying that?

"My people are brutal," he said.

"So are mine." She inhaled his heady scent, a combination of leather, soap, and musk. "I don't want to leave you. No matter how hard you try to convince me."

twenty-six

L ANTERNS AND FLOWERS brightened the courtyard in the palace. Lively music drifted from a corner where a few people were playing violins, harpsichords, and accordions. The celebration for the latest shipment and the defeat of Pearce was fully ongoing.

Elizabeth danced with Finn, an Irish dance that was all jumps and quick passages. She laughed when Finn held her hands and made her run in a wide circle. The whole world spun with her. If he let her go, she'd find herself sprawled against the wall. When the music ended, she clapped her hands along with the others. The warm night and the people dancing and laughing reminded her of when she'd lived with her brothers and sisters in Spencer Hall and played and danced with them. Another life. Now they wouldn't glance her way.

"Thank you, Finn." Breathless, she hugged the boy.

"Any time, miss."

She walked over to the table where the drinks and the food were set and tried a slice of the acorn cake Jane had baked. The not-too-sweet taste of the honey was perfectly balanced by the nutty flavour of the acorns. Jane might be a bitter woman, but she could cook.

Finn joined her. "I was thinking about going to the library to study."

"Good idea," she said between morsels. "It's quiet and has everything you need."

He poked her with an elbow. "Did you see the Guv?"

"Christopher is here? I thought he was still at the dock." Elizabeth gazed around, putting down her plate. "I want to dance with him. Where is he?"

He tilted his chin towards a corner. "He hasn't taken his eyes off you for a moment."

Elizabeth followed Finn's gaze. Christopher leant against one of the pillars in the dimly lit arcade, a mug in his hand. His heated blue gaze burned her. It cut through the crowd to find and claim her.

There was nothing kind in that stare, only raw desire about to explode.

The music started again, but as a woman dragged Finn towards the centre of the courtyard for another dance, she didn't join the dancers. She headed for the arcade and brushed past Christopher. He followed her with his gaze as if there were an invisible rope tying them together. Maybe there was.

She pressed her back against the wall in a dark corner, still breathless but for a reason other than the dance. He put the mug down and went to her, moving with rapacious intent, but she wasn't scared. The closer he came, the faster she breathed.

Standing a few inches from her, he placed both his hands on the sides of her head. He was so close a whiff of his heady scent made her dizzy. Maybe his desire was contagious because all of a sudden, she needed to feel his hands and lips on her body. He raked a slow gaze over her, and she felt that gaze on her skin, like a caress.

"Do you know what you do to me?" His voice was nothing but a low growl.

She licked her bottom lip, and he followed the gesture, his eyes growing wider. "No, I don't," she said among pants.

He dipped his head and paused, his lips a breath away from hers. "Shall I show you?"

Her skin tingled with his deep baritone, his words, and the dark hunger he radiated.

"Yes," she whispered.

He closed the little space between them, making her feel all the taut muscles in his powerful body. He'd always been well-built and strong, but the past years and his criminal life had made him magnificent.

She was effectively trapped between the wall and him, but she had no intention of escaping. Yet he didn't take advantage of his dominating position by touching her or kissing her. His breath mingled with hers as he devoured her with his gaze only.

Finally, he touched her, trailing his fingertips over her cheek and down her neck. He stopped on the neckline of her dress, sucking in a sharp breath. He closed his hand around her neck gently, but her pulse drummed a fast tempo against his palm.

"Go to my room and wait for me." It was an order she wasn't going to disobey. "Now."

He stepped back from her, staring at her. He gave her barely enough room to slip out of his grip. His stare followed her up the stairs, sending shivers down her back.

When she slipped into his bedroom, a moment of uncertainty caught her. She had no idea what she was supposed to do. Lie down in his bed, strip naked, or sit politely on the chair and wait?

The sound of the music and laughter came muffled through the thick door. She paced on the rug in front of the blazing fire and searched around for inspiration. But then again, he'd told her to wait, and she wasn't exactly a seductress.

She sat on the bed only to stand up again when the door opened and laughter roared from downstairs. He stepped into the room, and she couldn't suppress a shiver. His presence dominated the bedroom, choking the space. She remained still, trembling with anticipation.

He locked the door behind him without taking his eyes off her. His stare burned so intense she wouldn't be surprised if she found herself naked from it.

The world vanished, sucked into the warm light of the bedroom and the heated tension between them. He took his time crossing the room while shedding his long coat, like the wings of a fallen angel. He carefully removed the gun and dagger and placed them on his escritoire. Each movement was slow and deliberate, driving her mad with need. By the time he was again an inch from her, she was panting and throbbing.

"Undress." It was another order in a tone that didn't leave room for protests.

She shouldn't find that so intriguing.

Her fingers became suddenly clumsy as she hurried to unbutton her shirt. He watched her silently, doing nothing to speed up the process. The crackling of the fire and her uneven breathing were the only sounds.

When the shirt was open, she shrugged out of it impatiently. Unfastening the skirt and petticoats was a quick thing. Then she removed her corset, boots, and stockings, but when it was the moment to remove her chemise and drawers, she hesitated.

She had the thought it was the first time a man had seen her naked. But actually, Christopher was the only man who had seen her naked.

He regarded her from underneath hooded eyes. "Why did you stop?"

"I'm a little nervous."

He caressed her cheek, and the simple, tender touch sent a jolt through her. "You can leave whenever you want, or I can leave if you prefer."

"No." She leant into his hand.

"I want you naked."

She swallowed hard.

"Do you want me to finish?" he asked.

"No."

She untied her drawers and lowered the straps of her chemise with a quick gesture, lest her modesty stop her again. His eyes darkened with desire as the light from the fire was the only thing covering her skin.

"And now?" She ached everywhere. Even her lips tingled.

"Sit on the bed."

He didn't move though, so she had to brush against him to do as told. He hissed a breath when her breasts touched his arm. The mattress dipped when she perched on the bed.

"Loosen your hair," he said.

She made short work of removing the hairpins and undoing the chignon. Her curls fell over her shoulders and breasts in a soft *swish*.

He loomed over her, staring at every bare inch of her. "You're so beautiful."

She tilted her head back to look at him. "You make me feel beautiful."

He knelt in front of her and spread her legs wide, none too gently. That was all the warning she had before he dipped his head.

She wasn't ready for his deep kiss. She wasn't ready for the onslaught of pleasure. She wasn't ready for the shock.

The first lash of his tongue jolted her. The second made her gasp. The third caused her to shudder.

She closed her fists on the quilt, loud moans leaving her. He held her by the hips, going deeper with his expert tongue. The pleasure was so strong she had to close her eyes. He put her knees on his shoulders to get closer until his lips were the only thing she felt on her body.

All her focus gathered on the spot of her body where his

tongue stroked her, on his slow lapping, and his gentle lips against her.

The burst of energy rushing through her caused her back to arch. She closed her thighs around his neck in response, panting and burning for him. The release was a primordial force that coursed through her like lightning. She lay back, boneless and dizzy with pleasure. How was she supposed to know such a pleasure was possible? How could she live a normal life after that?

He kissed her inner thighs, grazing them with his teeth gently as he moved up her body, scattering kisses. He paused once he straightened up, his chest rising and falling quickly.

When he moved over her, she wrapped her legs around his hips. He licked his glistening lips, fluttering his eyelashes down.

"I haven't finished," he said in a coarse voice that made her achy again. He took her wrists and put her arms over her head. "Stay like this. Don't move."

The heat seemed to consume her body while he drank her in. He propped himself up on one elbow to caress her breasts. The first stroke was madly slow and incredibly powerful. But he used more strength after that, rubbing her nipple with his rough fingers until it became painfully taut. His rugged pads only amplified the wonderful sensation that shot a throb between her legs. She writhed, moaned, and arched her back, growing mad with need. When she lowered her arm to grab his shoulders, he stopped.

"Arms up."

She did as told without hesitation. But then he closed his hot mouth around her nipple, and she writhed again, rocking her hips and searching for more friction. He was still fully clothed, but if the fabric of his trousers or shirt chafed her skin, she didn't notice or care.

She wanted to tangle her fingers through his glorious hair, but he would stop kissing her. He worshipped her breasts with his wicked tongue and lips, switching between them when she grew too achy.

"Please," she whispered because she couldn't speak louder.

He slid a hand between her legs and found her wetness. She unashamedly cried out when he rubbed her slowly while rolling her nipple between his lips.

The pleasure was too much, overwhelming, unmanageable. She muffled her scream with his shoulder, wrapping her arms around him. Spasms rocked her body, and he held her through the release, giving her all the support she needed.

The burst of pleasure seemed to go on forever, more powerful than the first. When her breathing returned to normal, she sagged on the bed, happy and satiated. He stared at her again, but this time, there was a tenderness in his expression that melted her heart.

"So beautiful," he whispered, caressing the side of her breast. "Sleep here tonight. With me."

"Yes."

He rose only to unbutton his shirt and trousers.

The light of the fire agreed with him; it exalted all the sharp ridges and edges of his sculpted body. When he was fully naked, he gathered her in his arms and tucked her in bed, slipping in with her.

Lying naked with him under the covers felt familiar, safe, and exciting at the same time. She snuggled closer to him, and he wrapped his arms around her. His sweet hug and warm body were the perfect conclusion for the most powerful release of her life.

twenty-seven

FOR CHRISTOPHER, TIME could stop right there and then, in his warm, dark bedroom.

Spending a night with Elizabeth in his arms wasn't new, but he would never grow tired of holding her in his sleep. They'd slept through the night, holding each other with desperation, as it'd happened years ago in the cottage. But this time, no one would take her away from him. Only she had the power to decide to leave him, and if that was her choice, he'd accept it.

He caressed her silky hair, incapable of keeping his hands to himself while she was so close. Her shoulder felt silky under his fingers. The curve of her hip made him want to grab it, and her breast filled his hand nicely.

She opened her eyes and smiled. "What are you doing?"

She stretched out, thrusting her breasts towards him, and he couldn't stop himself.

He caught her nipple between his lips and drew it into his mouth. Her soft moan had him ready and aching for her in a moment. She moved under his lips, rolling her hips.

When he slid his hand between her legs, he found her deliciously wet. He burned to take her properly, make her feel how much he wanted her, but that had to wait.

The more he rubbed her, the wilder she became, breathing hard and jolting until she gripped his shoulders and pressed her mouth against his chest. He held her again, glad his touch gave her so much pleasure. Little pulses went through her. He watched her becoming flushed and glowing, utterly beautiful, completely devastating.

He kissed her forehead. "Good morning."

She laughed, running her hand down his chest. Her touch was like fire on his skin. Each finger marked him. Each touch made him hers. She stroked his hip and thigh before gripping him. His body gave an involuntary jerk.

She kissed his chest. Her spicy scent teased his nostrils as she fondled him. The movements were slow and gentle, but a fiery battle of emotions was going on inside him. He had to force himself to stay calm and still, instead of thrusting inside her like a beast in heat. Between her velvety lips on his chest and her gentle hand wrapped around him, he was bursting with need and pleasure. Energy erupted within him as quickly as a firework and just as powerful. She kept her grip on him when he spilt in her hand, a groan rumbling out of him.

She kissed his cheek, lips, and neck, this time in a sweet fashion that melted his heart. "You're beautiful, too."

"Great. Now that we've established we're both beautiful, I'd like to kiss you again." He slipped his hand between her thighs.

She giggled. "I like it when you do that."

"I like it, too." He spread her legs and watched her, licking his lips. He was about to taste her when footsteps pounded.

"Guv!" Smithy's loud voice and insistent banging on the door tore a curse out of Christopher.

"What in the bloody hell?" he shouted.

Elizabeth jolted.

"Them coppers again. They're searching the warehouse. They have a message from the duke for you."

"Bloody hell." He gritted his teeth.

"Guv!" More banging.

"Dammit, Smithy. Wait!"

The banging stopped.

He kissed the tip of Elizabeth's nose and slipped out of the warm bed. "Sorry."

"Go. Don't worry." She gathered the bedsheet up, covering herself, although she glowed more brightly than the morning star.

Pulling his trousers on, he smiled. She was just too beautiful, all pink, dishevelled, and wide-eyed.

"We aren't through yet," he whispered.

"I do hope we aren't."

He kissed her one last time before going out. He shut the door behind him, careful not to let Smithy catch a glimpse of a half-naked, glowing Elizabeth.

"When did they arrive?" he asked, going down the stairs and forcing himself to think about work.

"At dawn. They were looking for you."

"Guv." Finn hurried towards him, carrying a book under his arm. "What can I do?"

Christopher took his arm. "I need you to go to Pearce's house and interrogate the servants today. Ask them about the bloody ball."

Finn frowned. "The servants? I can come with you to the warehouse."

"No, go to the duke's house and question the servants. Stay away from trouble."

Finn exhaled through his teeth. "Yes, Guv."

A carriage was waiting for Christopher when he exited the palace. The drive was too short for him to analyse the situation in depth. After he'd managed to fool Pearce's men, retaliation was expected, only not that fast.

He strode to the warehouse with Smithy at his side. At least a dozen officers were there, batons in their hands, in a standoff with his men. His name was shouted, and a few people pointed at him. One of the peelers left the group and walked towards him. But the man wasn't a peeler, or at least he hadn't been one until recently. He was, Butch, the former leader of the Reapers, the brutal gang Christopher had dismantled and kicked out of Whitechapel.

"What the hell?" He stopped in front of Butch.

"Your highness." Butch performed a mocking bow. "We meet again."

"What are you doing here?"

Butch stroked his scarred chin. "We have a message to deliver to the King from the duke."

"What message?"

"This."

The blow was so quick he barely had time to dodge it. His men shouted a war cry before charging. Blades and guns were pulled out, and the chaos started.

So it was going to be one of those days.

THE PALACE TURNED into an improvised hospital in the span of an hour. Elizabeth walked through the courtyard where bleeding and groaning men kept arriving. It was amazing how the morning had changed from wonderful to nightmarish in a short period.

The news of a violent brawl at the docks had spread quickly, and the wounded had started to flow in the garrison. Although she hadn't done much aside from carrying buckets of warm water, clean cloths, and bottles of carbolic acid to those who took care of the wounded. There were men she'd never seen, but no trace of Christopher.

The coppery scent of blood combined with that of disinfectant gave her a headache, and she had to take deep breaths not to feel dizzy at the sight of slashes and cuts.

"Elizabeth!" Jane shouted from the other side of the courtyard. "I need hot water now."

She hurried to bring the bucket to Jane, averting her gaze from the wounded man. "Did you see Christopher?"

"No." From Jane's clipped answer, Elizabeth couldn't understand if the woman was worried or not.

Finn was stitching a wound on a man's arm, and she nearly gagged. She hated raw steaks because of the blood. She wasn't made for such carnage.

Sidestepping a pile of bloody rags, she spotted Smithy who had a bandage around his forehead. She rushed to him. "Where's Christopher?"

He jabbed a thumb over his shoulder. "He's coming."

She didn't have time to feel relieved. Shoulders hunched, Christopher came in, half-dragged by a tall man. Blood trickled down from his forehead, but with his black clothes, it was impossible to say if he was bleeding anywhere else.

"Christopher." She slid an arm under his, helping the man carry him. "What happened?"

"Nothing we haven't already seen." His voice sounded strained.

"Where to, Guv?" the man asked.

"My room."

She staggered under his weight when they went up the stairs. "Where are you wounded?"

He let out a raspy chuckle. "It'll be quicker to tell you where I am not." He groaned when the man laid him on the bed.

"What do you need, Guv?"

He waved him away. "Take care of the others. They're in worse condition."

"Worse condition? You can barely walk." Elizabeth prepared a bowl of hot water. "Let me see where you're hurt."

"I need help to get undressed."

She unbuttoned his shirt while he grimaced. Blood soaked his chest, but she didn't see any gush or gunshot wound.

"Where is the wound?" Her voice sounded high-pitched to her own ears.

"This isn't my blood." He rolled to his side. "My blood is on the back."

She pulled off his shirt to reveal a slash across his marred skin. The shock froze her for a moment. "Heavens."

There was so much blood she couldn't understand how serious the wound was.

Jane, barging into the room, broke the moment. "Guv, let me see." Blood stained her apron. She examined the wound, prodding it and ignoring Christopher's groans. "Not deep but nasty." She glanced at Elizabeth. "Clean it and stitch it. You should be knowledgeable by now."

Her pulse slammed in her veins. "I've never done anything like this before. I don't know where to start."

"It's like needlework."

Elizabeth shivered. "But ..."

Jane took her shoulders none too gently. "You decided to stay. Good. That's our life. That's what you have to deal with. Clean the wound and stitch it. You've seen me doing it a few times. Do it," she said to Elizabeth before leaving.

"Ah ..." She rubbed her forehead.

Christopher winced, propping himself up. "I'll guide you. Start with the hot water and wash the cut."

"I know a little, but I learnt recently, and I've never seen a wound like that."

"Don't worry."

"All ... right." She cleaned the wound with water first then with carbolic acid.

He shouted into the pillow when she applied the disinfectant to the cut.

"I'm sorry."

He waved dismissively although all his muscles contracted and spasmed.

She rummaged through the box that contained the necessary supplies for dealing with a wound. The stitching was the biggest problem. She'd seen it done a few times, but that was it. And what was the difference between the straight needle and the curved one? What type of thread should she use? There were different types of them, some thick, others thin.

"I can't do it." She panted, her hands trembling. "I don't know how to do it."

"Stay calm. It's all right."

But it wasn't all right, and there was so much blood. What if he died? What if she made a mistake and the wound wouldn't heal or became infected? Her vision darkened at the edges. Her legs quivered.

"Sit down, Elizabeth." His commanding voice couldn't be ignored.

She did as told, choking on air. "I'm sorry."

"Shush. Take deep breaths and don't faint, please." He whistled, and Darko rushed inside, twitching his nose at the smell of blood. "Fetch Finn."

Darko raced out of the room and returned a few moments later, barking. Finn followed him.

"Guv." He glanced at her and at Christopher. "Are you all right, miss? You're so pale. Let me get you something."

"Excuse me." Christopher waved a hand, stopping Finn. "I'm bleeding and need stitches."

"Yes, Guv." Finn searched through the medical box without flinching while checking the wound.

"What type of needle and thread are you going to use?" she said, swallowing the bitter taste in her mouth.

"You can ignore straight needles. They're for easy cuts. I always use curved needles. The thick ones are for seriously deep wounds, but for this one ..." He leant over to examine the slash. "A medium width needle with a type four thread. You were lucky, Guv. It could be worse. Shall I give you laudanum?"

"Just bloody stitch it."

She averted her gaze as Finn stitched the wound while Christopher clenched his fists and squeezed his eyes shut.

"Nearly done, Guv," Finn said, completely focused on the task.

She distracted herself by trying to pet Darko. The dog didn't bark or growl, but he seemed preoccupied with his master's health.

Christopher groaned in pain.

Finn clicked his tongue. "Sorry, Guv."

She took Christopher's hand. "Why don't you take the laudanum?"

He drew in a few deep breaths. "It makes me sleepy, and I need to be awake to make decisions."

"Done." Finn cleaned the wound again before bandaging it with a long white strip of fabric. "You can't move too much, or it'll start bleeding again. I'll check it later. I have other people to stitch."

"Go." Christopher rested his head on the pillow.

Elizabeth covered him when Finn left. "Finn was incredible. I'm sorry I was useless."

He licked his lips. "You're shocked."

"I am." Her voice cracked. "Just thinking you could have died while I was completely useless fills me with fear, and I can't stand the blood. I might get used to it, but I can't now."

"Elizabeth." He held her hand, leaving a smear of blood on her skin. "What happened today is a natural occurrence in my life. This is what it means to be next to me."

"I'll get better at this. I promise."

He closed his eyes for a moment, muttering something she didn't catch. "You don't have to do anything you don't want."

"I do, because I want to stay here."

He pushed himself up, pain straining his features. "Would you help me get downstairs?"

"You need to rest."

"I must see how the others are faring. That's another natural occurrence in my life."

She swallowed past the knot in her throat. "I'll help you."

ELIZABETH STROKED Christopher's head as he finally slept soundly. He'd spent a few hours with his men, talking and discussing with his lieutenants before allowing himself to rest. She'd watched horrified as he'd pushed himself to the limit, disregarding his own well-being to take care of his men. Thinking she could have lost him made her feel as if she were falling from a high cliff. And she hadn't been able to help him.

Jane entered the room, quiet on her feet. Without telling her anything, she examined his face and took a sniff of his back, lifting the blanket. "No infection. He finally accepted the laudanum, I gather."

"He did. He fell asleep immediately."

Jane pulled the cover up and exhaled. "This is what I mean. I don't hate you, but as you must have seen, you aren't made for this life, girl. Finn told me he'd stitched the Guv because you couldn't do it."

She sat on the chair. Could she feel more useless?

For the first time, Jane's expression softened into something almost maternal. "You should leave while you can. I'm telling you for your own good."

"I won't leave him."

Jane grinned. "You will. You're too spoiled not to."

A flicker of annoyance shot through her exhaustion. "You don't know me. Yes, I've never stitched a wound or seen the aftermath of a bloody battle, but Christopher is everything to me."

"Because he gave you a home and helped you when no one did."

"Because I love him!"

The words came out of her without her thinking, but they were true. She felt them deep in her soul. She loved Christopher. She didn't want to go anywhere without him. She wanted to stay with him, whatever that meant.

That shut Jane up for a full minute. "I hope you mean it."

"I do. In my world, a man like him, an illegitimate son of a duke, is scorned and despised. My mother forbade me from talking to him and warned me to stay away from him. When my parents kicked me out, they told me that if I would accuse Christopher of attacking and forcing me, they would forgive me."

Jane gasped. "They wanted you to blame him, even though he hadn't done anything wrong?"

"Yes. They said it was the only way to save my family's reputation."

"And what did you do?"

She touched Christopher's hand. "Well, I'm here, am I not?"

Jane smiled again, but her smile didn't hold contempt. "You're one strong lady."

"I'm trying to be one, but I'm not like you. You were right about that."

Jane fiddled with her apron, seemingly incapable of meeting her gaze. "Do you think I'm strong?"

"I haven't met a woman stronger than you are. I mean it." Elizabeth gave her a nod. "You have my respect."

Jane lowered her gaze. "I'm not strong," she whispered. "When I was a governess in Lord Latymer's house, I tried many times to defend myself from his prowling hands. He would catch me off guard when I was alone and touch me inappropriately." She drew a shuddering breath. "Sometimes I froze, so shocked I was. But even when I shoved him and rejected him, he would insist, saying I was only playing with him. And the ironic thing is I was the one to lose everything and branded as a trollop."

"You aren't weak, Jane, and what happened wasn't your fault. Sometimes fear paralyses us. It doesn't mean you aren't strong. That man was a swine, and you did your best in a very difficult situation. You needed the job and money. Don't blame yourself."

Jane raised her gaze, and there wasn't hostility as she stared at Elizabeth. "Thank you," she whispered. She opened the door and paused. "I'll teach you how to stitch a wound."

twenty-eight

CHRISTOPHER MIGHT HAVE underestimated the seriousness of his injuries.

The cut on his back was so painful that for two weeks, he'd found it difficult to sleep, sit, walk, breathe ... anything, really, and the punches he'd received during the brawl made him sore.

His head had felt the size of a watermelon and throbbed with a passion. He'd had no choice but to take laudanum, which drastically reduced the time he was conscious and rational.

Almost three weeks had passed since the fight at the warehouse, and finally, he had recovered his strength. Because many of his men were equally injured, yet another shipment had to be delayed. Of course, the official version was another battle between two rival gangs had ensued.

Sod Pearce to hell.

On top of that, Elizabeth worried him. She'd spent every day next to him, staring at him as if she expected him to die at any moment. Her fear was palpable. She wasn't made for this life. Few were. He couldn't demand she live as he did and be happy. She wouldn't want to build a family with him in this precarious life.

He was ready to renounce his criminal throne for her, but it would take time.

"Here's your tea." She entered the bedroom, carrying a tray with a fresh pot of tea, oat biscuits, bread, and ham. "I'll apply the salve to your wound again. It's getting better quickly. That's a good sign."

"Wait." He propped himself up, twitching his nose at the smell of carbolic acid wafting from his clothes.

No matter how much soap he used to wash himself, the stink of carbolic acid remained on his skin, bedsheets, and food.

"What is it? Your back again?" Her pallor hadn't improved in the past weeks.

"No." He grabbed her trembling hand. "These past weeks, I've been either unconscious or busy with my men, and we didn't have the chance to talk."

She pressed her lips. "I know what you want to say. I nearly fainted, and I couldn't watch when Finn stitched the wound. Without him, I'm not sure what would have happened to you. I'll get better. I need time. I promise. Jane will teach me how to stitch wounds."

"No." He regretted the sharp tone he used. "You don't have to change or get better. But you should ask yourself if this life is for you."

"Christopher—"

"Really for you. You might get used to the blood, but life here will always be violent, and you can't get used to that. Sooner or later, it'll be too much, and either a part of you will die, or you'll regret having stayed. And I'd rather see you lead a happy, normal life without me than watch a part of you being murdered by this life and learning to hate me."

"You're too dramatic. I want to stay here."

"I want you to stay here, too. But I want you to make a choice you won't regret. I can live, knowing you're safe and happy without me. I can't live if you're by my side but resent me."

She lowered her gaze. "I grew up in a wealthy family. That's true. My life was without danger or worries about where I would get my next meal. My parents spoiled me. All this is true. In the past months, I learnt first-hand what poverty means. For the first time, I've worked to earn money, and I had to defend myself from men who tried to grope me."

"What?" He sat bolt upright, ignoring the shot of pain in his back. "When did this happen?"

She smiled and put a hand on his chest. "Don't worry. Nothing happened."

"The hell nothing happened. Who were these men?"

She pressed a finger to his lips. "You're getting distracted. What I mean to say is that I survived. Those lessons were hard to learn, but I survived. And I want to stay here."

"Learning to work with your hands is not the same thing as dealing with criminals and risking getting arrested."

Her delicate eyebrows drew together. "I know what I'm doing."

He begged to differ. What she'd seen was but a glimpse of what her life with him would be. He wondered if he had the right to drag her into his dangerous world. The least he could do was to be honest with her.

"I'm ready to leave this life for you," he said.

Her eyes flared wide. "Would you really?"

"Yes. Hell, I enjoy the excitement, I'm not going to lie, but it's tiring. But it'll take time. I can't leave my men unprotected, and all my businesses need to be settled."

"Oh, Christopher."

"If my plan to turn my business into a legal company doesn't work, leaving this life behind might take years." He couldn't express himself further as Finn appeared on the threshold, wearing a nice brown tweed suit.

"May I come in, Guv?"

"Come in."

"I have news." Finn waved a piece of paper. "It took me an embarrassing amount of time, what with the battle and everything else, but I have the list of people who were at the duke's ball in June." He put it on the bed. "The duke's servants are fiercely loyal to him, or maybe scared, but I found a maid who trusted me."

"Well done." Christopher showed the list to Elizabeth. "Did you write down all the names?"

He thrust his chest out. "I did, Guv. I copied them from the list the duke's maid had in a drawer."

"Excellent." Christopher studied the list. "I don't know half of these people."

"I know many of them," Elizabeth said, "but I don't see what any of them would gain from discrediting us."

"Is there any jealous woman who wanted Pearce for herself?"

She sank her teeth into her bottom lip, looking adorable. "The majority of the women on the list are married or engaged. Others are barely débutantes. Again, Rebecca is the only name I can think of."

"But you said she didn't come."

"She didn't." She frowned. "She knows I lied about the Great Blizzard. I told my parents I took shelter in our hunting lodge, but instead, Lady Bletchley said she'd been there with her family. Rebecca Norton was present when we discussed that."

He nodded. "She understood you lied because you were with someone else, and it wouldn't take long to guess that someone was me."

"She must have seen us together at the ball, but again, she declined Pearce's invitation."

"The maid said that some guests arrived late," Finn said. "I can ask her again for this Rebecca."

"Yes, do it," Christopher said.

"Great," Finn said. "If this is all, I'd like to go." He started to walk out, but Christopher stopped him.

"Where are you going in your finest?"

Finn flushed to the roots of his nicely styled hair. "The library."

"You don't usually wear a nice suit for that," he said.

Finn fiddled with his flat hat. "Yes, well, this library is close to the toffs' houses, and people wear fine clothes there."

Christopher raised his eyebrows. "What's her name?"

"Christopher, leave the boy alone." Elizabeth shook her head.

"I care about him. I want to know what he's up to. Finn?"

The boy flashed a shy smile. "Odette. She's very pretty and very clever. We talked a bit in the library, but we shouldn't. So we now meet in the library when it's not too busy."

"I'm happy you found someone to share your studies with," she said.

"I think Finn wants to share something with Odette other than books." Christopher grinned.

"Shush," she chided him.

Finn blushed again, scrubbing the back of his neck. "Well, I have to go now." He ran out of the room as if followed by the coppers.

"You helped him a lot," Christopher said, stroking her hand.

"Helping him with mathematics was easy for me. Helping you with the cut and blood wasn't."

He pulled her close for a kiss he knew he didn't deserve. She sagged against his chest, and he deepened the kiss, deliberately forgetting about the future for a moment.

She moaned in the kiss when he cupped her breast through the fabric of her shirt. Her nipple hardened under the pad of his thumb.

"We must be careful," she whispered against his lips. "You haven't recovered yet."

"Sleep with me tonight."

"I've been sleeping here every night."

"Yes. On the sofa."

"You were in pain, and I didn't want to hurt you by accident in my sleep." Her eyes became suspiciously shiny. "I don't want to hurt you."

He kissed her cheek and neck. "Neither do I."

He swore an oath, right then and there. Her safety and happiness came before everything else, and if his illegal business made his life too complicated and that meant letting her go, he would.

ELIZABETH WAS MAKING progress with the accounting job for Christopher and with Darko.

Her situation with the hound was a far cry from being extremely friendly, but Darko had stayed without growling at her while she'd worked in Christopher's study.

Darko half-slept, half-watched her from his thick bedding. His pointed ears turned around every time she made a noise. She dropped the pen, and his head went up.

"Do not fret. It's only the pen." As she leant over to pick it up, he padded across the room towards her.

She moved very slowly as he sniffed the floor where the pen had fallen and then her fingers. He made a noise like a snort, a sign he was disappointed. No treats.

But she had a secret weapon. With her free hand, she fished out a slice of bacon from a container on the desk.

"We are friends, aren't we?"

He sat, his amber eyes on the bacon.

"Good boy." She handed him the treat and giggled when his raspy tongue tickled her hand.

When he finished cleaning the grease from her fingers, he straightened and stared at her as if he were making a decision. She remained still, returning the stare although they said a dog considered a prolonged stare as a challenge. He made a funny noise before rising on his hind legs and running his tongue over her face, one long lick from her chin to her forehead that left her whole face wet. It had to be a sort of initiation or baptism.

"Eww." She did her best to stay still.

He lazily returned to his bedding and curled up with a sigh. She guessed it was his way of telling her she was tolerable.

After she discreetly wiped her face—lest Darko get offended by her ingratitude—she resumed her work, recording all the transactions and balances of Christopher's lucrative activities. At least she didn't need to worry about tax calculations. And to think Christopher was ready to renounce his life for her. It didn't matter if it'd take him years. She would wait for him.

Sometimes when she closed her eyes, visions of the bleeding gash on Christopher's back would flash across her mind. The blood and shouts of pain of the wounded would forever be impressed in her memories. What would she do the next time when Christopher's injuries were more serious?

"Miss?" Finn entered with a tray of steaming tea. "I brought tea and some news."

"Thank you. What news?"

He took a chair and sat on it backwards. "The duke's maid told me that Miss Rebecca Norton actually came to the ball."

She held her breath. "Is she certain?"

"Absolutely. The maid remembers it because Rebecca arrived late and dropped a glass of wine on her dress. The maid escorted her to a room upstairs where Rebecca removed her dress so the maid could clean the stain. Rebecca remained in that room for a while, and after the maid returned the gown, she decided to leave the ball in a hurry. Hardly anyone saw her."

"Dash it all. So it must be her. She must have seen Christopher and me while she was upstairs, and after she saw us, she decided to leave, surely to plan what to do next."

"It doesn't prove she's the gossipmonger, but it proves she lied to you."

"Indeed." She folded her arms on her chest. Her instincts had been right. "Thank you, Finn. You've been wonderful."

"You're welcome." He poured her a cup and opened his mouth, but then closed it again.

"What is it?"

His smile seemed forced, but it didn't last, and he turned serious. "May I talk to you?"

"Certainly."

He ran a hand through his hair. "It's about Odette. She's one of the toffs, as you are. No offence, miss."

"None taken."

"She has a chaperone, velvet dresses, an elegant accent, and a shiny carriage, and all that. I didn't tell her who I am, an orphan who lives in Whitechapel with the King." He hunched his shoulders. "Would the Guv be disappointed?"

"No, darling. Christopher would understand, but you can't lie to Odette. It's not right."

"But if she knows I'm a criminal, she won't want to see me again, will she? You're a lady. A lady doesn't spend time with people like me."

What was she supposed to say? She didn't want to encourage him to lie. The lie would be discovered sooner or later, and Odette would surely be upset. But she couldn't lie either and tell him Odette wouldn't care about who he was.

"Even if Odette doesn't care about what you do and wants to see you, her parents will forbid her to. It's a complicated world."

"Why do you stay with the Guv?" he asked.

"Because I care about him. Very much. And my situation is different from Odette's. I'm not a lady anymore."

He frowned, looking older. "So you want to stay here because you can't live with your family anymore?"

"No, it's ..." Difficult. The incident with her family had pushed her out of her house, but she didn't regret her decision to stay with Christopher. "I've always known that my parents didn't approve of Christopher. They did everything in their power to keep us apart. An argument with them was inevitable, as it was my decision to stay with him. What I can tell you is not to lie to her. Let her decide what she wants."

He nodded solemnly. "Will you come with me? I am supposed to meet her in Hyde Park for a promenade, and I don't want to go alone. You're a lady and know how I should behave."

"Of course I'll come."

twenty-nine

"YOU LOOK VERY handsome, Finn." Elizabeth straightened Finn's bow tie as they crossed Hyde Park on a bright, sunny afternoon.

"I'm so nervous. My hands are all sweaty." He showed her his palms.

"Do not worry. We'll take a nice stroll through the park, have a chat with Odette, and that's it. I'll keep her chaperone busy while you'll have the opportunity to have a private talk with Odette."

"Thank you for being with me. I couldn't have done it without you."

She patted his shoulder. "Let's go. A gentleman doesn't make a lady wait."

He shrugged. "I'm not a gentleman, anyway, am I?"

"You're a good young man, Finn. That matters more."

He showed her a wide grin. "I know there isn't a single possibility I might court Odette, but at least I want her to know me for who I am."

"Right choice."

"And who knows, maybe she'll be as brave as you and decide to be with me, anyway."

Elizabeth felt anything but brave.

She paused along the Serpentine, remembering a time when she'd walked that very path with her mother, sisters, friends. She hadn't appreciated the privileges she'd enjoyed back then. The free time, luxuries, and nice meals had been taken for granted. If anything, she was grateful to have learnt that important lesson.

"That's her." Finn fiddled with the collar of his shirt. "Isn't she lovely?"

Elizabeth watched the pretty blonde girl in a dark-blue capelet walking towards them. Her expensive shoes and gown marked her as a girl from a wealthy family. Unbidden, a pang of nostalgia hit her because there had been a time when her mother had cared about her and spent time with her before caring about their reputation more than her daughter.

"Yes, she's very pretty."

An older woman, who had to be Odette's chaperone, narrowed her gaze the closer she came.

Odette beamed when she saw Finn and waved at him. "Finn. I'm so happy to see you."

Finn bowed from the waist. "Odette, ma'am."

"I'm—" Elizabeth was cut off by the woman.

"I beg your pardon, miss, but are you Lady Elizabeth, the daughter of the Earl of Lincoln?"

"Yes, I am she." No point in lying.

Odette bowed her head. "It's a pleasure to meet you, Lady Elizabeth."

The woman put an arm around Odette's shoulders, pulling her closer. "I'm afraid we must leave."

"Mrs. Dupont," Odette said. "We've just arrived."

"It doesn't matter," Mrs. Dupont said. "We can't stay."

"Finn and I have planned this walk for a while." Odette slid out of her chaperone's grip. "We can't leave."

"Why do you need to leave?" Finn asked.

Oh, Elizabeth had a hunch. She also guessed Mrs. Dupont

didn't want to divulge the full story of the disgraced lady, daughter of an earl, in front of her charge. Mrs. Dupont gave her a pointed look, confirming Elizabeth's suspicions.

"If the ladies are busy, we won't keep them," Elizabeth said.

"But I waited for today for a long time," Finn said at the same time as Odette protested, "I don't want to go."

"Come, Odette. Don't be difficult. Your mother told you to obey me." Mrs. Dupont's firm tone matched her expression. She half-pushed, half-dragged Odette away. "Have a nice day." From her tone, it sounded like she meant the opposite.

"I'm sorry, Finn." Odette waved at him, her eyes shining.

Finn's deep frown made him look older. "I don't understand. Am I so repulsive? I put my best suit on and ... I must be the most disgusting man they've ever seen."

"Good gracious, no. You're perfectly all right. It's because of me," she said. "Mrs. Dupont recognised me as the disgraced daughter of an earl. No one wants anything to do with me, and she doesn't want to be associated with me. She has to protect her charge as well."

"That's unfair." He shoved his hands in his pockets.

"Don't blame Mrs. Dupont. She surely has orders from Odette's parents not to put Odette in any compromising situations. I'm sorry, Finn. If Jane had come instead of me, your day would have been different."

He kicked a stone. "This is an injustice. Your father is an ass." He glanced at her. "Sorry, but that's what I think."

That was what she thought as well.

THE MORE CHRISTOPHER listened to Elizabeth telling him about what had happened in Hyde Park, the more his urge to kick the toffs in their aristocratic arses grew.

"So Finn didn't have the chance to talk to Odette," she said, sitting on the chair next to him in his study. "I've never felt more humiliated and sorry for Finn. I thought being thrown out of my own house was the most embarrassing thing that ever happened to me. I was wrong."

He caressed her cheek with his knuckles. He had no words of comfort to offer because he'd been humiliated, beaten, and hated only because he was a bastard, and he hadn't found words to soothe the pain.

Through his years, he'd dealt in different ways with his sense of guilt for something he had no control over. Anger worked only for a short time. Hate was a good motivator, but indifference was better.

Let us not speak of them: look and pass on, Dante had said.

"You shouldn't care about what they think of you," he said, trailing his fingers down her neck. "You didn't do anything wrong."

"I hate the fact that, because of what happened to me, other people are suffering."

"Come here."

He hugged her, and she buried her face in the crook of his neck. He hated the feeling of impotence in front of her pain. Aside from holding her, he couldn't protect her from how people treated her, or from how she felt about that, and having experienced people's hatred on his own skin—literally—he felt even more frustrated.

"I have some news that might cheer you up," he said, kissing her forehead. "I asked Smithy to search Rebecca's life for secrets. He found something interesting."

She lifted her head.

"So Finn told us Rebecca was at the ball," he said. "Smithy discovered that her brother has some serious gambling debts he must settle."

"Why is that good news?"

"Because if her brother is in financial difficulty, Rebecca is looking for a wealthy match, and Pearce is a duke. Imagine if she went to him and told him you and I were lovers, and that we'd been together during the Great Blizzard. She could prove it. Pearce constantly fears to be overlooked and dismissed by those he cares about, so he didn't hesitate to believe you and I were lovers. She would play the part of the devoted friend, offering to be close to him in a moment of suffering. He needs to marry, and after the scandal, he needs to marry quickly. Nothing better than a wedding to distract the gossipmongers. And whom he's going to choose as his wife?"

"You're probably right."

"We should talk to Pearce and tell him about Rebecca."

She chuckled bitterly. "He won't believe us."

"No, but he would believe Rebecca. We can convince, or trick, her to confess what she did while Pearce is listening."

"How?"

Finn barged into the room like a battering ram, with a wide grin, as happy as Larry. "I have news!"

"Dammit, Finn, you scared me half to death." Christopher withdrew his hand from the gun.

Finn kept smiling. "What happens if you get scared half to death twice in a row?"

"Why did you teach him maths?" Christopher asked her.

Elizabeth laughed.

"So you have news. From the dock?" he asked.

"No, from the gambling den in Fulham." Finn dropped a heavy leather bag on the desk and opened it. Banknotes, pocket watches, and documents spilt from it. "I, dear Guv, won all of this."

"Damn me to hell and back." Christopher went through the banknotes. There had to be a few thousand pounds. "How did you do that?"

Finn sat on the chair and crossed his arms behind his head. "Maths. Statistics and probabilities, to be precise."

"Yes!" Christopher pointed at the money, grinning. "That's why you taught him maths!"

She opened her mouth, surveying the small fortune. "Actually, I didn't want him to use his knowledge to gamble. Finn, education is meant to elevate the spirit, not to rob people."

"I didn't rob anyone." He scowled, indignant. "I used my knowledge to not exactly cheat. I counted the cards and made a quick calculation to better my chances, yes, but it was for a good cause." He rummaged through the documents and selected a few of them. "I won the money and this place ..." He read from a document. "Spencer Hall, from none other than your not-so-esteemed father."

"What?" Christopher and Elizabeth said together.

Christopher quickly read the document. No doubt. The earl had gambled his unentailed estate in Dartmoor and lost against Finn.

He read the document again. "Unbelievable."

Finn clicked his tongue. "The earl was very upset, let me tell you. He's also a terrible player, lacks vision and strategy." He hooked his thumbs in his waistcoat. "All things I excel in."

Elizabeth sagged into a chair. "How did you do that? I didn't even know my father attended gambling dens."

"Maths aside, the earl can be easily provoked," Finn said in a smug tone. "He has a temper and is a sore loser, not to mention arrogant. It didn't take long for him to play one game after another just to prove he was so well off he could lose easily."

Christopher was impressed. "And why did you do this?"

Finn stretched out his hands towards Elizabeth. "Justice for Elizabeth. Her father kicked her out, left her with nothing, and didn't care about her. She was disgraced, and because of that, I can't see Odette anymore. Now Spencer Hall is yours, along with the money I won." He pushed the prize towards her.

She blinked a few times. "Finn, I can't accept it."

"The hell you can," Christopher said.

"Why not?" Finn lost his cocksure attitude, looking just like a boy.

"I appreciate what you did for me. I really do." She took Finn's hand. "But I have no interest in taking my father's estate or money. I don't want anything from him. He had the chance to show me his love and trust but failed me. He hurt me deeply. He was supposed to protect me but did the opposite. That's why I can't accept the offer."

"I don't understand. Exactly because he hurt you, you should take the money and the estate. You deserve them."

She shook her head. "I think we should give everything back to him."

"No!" Finn scraped his chair back and shot up to his feet. "I won against him fair and square. I won it for you!"

"Not exactly fair and square, and I don't want my father's money extorted with deceit. In my eyes, I wouldn't be better than he is, and I am."

"This doesn't make any sense. He deserves to lose his estate, and you deserve to be compensated."

She lowered her gaze. "I can't take this."

Finn stormed out of the room, leaving everything on the desk.

Elizabeth sighed, pressing two fingers on the bridge of her nose. "I'm sorry he got angry."

Christopher leant back in his chair, aware the situation was another normal occurrence in his underworld life. "I agree with Finn. You should take everything."

She glared at him. "My family rejected me. I don't want anything from them, and certainly, I don't want a gambling prize."

He held up a hand. "I understand, but what do you have to lose? Your father doesn't know Finn is associated with you. Just enjoy the loot."

"And what am I supposed to do with Spencer Hall? Spend the summer there?"

He shrugged. "Sell it. I reckon you'll make a fair amount of money."

"It's not about the money." She shoved the banknotes into the bag. "Why is money so important?"

Ah, that was the point, wasn't it? "With due respect, you don't understand where Finn comes from." He took her hand to stop her from filling the bag. "When I found Finn, he was a scrawny thing, dirty with grime, and halfway to an early grave. That's why I took him in. Seeing him so frail and scared broke my heart. It's always about the money for him. Money means life for him. I don't mean to be preachy, but you grew up wealthy, never worried about food or the cold."

"I lived on the streets as well. I'm not a spoiled girl anymore."

"I know." He squeezed her hands, desperate for her to understand. "What I mean is that you experienced both sides of life. He didn't. The only thing he knows and understands is surviving, and money makes the difference between life and death. You can afford to reject the offer, and you have my sympathy. I appreciate your decision, but he can't. Not now. In time, he'll see things differently. You can afford to be morally superior. He can't. So I think you should at least keep the money."

She fiddled with the strap of the bag. "Finn can have the money."

"Don't insult him. Please."

She exhaled. "All right. I'll keep the money, but I can't keep an over one hundred-thousand-acre estate."

"You can, but it's your decision. Hell, I would keep it and throw the biggest party Dartmoor has ever seen."

She smiled. "I want to give Spencer Hall back to my father. Will you come with me?"

He kissed her hand. "Always."

thirty

NAVIGATING THE ARISTOCRACY'S rules was easier than dealing with gangsters's etiquette for Elizabeth.

She had no idea her refusal to accept Finn's gift would cause such a reaction, and she had no idea that Christopher would agree with Finn. Yes, it was true that she didn't belong to their world.

She found the boy in his room, bent over a book on probability. How fitting. "Finn."

He rested his chin on his fist and didn't look up. "What?"

"I'm sorry." She sat next to him, but he kept his focus on the book. "I didn't mean to offend you."

"It doesn't matter.."

"It does." She touched his hand.

He faced her, his deep eyes hard. "Will you keep the gift?"

"I'll keep the money, but I can't accept Spencer Hall."

He scoffed, folding his arms over his chest. "So I wasted my time."

"No. I found what you did impressive." Wicked, but impressive. "I can't accept an estate."

"He deserves to be tricked."

"Maybe, but I don't want to be an executioner and deliver the killing blow."

His stance slackened. "I'm sorry I lost my temper."

"You have a talent for maths although you should be careful with cheating when playing cards. You might find your match."

"I'm careful. Besides, I only count the cards and do a quick calculation of the probabilities. I don't hide an ace up my sleeve. People don't take me seriously. They underestimate me."

"I don't. You're a brilliant, caring young man, and I appreciate what you did for me. I think that losing Spencer Hall while gambling is enough punishment for my father. My mother must be furious. She loves Spencer Hall."

"I did it for Odette as well. Your father has destroyed my life." He jabbed a finger at himself.

"Don't be so dramatic. There will be other opportunities to see Odette. She's still interested in seeing you."

"Until she knows I work for the King."

"That's another matter." She gave him her hand. "Do we have an agreement? Please don't be angry with me. I promise I'll help you see Odette again."

He flashed a timid smile. "We do have an agreement."

ELIZABETH'S LEGS quivered as she stood on the pavement in front of her parents' townhouse. The house where she'd slept, spent her afternoons laughing with her sisters, and played the piano at Christmas with her grandmother. Now it was a strange place, cold and unforgiving. Returning here was like meeting someone who had been her best friend but was now a stranger.

She'd never found the white-walled, three-storey house intimidating, but standing under its shadow before she talked with her parents chilled her to the bone.

"Are you sure you want to see your parents?" Christopher asked. "You can just leave the document and be done with it."

She held the envelope with the promissory note of Spencer Hall. "No, I want to talk to them. I won't behave like a thief. I didn't do anything wrong, and they should be ashamed of themselves, not me."

Christopher nodded. "That's the spirit, and I'm so proud of you."

She smiled with a confidence she didn't feel.

"I'll wait for you here," he said. "I guess they wouldn't be happy to see me."

She took a deep breath and walked around the house to the rear entrance. Knowing her parents, her chances of being let in would be greater if she didn't knock on the front door and risk being turned away.

Despite the fact she was confident of her integrity and was aware she hadn't been unfaithful to Pearce, a cold quiver took hold of her.

"Who's there?" The scullery maid pulled the door open and stared at her. A riot of emotions displayed on her face, none of them inviting. "My lady?"

"Good morning. I must see my father immediately." Her voice quivered a little.

The maid shook her head. "I can't let you in. I'm sorry. You shouldn't be here."

"I'll be quick." She walked past the maid, ignoring her protests.

"My lady, I can't let you in."

"I won't be long."

She walked with determination along the hallway, pretending not to see the servants' sideways glances or hear their mutters. Her father was likely to be in the sunroom, having his breakfast. He was a creature of habit, very predictable. Well, aside from his secret gambling vice.

"My lady." George, the footman, followed her, stomping behind her in the corridor. "I must ask you to leave."

She was surprised her father's servants still addressed her with respect.

"It's all right. It will be a quick visit."

George seemed torn between obeying and tossing her out. "I …"

"I'll take the blame. Don't worry."

She pushed the door to the sunroom open, and as predicted, her parents were drinking tea at the pretty white table surrounded by pots of fresh flowers. Porridge and kippers were always present for breakfast, along with Cook's scones and fresh butter. The scent teased her nostrils and brought her back to those lazy mornings when she'd enjoyed a long breakfast in this very room, surrounded by sunlight.

For a moment, no one spoke. They stared at each other in frozen shock. Mother remained with her cup halfway to her mouth. Even George stood petrified behind Elizabeth, and Father's eyes widened.

He was the first to recover. "What is the meaning of this?"

"I'm sorry, my lord." George made a half-hearted attempt at grabbing her arm, but she stepped out of his reach.

She opened the envelope with shaky fingers. "Do not worry. I'm leaving. I'm here only to give you Spencer Hall back."

"What are you talking about?" Mother thawed as well.

Elizabeth put the promissory note on the table. "I could have sold the estate or taken it for myself, but I didn't."

Father paled, gazing everywhere but in her direction. "Well …"

"I don't understand. What is this?" Mother snatched the document and read it. When she finished, she lowered it slowly, her eyebrows rising to her hairline. "Charles, tell me there's a mistake. You gambled Spencer Hall and lost it?"

Elizabeth was shocked, too. She'd assumed Mother had been

aware of Father's gambling, or at the very least that Father had confessed to having lost Spencer Hall.

"Charles!" Mother said. "Explain yourself."

He fiddled with his bow tie. "Yes, I did lose Spencer Hall at a card game."

Mother gasped so deeply and loudly that Elizabeth feared she might faint.

"But," he hurried to say, "it's not what it seems. Obviously, Elizabeth planned all this to make me lose. She must have devised a plan to cheat and force me to hand her Spencer Hall. It's her doing."

"How dare you!" Elizabeth slammed a hand against the table, ignoring the pain. After the cups rattled in their saucers, silence dropped. "I didn't devise any plans. You lost Spencer Hall because you're a gambler. You did this. I didn't do anything." She tapped her fingers on the document. "The person who won Spencer Hall offered it to me. I came here to give it back to you because I didn't want it."

Mother folded the contract carefully. "I think she's telling the truth."

"Margaret—"

"Don't say a word. We'll talk about that later." Mother pressed her lips in a flat line. "Elizabeth, while I think your father is responsible for this incident, I do question how you came into possession of this document."

"By chance, because from the moment you threw me out, I barely survived, and ironically, the places Father attends to gamble are the same dangerous places where I live now, and if you had cared to read my letters, you would know."

"She planned this," he said. "I told you."

Sadness came to the fore, and she couldn't contain it. "I'm so disappointed by you."

It pained her saying that, but it was true.

"Elizabeth," Mother said, "he's your father."

"Not anymore. I disown you." She took in a deep breath because she didn't want to cry in front of them. But since she was there, she could voice her opinion. "You didn't protect me when I needed you. A parent should do more, a parent should be ready to defend their child. You hurt me and disappointed me. You are no longer my family." She couldn't go on without sobbing.

She strode out of the house, her eyes burning with desperation. This time, she used the front door. Let the neighbours see her leave.

Christopher was next to her in a moment. She hadn't seen him coming.

"How are you?" He cupped her face and searched her eyes.

"I'm all right. Really, I am."

He hailed a cab and hugged her once they were inside. "You aren't all right."

She rested her head on his chest, fighting the tears she wouldn't shed for those who didn't care about her.

thirty-one

CHRISTOPHER HAD SPENT the afternoon with Elizabeth in his arms. They hadn't talked. They'd just held each other. Even dinner was a quiet affair. Only the two of them were in the dining room. Darko was playing fetch with Finn. When they went up the stairs to his bedroom, she leant against him, sniffling.

"The pain will go away," he said, caressing her hair. "One day, you'll wake up and realise it doesn't hurt anymore."

"It's not the pain. It's the certainty I don't have a family anymore. I didn't realise how safe having my parents by my side made me feel. Now their protection and love are gone. It's like I'm mourning a loved one."

"You have me." For as long as she wanted him.

He still believed that, if her parents apologised, she would forgive them and decide to return home. Every instinct ordered him to keep her with him, but her life would be simpler with her parents. Safer. But at the same time, he was her family, and he was more than willing to take care of her.

"I'm so grateful for having you." She slipped a hand under his shirt. "And I don't want to be sad anymore. I spent months being scared and sad." She smiled before leaving the bed. "I want a new life with you."

"It sounds wonderful." He followed her as she slid behind the screen.

"It is, and I'm going to show you just how much."

The shuffling of fabric came.

"What are you doing?" he asked.

She came out wearing only her dressing gown. She didn't answer, and it was fine with him, as his attention was completely focused on her slipping into the bed.

Before ripping the garment off her lovely body and kissing her, he held her tightly, needing to feel her next to him and to make her understand how precious she was to him. She coiled her arms around his neck, her soft breathing tickling his skin.

"You know that after we're truly together, it can't be undone, don't you?" He caressed her loose hair, letting the silky curls spill through his fingers. "Everything will change."

"My family disowned me. Everyone thinks I'm a trollop. I want to be with you. And that's not going to change."

"I don't mean that." He cupped her face to stare into her eyes. "I don't care about your family, and certainly I don't care about what people think. I'm talking about us." He brushed a curl from her cheek. "I won't be able to let you go after we're together. Ever. To me, it's a vow. I don't take being with you lightly. If that scares you, I understand. You're free to leave my bed at any time."

"I don't want to leave." She pressed her thumb to his bottom lip. "I want to be with you, too."

He hesitated before speaking again. "If you change your mind and want to return to your old life—"

"Christopher."

"Please listen. If that happens, unfortunately not being a virgin will make your life more difficult. If you want to remain a virgin ... well, you know what to do. I'll do everything you want me to."

The idea of Elizabeth marrying a toff was like a stab in his chest, but she wanted a life of safety and leisure as she'd been used to. Then he'd do everything she wanted.

She put her soft hand on his cheek. "I love you, Christopher. I want to be with you. Only you."

It took him a moment to recover from the shock of her words. They were that powerful. They reached a deep part of his soul that desperately needed to hear them from her, and the love bursting within him couldn't be contained anymore. He'd held his love back for fear she didn't want him as much as he wanted her. But now he let it flow freely.

"I love you, Elizabeth." He put everything he felt for her into those words.

The worry and turmoil that had bothered him since he'd met her lifted with a surge of happiness. Finally, all those years spent wondering if he could ever have her found an answer.

They hugged each other again but with more desperation than passion. Her heartbeat thumped against his chest, and their love suffused the air.

"Take me, Christopher," she whispered.

He slowly untied the knot of her dressing gown because, as much as he wanted her, he meant to enjoy this moment. The fabric slid off her shoulders with a light tug.

The glow from the lamps turned her smooth skin into gold. He paused to admire her beauty. With her chestnut curls and golden skin, she was an autumn goddess.

He slipped a hand on her nape and pulled her closer, pausing again to breathe in her rosewood scent. The kiss started slow; he wanted to savour every inch of her delicious lips. But when she parted them for him, he thrust his tongue inside her hot mouth and became lost.

A battle of tongues and lips began. He tangled his fingers through her hair to pull her closer to him until her breasts were squashed against his chest.

He broke the kiss, only to gently lay her on the bed. She

panted, her lips reddened by the kiss and glistening. She grabbed his shoulders, making him feel her nails on his skin.

A shot of pleasure went through him the moment he stretched over her, careful not to crush her. He kissed her neck and collarbone, going lower. She moaned when he drew her nipple into his mouth while running a hand over the curve of her hips. He moved lower, pausing to kiss her belly.

The scent of the soap she used to bathe lingered on her skin and mingled with his own scent. The thought of smelling her scent on him sent a fresh jolt of energy down his body. He spread her legs to kiss her inner thighs. Her breathing quickened when he reached her wet core.

As he kissed her deeply and slowly, her hips writhed and rolled in sensual circles. He stretched her with two fingers, readying her for him. The last thing he wanted was to hurt her. So even though every instinct in him urged him on, he forced himself to go slowly. He rubbed and lapped at her, tasting her as deeply as possible. Breathy little noises came out of her, and they were the most erotic sounds he'd ever heard.

When she cried out in ecstasy, he kissed his way up her delicious body. Sheer pleasure clouded her wide eyes, and the release had brightened her cheeks.

After taking care of donning a clean sheath, he propped himself on his elbows, careful to keep his weight off her. He paused again to stare at her flushed face and glistening lips before moving his hips forwards. She closed her eyes, reclining her head, and her slender neck with the swift pulse tempted him too much. He trailed his lips down her jaw and neck before thrusting deeper.

She welcomed him with a sigh and a tight velvet grip. The strength of the burst of pleasure was unexpected. He had to pause again. For a moment, they shared heat and breath. Only they existed in the world. Only she mattered.

Then he started moving, gently at first, to let her body adjust.

"Does it hurt?" he whispered.

"No, and I trust you."

Those were likely the best words he'd ever heard. He eased forth, watching her reaction for any sign of pain. Inch by inch, he sheathed himself completely, and it was heaven and hell mingled together. Heaven, because only she could give him so much pleasure, and hell, because he was burning from the inside out. When she moaned again, he sped up.

They found a rhythm made of thrusting hips and shifts. She arched her back, crying out her release and gripping his shoulders hard. The more she sank her fingers into his skin, the closer he was to finding his own release. After watching the pleasure parting her lips, he couldn't go on much longer.

The power of the release made him quiver, leaving a trail of fire down his back and endless love in his heart. He rolled off her and hugged her from behind, pressing his chest to her back. Her breathing was uneven, and her chest rose and fell quickly.

"There's only you." He kissed her shoulder. "There's always been only you from the moment we shared the cottage. You marked my soul, took my heart, and filled my mind with thoughts of you. You filled my miserable life with light and happiness, and there won't be anyone else."

She snuggled closer, covering his hand with hers. "There won't be anyone else for me as well, and that's my vow to you."

thirty-two

A SHOT OF tension went down Christopher's spine when Pearce entered the common room in the palace. The Duke of Grafton was here in the headquarters of Christopher's criminal organisation! He'd be less shocked if the queen had entered.

A day ago, he'd sent a short but polite invitation to his brother, and surprisingly, Pearce had agreed to see him. So here he was with his beautiful Elizabeth, ready to see if their plan would work.

Wrapped in a long dark cloak that matched his dark soul, Pearce could be mistaken for one of those thugs who prowled the alleyways of Whitechapel at night. Certainly, his harsh expression added to his menacing persona and didn't invite kindness.

Pearce stopped in the middle of the room to survey it as if he were trying to decide if the place was to his liking. Indeed, the simple, sturdy furniture, the cheap glass lamps, and the cotton curtains had to be a shock for his ducal sensibilities, compared to his luxurious house. His gaze flared when he spotted Elizabeth, the only sign he felt an emotion, although he lacked his usual arrogance.

"Thank you for being here," Elizabeth said, bowing her head gracefully.

Pearce removed his gloves acknowledging her greeting with a bow of his head. "You're welcome."

Christopher opened his mouth to say something, but Pearce's politeness shocked him into silence.

"I'm glad to see you're well," Pearce said. "I was worried about you after you left."

"I didn't leave. My father kicked me out because of your accusations." Elizabeth didn't give him time to reply. "Did you take a cab as we asked you?"

Pearce nodded. "Yes. My carriage is nowhere near here, and I came alone not to attract attention."

"So, Rebecca will be here shortly," she said.

"Rebecca?" Pearce tensed immediately.

Elizabeth held up a hand. "Please bear with us. We have reason to believe Rebecca spread lies about Christopher and me with the intention of deceiving you. She likely wants to marry you. We invited her here in the hope that she would confess to her lies."

Pearce's eyebrows drew together. "What are you talking about?"

"Everything will be clear in a moment. I must ask you to trust me. Just this once." She held open the curtains that covered the nook. "If you hide here and make sure to remain still and quiet, we would be most grateful. We ask you only to listen to the conversation. There's the chance Rebecca won't confess to what she did, but I'm confident I can persuade her to talk."

"We know Rebecca was the witness who informed you of Elizabeth and my presumptive affair." Christopher exchanged a glance with Elizabeth. "And we know she lied."

"All right. I'll be quiet." Pearce did as told. He hid behind the curtains and stepped back against the wall so as not to be spotted.

"Thank you." Elizabeth closed the curtains and draped them carefully to conceal the duke completely. "We're ready."

They didn't need to wait long. Rebecca strode into the room with an arrogant attitude as he had thought Pearce would have done. They did have many things in common. Perhaps they'd be a good match. She, too, surveyed the room, gazing from Elizabeth to Christopher with disdain.

"Rebecca, thank you for coming." Elizabeth's voice sounded strained.

Christopher had to bow, only because he didn't want to give Rebecca a reason to leave.

"I'm here. What did you want to discuss?" She didn't sit or remove her coat or hat.

"I want to clear my name," Elizabeth said, matching Rebecca's stiff stance. "I know you lied to the duke and told him you saw Christopher and me together. I'm asking you to tell the truth."

Rebecca remained silent long enough to make Christopher worry. He couldn't offer to help her brother pay off his debts until she admitted to having lied, or Pearce would think Rebecca's confession was disingenuous and driven only by her wish to protect her brother. Christopher needed only a word from her. A word that would reveal the truth.

Finally, she cleared her throat. "Why would I do that?"

"Because your lie destroyed my reputation and my life." Elizabeth narrowed her eyes to slits. "And because your plan didn't work as you wanted, anyway. The duke isn't courting you, is he?"

"An engagement with the duke was what you wanted," Christopher said. "Push Elizabeth away to have the opportunity to be courted by Pearce and marry him."

"You're wrong." Rebecca's stance slackened a fraction. "The duke and I are growing closer with each passing day. He shows signs of affection and care towards me. I don't expect to be engaged to him in a matter of weeks, of course. The sordid incident involving you upset him deeply, but my plan did work."

Elizabeth's chest heaved. "There was no need to lie. The duke was only agreeing to court me. There was no engagement."

"Don't make me laugh. It was obvious to everyone he was deeply taken by you. I know he searched for you after you left. I saw him buy an expensive engagement ring for you. He agreed to start with a simple courtship because he knew you weren't interested in him. You didn't deserve his attention. You would have rejected his marriage proposal and humiliated him after the courtship ended. So I humiliated *you*."

Christopher chuckled bitterly. "You don't really think that making him believe Elizabeth was being unfaithful to him didn't humiliate him, do you?"

Rebecca blinked a couple of times. "Elizabeth didn't care about him. She would have never loved him, and the little scene between you two I witnessed at the ball proved it. I saved him from a miserable match and a broken heart."

"I'm quite sure his heart broke when you gave him that false news," he said.

"He's more than happy now." Rebecca straightened again.

"Did you pay other people to spread the same lie?" Elizabeth asked. "Or did they volunteer?"

"Don't be ridiculous. Irene agreed with me you weren't the right woman for the duke, and your association with Blackwood is no lie, and Maude was with her parents in your father's hunting lodge during the Great Blizzard. We knew you were lying. You're so ready to judge and condemn others when you lie, too. You weren't in the hunting lodge. You were with Blackwood, likely in that small cottage at the edge of town. People saw smoke coming out of the cottage's chimney. Then the day after the ball, my lady's maid learnt from your footman that you were planning to stay out the whole day. It was obvious you were meeting with your lover."

"But I didn't," Elizabeth said.

"It doesn't matter. As I said, you don't deserve the duke's affection. So no. I'm not going to tell him the truth. Why would I?"

Christopher glanced at the curtains as a muffled noise came.

"You might change your mind, Miss Norton. Your brother has an obsession with gambling, doesn't he?"

Rebecca gripped her reticule. "That's none of your business."

"Oh, but it is, since he gambles in one of my dens. He has a huge debt with his creditors. Trust me when I say that you don't want to upset those people. They aren't very understanding when it comes to money." He lifted a shoulder. "I can make sure your brother's debt is cancelled today. His creditors aren't my men, but they won't care where the money comes from."

She fiddled with her hands, shifting her stance.

"I can do more," Christopher went on. "I can also make sure that no gambling den will ever let him in, so you'll have time to convince your brother to stop gambling once and for all, which actually goes against my own interest because he keeps filling my coffers, thank you very much. Tell the truth to her parents and the duke, and your brother will be spared a slow, painful death by the hand of his creditors."

Rebecca lowered her gaze. "The duke will be furious. He'll ruin my reputation."

"You have to choose, Miss Norton." Christopher used a harsh tone. "Your brother's life, or the duke's wrath."

"As unpleasant as talking to the duke might be," Elizabeth said, "he would never hurt you or your brother, as those thugs would do."

A sob shuddered through Rebecca, and she clamped a hand over her mouth. "This is unfair. I'm going to lose Pearce if I tell him the truth."

"You shouldn't have lied to him to start with." Elizabeth folded her arms over her chest. "What do you choose?"

Christopher did feel some pity for her. "I need an answer, miss."

"All right." She swallowed hard. "I will tell the truth to the duke, but you must promise me that my brother will be safe."

Christopher nodded. "You have my word. The moment the duke is informed of the truth, your brother's debt will vanish."

"Very well. Then the conversation is over." Miss Norton spun towards the door and left the room as if it were on fire.

Once she slammed the door behind her, Pearce shoved the curtains aside, his eyes wild with fury. "I can't believe this."

"Exactly." Elizabeth's determined expression wasn't less fierce than Pearce's. "You refused to believe me. I told you those rumours were only lies, but you didn't listen to me. You had no doubt I was to blame." Her voice cracked. "You didn't let me talk, and I risked my life on the streets because no one believed me. Only Christopher helped me." A sob escaped her, and she walked out of the room. Her footsteps thundered in the small space.

Christopher's chest clenched for her pain, but at least the truth was out.

Then he was alone with his brother in an uncomfortable silence so thick he could grow potatoes in it.

Pearce hung his head in a defeated fashion unfit for a duke. "Why did you offer Rebecca a deal? I was listening. I know the truth, no matter what she decides. You didn't need to help her brother."

"Because she must confess, so everyone will know Elizabeth is innocent. If Rebecca doesn't confess and you shun her, she'll spread rumours about your credibility. It's better if you pretend not to know anything until she tells you. There must be no doubt or shadow over Elizabeth's reputation."

He nodded. "I wronged her. Deeply."

"You should take responsibility for what you did. But," he added when Pearce shot him a glare, "she has a very good heart. If you give her time and apologise profusely and sincerely, I'm sure she'll forgive you." He wasn't sure, but Pearce had to apologise to her.

"I'll apologise anyway, whether she forgives me or not. It's the least I can do."

"Another thing you can do is call your dogs off my back."

Pearce nodded without hesitation. "I didn't order them to beat you and your men. They acted without my permission. I want you to know that."

The news surprised Christopher. "Half of those men were thugs from one of the most violent gangs Whitechapel has ever seen. I'm not surprised they attacked us."

"I'm sorry. Really. When I employed those men, I only cared about their knowledge of your routine. I was wrong. As I was wrong about too many other things. I thought Elizabeth was one of the many people who betrayed me." Pearce raked a hand through his hair.

"No, Pearce. You're hurt because you believe Father loved me more than he loved you, and you think every relationship in your life is the same, but it's not true."

Pearce composed himself, and his cold attitude returned. "He did love you more than me. He certainly loved your mother more than mine."

"Yes, Father was in love with my mother, but he loved us both equally. You mistake his sense of guilt towards me with love. The special attention he gave me was driven by his guilt, not love."

For the first time in Christopher's life, Pearce hadn't lashed out at him when talking about their father.

"I missed him when he was with you," he whispered. "Mother was desperate. She kept crying whenever Father left her to be with you. I did my best to comfort her, but she suffered greatly."

"So did I when he was with you. That's why he wanted us to care for each other and be brothers."

"Mother would have never allowed it." Pearce scratched his chin. "I admit her opinions on you and your relationship with Father influenced me. I wasn't kind to you."

"Kind? You were a bloody ass." Christopher folded his arms over his chest. "They kicked me out of Eton because of you. You gave me the sack when Father died. You barely allowed me to say goodbye to him. I couldn't find a job because of you. Shall I continue? The list is rather long."

Pearce stretched out his hand to him, his expression determined. "I'll do better, and I apologise."

Christopher shook his brother's hand. "It's not me you should apologise to. Sarah and Arthur need you."

A muscle bunched in Pearce's jaw. For a long, horrifying moment, Christopher thought Pearce would tell him to go to hell. But then his expression softened. "Can you take me to them?"

"It'll be my pleasure."

"See, it was Rebecca's brother who told me Sarah was seeing someone else behind my back." Pearce exhaled, and some of his pain reached Christopher. "I wronged her, too."

The drive to Sarah's house was a quiet one, but the air between Christopher and Pearce wasn't charged with the usual hostility. Not that Christopher believed he'd soon be his brother's best mate, but at least they weren't at each other's throat anymore.

He hadn't realised how strongly he wanted to have a normal, civil relationship with Pearce until that moment.

Pearce glanced at the house before getting out of the cab. "The place is better than I thought."

"I wanted my nephew to live in a decent place." He knocked on the door. "Sarah, it's me, Christopher."

Footsteps sounded along with Arthur's happy giggling. The door was flung open, revealing a wide-smiled, pink-cheeked Sarah.

"What a surprise." Her smile vanished when she stared at Pearce. "What is he doing here?"

"Pearce wanted to see you." Christopher nudged him with his elbow and nodded at the hat.

Pearce removed his tall hat. "I know this is sudden, but I would like a moment with you. Please."

Sarah didn't move at first, but another sound, halfway between a snort and a laugh, from Arthur distracted her.

"I'm sorry, Sarah," Pearce said. "I'd be extremely grateful if you'd allow me to talk to you for a moment. After that, I'll do anything you ask. If you want to be left alone, I'll do that."

Sarah's eyes filled with unshed tears, and Christopher wanted to kick himself for having taken Pearce here.

But then she jutted out her chin. "Come in."

Christopher let Pearce go first. The house wasn't big, merely a sitting room, a small kitchen, and a bedroom, but it was warm and dry with plenty of sunlight. Arthur was sitting on the thick rug, smashing two coloured wooden blocks together with enthusiasm. Whatever the purpose of that exercise was, Arthur seemed more than satisfied with the result, despite the fact his small hands barely held the blocks.

Pearce sucked in a deep breath when he focused on Arthur. There was no mistaking the resemblance between Pearce, Christopher, and Arthur. They shared the same blond-silver hair and blue eyes.

"He's beautiful," Pearce said, seemingly choking on his words.

"And healthy, thanks to Christopher." Sarah picked Arthur up who let out a delighted squeal. "He doesn't cough anymore since we moved here, and he's putting on weight as babes should do. Christopher has taken good care of us. I'll always be grateful to him. He saved our lives."

"It was my pleasure." Christopher stepped closer to the door, uncomfortable with all the compliments. "I'll leave you two alone to have a chat if Sarah agrees."

Sarah kissed Arthur's head and nodded. "Thank you."

Christopher pinned his brother with a glare, meaning to warn him not to hurt Sarah. Pearce bowed his head in acknowledgement.

When Christopher shut the door behind him, he exhaled, a weight lifting from his chest. Surely Pearce wouldn't change in a day, but what mattered was that Arthur wouldn't grow up believing his father hated him, and that made the whole difference.

thirty-three

INSTEAD OF BEING relieved at Rebecca's confession, sadness had grown in Elizabeth's head for days. Suspecting something and hearing the truth of it were two different things. Silly of her, but a tiny part of her had wished, hoped beyond hope that Rebecca hadn't purposely wanted to destroy her life. She'd hoped it had been a mistake or a misunderstanding. She ought to learn not to be so naïve. One might say that living on the streets should have cured her of naivety. Apparently, not.

So when Christopher told her that Pearce had come to talk to her, she wasn't sure she should agree to see him. He was to blame as much as Rebecca for her predicament.

She paced in her bedroom, aware that Pearce was outside, waiting for her decision. To add insult to injury, Darko seemed to adore Pearce. The hound was yapping and making delightful noises while in the walkway with Pearce who spoke to him with soft tones and kind words. Love at first sight.

"Give him the possibility to talk," Christopher said, holding her hands.

"As he gave it to me?"

He kissed her knuckles. "You're right to be resentful, but he grew up with a mother who suffered from Father's absence and blamed her pain on Father and me. He's an insecure man."

"Why are you defending him all of a sudden?" she asked, genuinely curious.

"Believe it or not, I feel sorry for him. He doesn't have anyone while I have you and my friends here in the royal palace. He thinks that everyone lies to him, but he's sorry for what he did."

"Honestly, I'm confused." She frowned. "One moment, he wanted to marry me. The next, he was happy to see me kicked out of my house. Now he wants to apologise."

He stepped closer, his eyes pleading. "You didn't want to accept Finn's money because you said you were better than your father. You returned the contract to him because of your integrity. Don't you think you should show the same integrity to Pearce?"

"I'm still debating."

He chuckled and took her face. "Just hear what he has to say. It'll be another opportunity for you to tell him to go to hell."

Being resentful was exhausting, and perhaps he had a point. A small one, but still a point.

She would find closure and move on once and for all. "All right. I'll talk to him, but I'm not sure how I feel. Too many emotions in a short time."

"You're an amazing woman." He kissed her lips before leaving the room.

She mentally braced herself to meet Pearce again.

There was some truth in what Rebecca had said, though. Elizabeth had never wished to marry Pearce. She'd agreed to be courted, but deep down, she'd been aware she would have rejected him, no matter how the courtship would have gone.

The fact she didn't love him didn't mean his cruelty hadn't hurt her deeply. He'd been aware of the risks and dangers she would have faced in the streets, yet he had done nothing to stop Father.

Christopher opened the door, and Pearce walked in with measured steps. Darko stared at him as if he'd invented bacon.

"Elizabeth." Pearce didn't show his usual cocksure bearing. "Thank you for agreeing to see me."

"I'll leave you alone." Christopher left the room, smiling at her.

"You should thank Christopher. He convinced me to see you." She sat on the armchair. "I wasn't sure I wanted to see you. I'm quite confused."

He sat in front of her, his gaze guarded. "You were right. I didn't give you the opportunity to talk. I jumped to conclusions. I didn't trust you. I have no excuses for my behaviour."

Darko rested his chin on Pearce's thigh, tail drawing circles, and Pearce scratched his head.

"I'm glad you acknowledge that."

"I'll do everything in my power to become a better man. I promise."

She gave him a nod. "Again, I'm glad for you. I mean it."

"That's why I'm here to tell you my offer is still up." He gently took her hand and held it.

She was too stunned to snatch her hand back. "Offer?"

"Marriage. I lost you because of my stupidity. I want you again in my life. I won't make the same mistakes. I'll spend the rest of our life together, making you happy."

For a split moment, a vision of her life as a duchess flashed across her mind. Being a powerful lady had its charm. But above all, she would have the respect that had been denied to her by a lie. Still, she preferred to be the Queen of Whitechapel than the Duchess of Grafton.

"Pearce." She didn't look forward to hurting him. "There's something you need to know." She licked her dry lips. "I love Christopher, and he loves me."

He blanched, straightening on the armchair. "You love him."

"After my parents threw me out, I worked as a waitress in

taverns and a restaurant until Christopher found me and took me here. He had no idea what had happened to me, and there wasn't anything between us until that moment."

Her words were a stretch of the truth. While she and Christopher hadn't become lovers until she'd moved to the palace, she couldn't honestly say she hadn't felt anything for him before that.

Pearce narrowed his eyes. "So it was true. You were lovers."

"For heaven's sake!" She shot up to her feet, and he rose as well. It was amazing how he kept doubting her word. "Are you telling me I'm a liar *again*? I'm being honest. Before the whole incident started, Christopher and I hadn't seen each other in years. You rejecting me and my parents disowning me are the reasons I saw him again and fell in love with him. It's because of *you* that I'm here. So no, Pearce. I can't marry you. I could easily take advantage of your offer to lead an easy life, but I'm not doing that because I'm in love with Christopher. And if you accuse me of lying again, I swear I'm not going to talk to you again."

Pearce worked his jaw. "I believe you."

"Thank you."

"So I did lose you."

"I'm sorry, Pearce. I don't want to return to my old life, and I don't want to see my parents at the moment. If they threw me out once, they could do it again. If you really want to change and become a better person, then you should take care of your son."

His pain was tangible; it thickened the air between them. Her chest tightened for him, but honesty was the only thing she could give him.

She put a hand on his arm. "I'm sorry to cause you pain. I feel no joy in it. But I have to follow my heart."

"No, you're right. I have to do better than that, and I deserve your resentment." He held her hand again, but there was a tenderness in the gesture she appreciated. "I wish you all the joy you and Christopher deserve."

"I wish you joy, too." She hoped to put behind the cruel words, the pain, and the humiliation, for the sake of both of them.

epilogue

T HE CHRISTMAS DECORATIONS and lights brightened the palace. Large wreaths and red lanterns were scattered around the courtyard while the tallest Christmas tree Elizabeth had ever seen towered in the middle.

Cold gusts blew from the north, carrying the promise of snow, not something she looked forward to. Since after the Great Blizzard, her appreciation for the snow had dwindled. Sometimes she loved it. Other times, it bothered her.

Christopher wrapped his arms around her from behind. "It's getting cold. We should be inside. Everyone is there."

"I checked the mail." She rested her head on his chest. "There's another letter from my parents. The third in a week. Can you believe it? Just because it's Christmas."

They'd sent her a Christmas card as a peace offering, then a short letter, and then another Christmas card. She didn't want to see them yet, especially since Father had tried to blame her for the loss of Spencer Hall, but all the same, they asked to have a civil relationship with her, hoping they might apologise for the pain they'd caused her.

Rebecca had kept her word and told the truth to Pearce who

had cleared Elizabeth's name with a formal apology. Thus her parents were more than aware of her innocence, as they were aware that Christopher was now a rich businessman with a successful company. Pearce had helped him speed up the process of legalising the company.

She believed those were the only reasons for their sudden wish to see her. But she wasn't sure they really cared about her.

"Don't be too upset. We're your family now." He kissed her cheek, and the cold tip of his nose on her cheek made her giggle.

The air in the large common room was thick with the smell of cinnamon and mulled wine. Finn sat at one end of the long table covered with a bright-red tablecloth. Crumpled pieces of paper surrounded him.

"I told you to stop, Finn," Jane said, lighting the candles on the table. "You'll stain the tablecloth with ink, and dinner is ready."

"I've almost finished." He crushed another piece of paper and tossed it in the warm hearth.

"What are you doing?" Elizabeth asked.

"Trying to write a letter to Odette. She sent me a Christmas card, telling me that she'd like to see me again now that the duke made it clear that you were innocent and her parents aren't against you anymore, but I don't know where to start."

"By being honest," Pearce said from the sofa.

He was playing with Arthur, bouncing him up and down on his knee. Arthur laughed out loud, opening and closing his small hands in absolute delight. He grabbed a long curl of his father's hair and pulled.

"Careful." Sarah gently opened Arthur's hand.

"It's all right." Pearce smiled at her.

The large diamond ring Pearce had offered to Elizabeth was on Sarah's finger, and it was fitting, because Sarah truly loved Pearce.

"Being honest is good advice," Christopher said.

Finn propped his elbow on the table and rested his chin on his fist. "I can't be honest. She'll run for the hills."

"Then honest and polite," Elizabeth said.

"Elbows off the table." Jane clapped her hands, jolting Finn. "Honestly. And His Grace is present."

Darko gave out a snort as if in agreement with Jane. His infatuation for Pearce was still ongoing without the need for bacon bribes. She would never understand that dog.

Pearce came to the palace often to spend time with Christopher, Sarah, and Arthur, but officially, no one knew about his son, which never failed to sadden Elizabeth.

But some aristocrats managed to give bright futures to their illegitimate sons, gifting them with unentailed estates and, in rare cases through the queen, even a title. Whatever happened, Arthur would always have the support of his loving uncle and his father.

"Arthur will have a share of my enterprise if you're happy with that, Sarah," Christopher said.

She smiled. "Your company has been legal for a matter of months, and you already plan to share it?"

He shrugged. "Good planning. The little one will have a safe future."

"He'll never be alone," Pearce said, holding the baby. "I swear it on my honour in front of these witnesses on this holy day, Arthur will have all the opportunities I had."

Christopher grimaced. "Hell, even being beaten up in Eton?"

"No swearing, please," Jane said. "Not in front of the babe and at Christmas."

"Eton was a sheer nightmare for me," Christopher added.

"Because of me, mostly." Pearce handed Arthur to Sarah. "I behaved horribly with you. I'm sorry."

Christopher didn't flash his usual cocky grin. Elizabeth could swear there was a suspicious shine in his eyes.

"It's in the past," he said.

Pearce stood up and put a hand on Christopher's shoulder. He didn't say anything, but she suspected the two brothers didn't need many words. They patted each other's shoulders, and that was it.

"Did you write back to your parents?" Sarah asked, cuddling Arthur.

"I'm still upset. Putting the past behind me is harder than I thought."

Pearce caught her gaze. "If I may give a piece of advice. I was angry with my father because he used to spend so much time with Christopher. I didn't have time to tell him how much I cared about him. Your reluctance to see them again is justified, but one day, your parents will be gone, and you won't have the chance to make peace with them."

"Since when are you so wise?" Christopher asked.

"Since I'm a father." He smiled fondly at Arthur and Sarah.

That tender smile melted Elizabeth's heart.

"Dinner is ready." Jane carried a large bowl of steaming white soup to the table.

"I'm starving," Finn said.

"Quickly, before it gets cold. Not you, Your Grace. You take your time," Jane said.

Christopher rolled his eyes, muttering, "Favouritism."

Elizabeth sat next to him among the scraping of chairs, the laughter, and Arthur's cooing sounds. The warmth of her new family touched her heart, but Pearce was right. She could try to reconcile with her parents. The situation between them would never be as it was before the incident, but she'd try to get them back into her life, or at least not to resent them.

"I think I'm going to follow Pearce's suggestion and write to my parents," she said.

Christopher leant closer and whispered, "Do you think they'd approve of me as their new son if you marry me?"

She beamed, closing her hand around his. "They wouldn't, but I don't care."

"So you agree to be my queen?"

"Absolutely, Your Highness."

about me

Love stories have always captured my imagination. What's better than two people falling in love with each other? I write steamy romance, usually with a paranormal twist in an historical setting. Add a touch of suspense and mystery and a pinch of darkness. I love stories with  strong, sexy heroes and mischievous heroines who pull no punches.

I live in the City of Sails, New Zealand, drinking tea (coffee gives me anxiety) and devouring books.

Join my newsletter for exclusive content and the chance to receive an ARC copy of my books. Just copy and paste this link into your browser:

Barbara's Newsletter: https://bit.ly/39yZ4Lw

also by barbara russell

If you want historical romance:

Victorian Outcasts

If you love steamy paranormal romance set in Victorian London, my Royal Occult Bureau series is for you:

The Royal Occult Bureau Series

Are you into shape-shifter romance? Check out my da Vinci's Beasts series, set in WW2:

da Vinci's Beasts Series

For more Victorian paranormal romance with witches and sexy warriors, see the Knights of the White Blade series:

The White Order Series